NORTH GLADIOLA

Also by James Wilcox:

MODERN BAPTISTS

NORTH GLADIOLA

James Wilcox

1817

HARPER & ROW, PUBLISHERS, New York
Cambridge, Philadelphia, San Francisco, London
Mexico City, São Paulo, Singapore, Sydney

FIRST EDITION
Designer: C. Linda Dingler

Library of Congress Cataloging in Publication Data

Wilcox, James.
  North gladiola.

  I. Title.
PS3573.I396N6 1985   813'.54   84-48633
ISBN 0-06-015441-1

85 86 87 88 89 RRD 10 9 8 7 6 5 4 3 2 1

For
Steve, Joan, Patricia,
John, Laurie, and Suzanne

These all died in faith, not having received what was promised . . . having acknowledged that they were strangers and exiles on the earth.

—HEBREWS 11:13

I

E nulla! nulla!
Arida landa . . . non un filo d'acqua

—*Manon Lescaut*

1
❁

For Manon, Louisiana was the end of the world, France's Siberia, and so, on some days, did it also seem to Mrs. Coco, who fancied herself an exile of sorts, even though Brookhaven, Mississippi, where she was born and where her brother and sister still lived, was only an hour's drive north. Denmark and Quailie, the brother and sister, had never really forgiven her for eloping with The Italian, which is how they referred to Mr. Coco, who was in fact about as Italian as the Queen Mother. Oh, he had Italian blood in him, all right, on both sides, and his grandfather never did learn English. But it was a rarefied North Italian blood, which gave him the temperament, she soon discovered once the fever of the elopement had subsided, of a Victorian dowager. For a few years she managed to stay in love with him, fervently imitating his tight-lipped restraint while adopting a nunlike wardrobe of ill-fitting blacks and browns. After the first two children love waned to devotion; with number three, devotion dimmed until, after four, five, and six, all that remained was a vague sense of duty. With the last child away from home—in New York City, studying nutrition at Columbia Teachers College—Mrs. Coco found herself daydreaming about Mississippi, wondering what it would have been like if that foolish seventeen-year-old hadn't fallen in love with The Italian, if she had stayed where she was loved and understood, among her own people, good Baptists who would have killed for her. Would life seem such a burden in Mississippi? No, there was something about Louisiana, something oppressive that she felt every time she crossed the state line on her way back from the mall in Mississippi, where everyone in Tula Springs, Louisiana, did their serious shopping. The nice divider that Mississippi had in its highway, planted with azaleas and camellias, suddenly disappeared in Louisiana, leaving a two-lane that bumped up and down rises that weren't really hills, past rough pastures or meadows—it was hard to tell what was farm or wild in Louisiana, everything was so untidy—and clumps of starved-looking pines that didn't really qualify as woods. Perhaps Manon was lucky, after all, to have died young and escaped growing old in such a place.

Of course, Mrs. Coco never mentioned any of this to her husband, who held Mississippi in the greatest disdain. To him it was a land of boors and rednecks, from which she had been rescued in the nick of time, giving him a chance to do a little molding before she hardened into a mature adult; indeed, whenever Mr. Coco was displeased with something she said, his comment would be, "That sounds like Mississippi talking." Early in the marriage, hoping to smother any trace of Mississippi, the former Ethyl Mae Bickford had immersed herself in culture, studying French with a retired lady professor who, during a field trip to the opera in New Orleans, ate an innocent-looking oyster that led, via several complications, to her demise.

Along with French, Mrs. Coco had taken up the violin, but after several years of struggle, when her eight-year-old son's technique began to outstrip her own, she switched to the cello. Mr. Coco never did approve of this instrument because of the way a lady had to sit; he tried to persuade his wife to play sidesaddle. But Mrs. Coco stuck to her guns. She was enamored of the bass clef, the way the thick G and thicker C strings made her body resonate with a furtive masculine warmth. Such was her dedication that after five years of practicing two to three hours a day she discovered a lump where the varnished maple pressed against her left breast. In a panic Mr. Coco made a special novena for the lump, which turned out to be only a benign cyst. The scar from the operation—Mrs. Coco's only regret was that it was not larger—did not fade with time, but remained livid enough to make Mr. Coco a little uncomfortable when, with that peculiar moan of his, he would fumble with the frogs of her nightgown while she feigned sleep.

On her fifty-seventh birthday Mrs. Coco had an early dinner at home with her husband, who was always depressed on her birthday because his—and this would be his seventy-first—was just a week later. She did not have time for cake and ice cream, since she was due at Tula Springs' new BurgerMat, where her string quartet, the Pro Arts, was engaged for the Grand Opening ceremonies. After hurriedly pecking Mr. Coco on the eyebrow and thanking him for the present—a book that trained you to look on the bright side of life—she lugged her shabby pasteboard cello case to the car. She was saving up for a decent-looking fiberglass case with the money the quartet earned, but this was a slow process since, number one, the quartet didn't have all that many engagements, and number two, not everyone paid their bills. Jack Fairs of Baton Rouge, for instance, still hadn't coughed up a cent for the redfish rodeo that the quartet had played for back in September. All they had gotten out of Jack was a case of Butch Wax Control Stick, which Mrs. Coco had tried in vain to sell to the Tiger Unisex Hair Styling Salon across the street from her house.

As she pulled into the BurgerMat parking lot, the headlights swept over George Henry, who was lounging against the red, white, and blue bunting draped over the drive-in's glass doors. Her third child, George Henry lived in Baton Rouge, where he taught high-school civics and repaired computers on the side. Beer, two six-packs a day, had swollen him up to a hefty two-twenty, and that, along with his being nearly bald—except for a tonsure of frizzy gray hair—made him appear much older than thirty-seven. Indeed, his mother, who was petite and svelte, with only a touch of gray, had a difficult time thinking of him as her son. Could she really be responsible for anything that big and old?

"Look at your fiddle," she said as she got out of the car. George Henry, the first violin in the quartet, did not look as his mother picked the violin up off a newspaper vending machine.

"It was going to fall," she said and then added quickly, "How are you, sug? You look nice." He was wearing scuffed work boots with his tuxedo, but she decided to overlook this for now. "You're smoking," she observed instead.

"Mmm," George Henry said, the same George Henry who had sent her a Hallmark card the other day saying that for her birthday he was going to give up smoking.

"I thought you promised to give up smoking?"

He shrugged and flicked the ashes.

"Then why are you smoking?"

"Your birthday was yesterday. I didn't smoke yesterday."

Mrs. Coco sighed; she should have known it was too good to be true. "For your information, my birthday is today."

"Oh."

Her lips pursed, she went over to try the BurgerMat door and, finding it locked, rapped with her car keys on the glass. "Where *is* that man?" She had told the manager, Mr. Qumquist, that the Pro Arts would need an hour to warm up and test the acoustics, but here it was nearly seven and there weren't even any lights on inside, except for a dull red glow behind the stainless steel counter.

"George Henry, go round back and see if—"

"There's no one here, Ma."

In the lot next door, the site of a defunct insect museum that was going to be turned into a 7 Eleven, a goat tethered to a gas pump gave out a vague bleat that sounded like a car braking. Checking her cropped blond hair in the reflection of the glass door, Mrs. Coco muttered, "Well, it's about time," then turned and realized, as the goat bleated again, her mistake. This, on top of George Henry's smoking and the fact that one of the beads had come loose on the collar of her ankle-length black jersey dress, made her mention something she had promised herself not to bring up this evening: "George Henry, I'm not going to your wedding."

She had planned to write and explain her views to him in a thoughtful, rational discourse on the sacrament of marriage, which, as a convert from the days of Pius XII, Mrs. Coco took quite seriously. Already she had compromised herself by attending the wedding, a second marriage, of Larry, her oldest son, back in February. She had even shelled out two hundred dollars from her cello case fund for a rehearsal supper at the Ramada Inn, something the bride never did thank her for, acting as if it were her due. Then there was Nancy, the baby of the family, barely twenty-four years old and already divorced. Mrs. Coco felt she had to put her foot down somewhere; either she was a Catholic or she wasn't. If she wasn't, why, then there was no reason for her sister, Quailie, to be furious at her for quitting the Baptists.

"Did you hear me?" she said as George Henry gazed vacantly at the museum.

"Yeah, Ma, I heard." He struck a match and deftly applied it to the cigarette hanging from his lower lip. "Larry gets a reception, a new car, a trip to Disney World, and me, you won't even—"

"Larry is going to pay your father back for the car."

"Sure."

"And it was the Cahills who sent them to Orlando." She discreetly removed a small bug that had darted into her mouth before continuing: "Anyway, this is all beside the point. The point is, in the eyes of the Church, you're still married to Connie, who, by the way, sent me a lovely philodendron for my birthday."

"Is it because she sells hot tubs? Is that why you won't meet her?"

"I don't care if Heidi sells bananas," Mrs. Coco said, not quite truthfully, for it did disturb her that Heidi, George Henry's fiancée, sold hot tubs. No one who thought right would sell hot tubs.

"Ma, I love her. Doesn't that mean anything?"

"Oh, love—what do you know about love?" Mrs. Coco waved away some nonexistent smoke; her son was careful to turn his head when he exhaled. "I don't see why you two can't simply live together like everyone else nowadays. Why must you get married?"

"Heidi just happens to have certain principles, and I respect them."

Finding herself on the wrong side of the argument, Mrs. Coco countered with a sudden offensive: "You shouldn't drink so much."

"What?"

"It's ruining your looks."

"Ma, what are you . . . I'm trying to . . ."

"Oh, here's Duk-Soo," she said, waving at the orange motor scooter that had just pulled in off the highway.

Duk-Soo Yoon, the second violin in the Pro Arts, was under tremendous pressure this week, engaged as he was in completing an approved bibliography for his dissertation on tourism, at St. Jude State College in Ozone. Though forty-nine years old, Duk-Soo had the sensitivity of a teenager, making it something of a chore for Mrs. Coco to correct him when he played flat, which was often, or sharp, which was even more often. He took everything to heart, his full, fleshy face contracting with pain at the slightest hint of criticism. Unlike George Henry, who always found an excuse not to practice, Duk-Soo ground out his scales and arpeggios every day, bibliography or no bibliography, and yet he never improved. Several times in the past year Mrs. Coco had resolved to ease him out, turning the quartet into a trio, which meant everyone would earn a little more per concert. But every time she broached the topic, a look of such distress clouded the Korean's lovely dark eyes that she hadn't the heart to continue.

After unstrapping his violin from the basket in back, Duk-Soo, a stolid gentleman whose silver hair was obscured by a bulbous yellow helmet, stooped to chain the scooter to a lamppost before joining Mrs. Coco and her son beneath the smiling hamburger that beckoned motorists to the drive-in.

"How can you see out of that thing?" Mrs. Coco fussed as she wiped the helmet's visor with a tissue. Rain had been falling off and on since early morning, bringing no relief, though, to the summerlike spring, one day hotter, more oppressive, than the next. Seeing what looked like the rental stub attached to the lapel of Duk-Soo's baby-blue dinner jacket, she unpinned it while he lifted off the helmet.

"No, please," the Korean said as she tossed the stub and the tissue into a nearby garbage can.

It was a note to himself, he explained. Something he must not forget before going back to St. Jude.

"Duk-Soo, what . . . Get out of there," Mrs. Coco said as he rooted in the garbage can.

"Mother," George Henry said.

"Look what he's doing to his jacket."

"Leave him alone."

Inside the BurgerMat the large white globes hanging from the ceiling flicked on and off, then on again as Mr. Qumquist and two black teenagers walked out from behind the stainless steel counter. Seeing the musicians outside, he unlocked the front door and asked them to stop messing around with his sanitary receptacles.

More teenagers arrived—three large white girls crammed into the front seat of a compact pickup and a lone boy dropped off by his mother—as George Henry and Mrs. Coco hauled in the music stands from the trunk of the car. While they arranged these on a small dais near the french frier, Mr. Qumquist handed out mums to the teenagers, who were slipping beige tunics over their T-shirts and blouses. "Stick them on your *left* side," he said, thrusting four mums at Duk-Soo, who was just standing there, getting in everyone's way.

A few legitimate guests had already begun to trickle in—would-be customers were turned away at the door—and still there was no sign of the viola. Using a pay phone, Mrs. Coco got in touch with the viola's husband, who told her that Myrtice had left the house an hour ago, and no, he had no idea why she hadn't shown up yet. Mrs. Coco's left eye was twitching by the time she got off the phone, and it continued to twitch throughout a protracted welcoming speech delivered by Mayor Binwanger, who, some twenty years ago, had carried on a notorious adulterous affair with Helen Ann, Mrs. Coco's oldest girl, who was then only a college student. Mrs. Coco had nearly died of shame that summer, quitting her volunteer job as a fourth-grade catechism teacher and switching from the A&P to the Jitney Jungle, which had higher prices but fewer shoppers who recognized her. Yet here she was, forced to listen to Mayor Binwanger rattle on about the 'gator bug his grandson had tied a string around and flown like a kite—as if anyone cared. She had often wondered if it were possible to attend a public function, a party, even a movie, without seeing him, but like the psalmist who once asked, "Whither shall I flee from thy presence?" Mrs. Coco knew deep down that the question was only rhetorical.

"All right, boys," she said when the mayor had finally finished his speech. Duk-Soo and George Henry had squeezed themselves onto the wooden dais and were tuning to the A of Duk-Soo's tuning fork. "We'll start with the slow movement of the Haydn, then the Mozart and the Boccherini, and after Mr. Qumquist makes his speech, we'll do the medley from *Cats*. George Henry, are you listening?"

"Hm?"

"Oh, where is that woman?" Mrs. Coco muttered as she gouged a hole in the dais with her jackknife. "I could crown her. Now, after *Cats*," she went on, placing the steel peg of her cello securely in the hole she had dug, "I'm going to say a few words to introduce the next—"

"Ma, no."

"Quiet, heart. Let me think."

"No. I'm not going to play if you give a talk." George Henry's bloodshot eyes gazed sullenly at a shapely redhead who was showing her invitation to Mr. Qumquist at the door. "There's no reason you got to talk. What the hell do you know about hamburgers?"

"I'm not going to talk about hamburgers."

"Then can it. No one wants to be lectured about music tonight. And your jokes aren't funny anyway."

"I disagree," Duk-Soo said, glancing warily at her. "Last week at the Tomato Festival they laughed at her anecdote about the three B's."

"Hey, Duk, give me a break," George Henry said.

Mr. Qumquist, whose left ear, because of a birth defect, was nothing but a pinkish nub, walked over to the dais to inquire when they were going to begin. The teenagers were already serving hors d'oeuvres and drinks as the BurgerMat filled with the first citizens of Tula Springs and Eutaw, the town across the state line in Mississippi where they had the mall.

"Well actually," Mrs. Coco said, "we're waiting on—"

"For Christ's sakes," George Henry muttered. "We don't need her. Let's get this thing over with."

"By the way," Mr. Qumquist said, turning his good ear to her while keeping an eye on the crowd, "were you really Miss Mississippi once? There's a fella from Eutaw told me he recognized you."

Mrs. Coco went red all over. She had never actually been crowned Miss Mississippi, but two years in a row she had won the swimsuit category, an appalling thought to her now. To think that she had ever paraded half-naked in front of all those people, including her future husband.

"Y'all play nice," Mr. Qumquist said; then, turning to a sullen-looking girl with a purple streak in her hair, he snapped, "Robinette, where's them pigs in a blanket?"

As they launched into the Haydn, minus the viola, Mrs. Coco could tell right away that her son hadn't been practicing. When he was twelve, George Henry used to put in three, four hours a day on the violin, which had paid off when he won the Music Teachers National Association regional auditions. What dreams she had for him then: Juilliard, a Carnegie Hall debut, European concert tours—nothing was too good for her boy. But in his teens George Henry not only lost interest in the violin, he actually became ashamed of it, thanks to his brother Larry. Two years older than George Henry, Larry had gotten nowhere with music, even though he practiced the trombone every other day until he got too big for his mother's whippings to have much effect, other than to make him laugh. By conscientiously teasing his brother at least twice a week Larry had finally succeeded in making George Henry despise music. As for the other children, Mrs. Coco had spent a small fortune on various instruments, from the bassoon—an infatuation of Nancy's that lasted about as long as her marriage—to Helen Ann's brief flirtation with a build-it-yourself harpsichord, which never got built, much less played. It was a bitter pill for Mrs. Coco, this feckless waste of time and money. She had always hoped for gifted children, slightly disabled by artistic genius which she would nourish and protect. Instead, what she wound up with was one child, George Henry, who returned to the violin as a hobby when he began to drink too much.

In the middle of the Mozart the microphone on a second dais loaded with dyed carnations squeaked loudly. Holding up his hand at the musicians like a cop at an intersection, Mr. Qumquist rewelcomed the guests with a joke about a young lady who walked out into the woods at the Bogue Falaya State Park and got chased by a bear, but the park ranger wouldn't let her hop back into the tour bus because Louisiana state law doesn't allow ladies aboard public transportation with a bear behind them. Then, getting serious, Mr. Qumquist extolled the Tula Springs Chamber of Commerce and the tremendous vitality that he was certain the BurgerMat Corporation would infuse into the economic life of the Florida Parishes. After the applause from the hundred or so guests, some in black tie and long gowns, and a few more words from Mayor Binwanger, Mr. Qumquist stood up again and invited everyone to dance to the fine music of the Pro Arts Quartet.

The globe above Mrs. Coco's head dimmed, blurring the handwritten notes of *Cats*. Duk-Soo had made a fuss last week about playing this medley since he claimed that the arrangement for string quartet, written by a friend of George Henry's, a music major at L.S.U., was illegal; if AS-CAP caught the Pro Arts, they would be severely fined and blacklisted. Mrs. Coco was leaning over, telling him to quit worrying and play, when she felt a little stab in her side. Looking up, she saw it was Myrtice Fitt, the viola.

"Move on over, hon," Myrtice said, poking Duk-Soo with her bow as she edged past Mrs. Coco's cello.

"Where have you been?" Mrs. Coco said coldly. In her eyes Myrtice was nothing but a vain, petty local housewife with all the wrong values in life, and she would have avoided the woman like the plague if she didn't just happen to play the viola surprisingly well and in tune. She was wearing a stylish pale gown that must have cost a fortune, and her auburn hair shone with a rich, lustrous glow that was not at all appropriate for a sixty-year-old.

"You told me McDonald's," Myrtice said with a petulant flick of her gold charm bracelet.

"But there isn't a McDonald's in Tula Springs," Duk-Soo said.

"I know. I went clear to Eutaw looking for one."

"I never said McDonald's," Mrs. Coco said.

"You did so. I have a photogenic memory, Ethyl Mae, so don't try and deny it."

"I did not say McDonald's."

"You probably did, Ma," George Henry put in. "I mean like you told me McDonald's, too. The only reason I knew to come here was because I talked to Dad, and he said—"

"I never, no. Why on earth would I say . . ."

From across the room Mr. Qumquist made a sawing motion at Mrs. Coco, who told everyone they better start playing if they wanted to get paid. It upset her to think that George Henry was taking Myrtice's side, and as a result Mrs. Coco forgot she was in A flat and played D natural all through the medley while pondering how much she was going to dock Myrtice for being late.

2

❁

Like a patient awaiting the surgeon's knife, the cello rested stiffly on a sheet draped over the dining room table, a keen light from a Tensor lamp bearing down on the maple's warm flesh tones. In the kitchen Mrs. Coco stirred a batch of glue in a saucepan, preparatory to the operation, while her husband, off in the pantry, which was now his workroom, punctuated the silence with the unnerving serial music of his home computer. Plan after plan would be devised on the terminal, elegant schemes for getting his store out of the red, all of them hopeless, of course. The only thing that would save McNair's, Mr. Coco's men's clothing emporium, was to move it to the mall in Mississippi. But Mr. Coco could not abide the thought of working in that state, and so his store languished, dependent upon a few loyal customers who felt guilty enough to buy an expensive shirt or tie to go with the suits they got at the mall.

When the glue reached the right consistency, Mrs. Coco brought it into the dining room and adjusted the lamp so that it shone on the almost invisible crack in the seam. She had traipsed all over the state trying to get it fixed properly, but whatever repair was done lasted only a week or two before the humidity made the seams swell and the cello buzz as if there were a penny loose inside it. Dipping a butter knife into the warm glue, she launched into another session of home repair with trembling hands. Working like this always put her on edge, for the cello was old and fragile, an eighteenth-century French instrument that Manon herself, if there ever was such a woman, might have listened to. Mrs. Coco had bought it in 1959 from a failed waiter in New Orleans, who subsequently blossomed out happily as a Mary Kay Cosmetics representative. The money for the cello, five hundred dollars, had been earned by teaching manners at the migrant school, where many of her pupils, white children, were introduced to the fork.

"Mae."

Mrs. Coco gasped. "Louis, please," she said, wiping off some glue which had skidded onto the maple, "I've asked you not to creep up on me like that."

Mr. Coco regarded her soberly for a moment. He was a quiet, distinguished-looking seventy-year-old with a slightly salty air about him that hinted of a past connected with the sea. Since the closest he had ever got to the ocean was when he took the wrong bus to Bogalusa and ended up in Biloxi, this impression of him—aided and abetted by the town librarian, who, as she would tell any and all within hearing range, always saw his face before her when she curled up every January with *Two Years Before the Mast*, her favorite book in all the world—was ill founded. Mr. Coco didn't even like fish, which made it hard to feed him on Fridays since he insisted on these remaining no-meat days.

"What about The Early Bird?"

Mrs. Coco frowned at the clamp she was screwing onto the side of the cello. "Louis, dear, can't you see I'm busy?" The quartet had another engagement the next day, and she didn't want Myrtice making any more comments about the buzz.

"The Early Bird—it has a nice ring to it," he mused aloud.

Although he was only moderately tall, standing next to his wife, who was rather compact, made him seem outsize, almost freakish, to her way of thinking. Age had not shrunk him, as she had hoped, to more suitable proportions.

"What are you talking about?"

"For the store. I think it needs a more upbeat name . . . that's what's wrong." He tugged at his eyebrow, an annoying habit that she feared was going to give him cancer. "All these years I thought I had to call it McNair's just because everybody was used to that name. But that's what's wrong—they're so used to it they don't even see it anymore."

"But sug, 'The Early Bird'? What do birds have to do with clothes? They make me think of peas."

"Peas?"

"Move your hand. You'll get burned."

His large nail-bitten hand, knotted with purple veins, remained beside the kettle of glue. "You don't understand, Mae. 'The Early Bird' suggests industry, opportunity, optimism. It's very upbeat. It has vigor."

From force of habit Mrs. Coco's free hand sought the scapular beneath her house smock. She had bought the Scapular of Mt. Carmel twenty years ago when she enrolled in the Blue Army, a worldwide organization operating nationally out of Washington, New Jersey, that prayed to the Blessed Virgin of Fatima for the conversion of Russia. Lately, though, she had found it hard to concentrate on the U.S.S.R. and was using the brown scapular for more personal petitions, for patience, forbearance, and some understanding of the mysterious ways in which her husband's mind moved.

Mr. Coco's narrow brown eyes—they had once reminded her of Adolphe Menjou, whom she used to have a crush on—dimmed with resentment. "Must you always find a way to undermine me? 'Peas.' Can't you just once . . . Oh, never mind."

Mrs. Coco applied another clamp, which she would remove in the morning when the glue dried. Her husband's shadow was obscuring her view of the cello, but she kept her mouth shut, hoping he would go away.

"Mae, would you mind telling me what that accomplishment you wrote down yesterday is supposed to mean— 'Pulled nail out of window frame'?"

She had a screw in her mouth, so she wasn't able to reply right away. A list of daily accomplishments was one of the exercises recommended in the remaindered book he had given her for her birthday last week. Mr. Coco was a fervid believer in self-improvement, which, to his wife, seemed somehow at odds with Catholicism. All this trust in positive thinking disturbed her; try as she might, she just couldn't make it jibe with the Cross that the nuns had taught her to visualize upon her back, the Cross that each of us must bear in order to be saved. How her husband, who professed to be a Catholic, who, unlike her, was born into the Church and didn't have to struggle every day to believe in it in the correct manner, how he could talk so seriously about the necessity of firm handshakes, bright smiles, self-confidence, believing in yourself—oh, no, no, the Nicene Creed did not begin, "I believe in Myself," there was no "me" in it—all this baffled her. Yet to keep the peace, she allowed him to tack up a Daily List of Accomplishments in her laundry room beneath a sign he had posted stating that words such as *don't, never, cannot, impossible, not, none, deny, negative, hard, difficult, nil,* and *nay* no longer existed in the lexicon of Ethyl Mae Coco, Number One wife in America. (The sign had originally read "Housewife," but she had crossed out "House.")

"What are you pulling nails out of window frames for?" he asked, still hovering.

"I was always catching my sleeve on that nail in the kitchen window." She squinted down at the cello. "Please, sug, you're in my light."

"You leave the mechanical stuff to me," he said, starting to leave. "That's my department."

Yes, she thought. Like when you tried to fix the rattle in the dishwasher by moving the refrigerator to the other side of the room.

"What?" he said, pausing at the door. "Oh, by the way, George Henry, you know—I told you, didn't I?" He cleared his throat and wandered out of the room.

"George Henry what?" she called after him, but not very loudly. Any mention of her son these days put her stomach in knots. George Henry was supposed to have gotten married last Tuesday, a few days after the BurgerMat opening, but when Mrs. Coco held firm, refusing to attend the ceremony in Baton Rouge, he had canceled and set another date for early June.

After swallowing a Sominex, which she always kept handy to calm her nerves, she wondered whether she should go to the pantry to find out what news he had of George Henry. She got as far as the door, then paused at the sight of her husband's broad back hunched in front of the computer keyboard.

"OK, now what?" he asked.

Surprised by the tenderness in his voice, she was about to reply when she realized that it was the computer he was talking to.

"Thank you," he said gently after a pause.

She turned away from the door. Five bleeps evenly spaced sounded, five electronic tones that almost made a theme, a strange, disjointed melody that brought the light-year distances of outer space to mind and made the climb upstairs to her room, where she was preparing for the trip tomorrow, seem immense.

Myrtice, late as usual, still hadn't shown up. Duk-Soo sat in the kitchen eating a prune Danish that Mrs. Coco coveted, but annoyed with the flab on her thighs, she contented herself with coffee and chicory. The quartet had an engagement that morning at Norris State Hospital, about an hour's drive from Tula Springs. She always insisted that they use one car, not so much in order to save gas, but because it made her nervous when each went his own way. Of course, there would have to be an exception today. George Henry, when she had gotten him on the phone last night to make sense of the garbled message relayed by her husband, said he was going to drive directly from Baton Rouge to the hospital. And furthermore, he didn't have time to rehearse beforehand, and yes, he did realize they had never played the Borodin in public before, but he was too busy to come all the way to Tula Springs, and that was that.

"Hon, would you mind calling Dr. Fitt again?" Mrs. Coco asked Duk-Soo, who had phoned him just a few minutes ago. Dr. Fitt used to teach criminology at St. Jude State College but was retired now and lived with his wife at his mother's elegant house on Newt Drive. Myrtice was obsessed with this sprawling pink-brick house, which was much nicer than anything she or her husband could afford on their own. It was one of the highlights of the tour the Episcopal ladies made every year for Home Show and Garden Week, during which Mrs. Fitt, Myrtice's ninety-two-year-old mother-in-law, was forbidden to net crawdads in the ditch out front.

"I know, I know," Mrs. Coco said after Duk-Soo said he would rather not bother Dr. Fitt again so soon. "But he might have heard from her since."

While the Korean called from the living room, Mrs. Coco left the sink, where she was washing out the skim milk cartons she used to fashion toys for the underprivileged, and ate the other prune Danish he had brought with him from the BurgerMat. She had decided that she was more concerned about his blood pressure—he was looking a little chunky—than her thighs.

"You sure you had two?" she said when Duk-Soo returned to the kitchen and inquired about the disappearance of his second Danish. "Well, never mind about that. What did Dr. Fitt say?"

"It was in the bag," he said, peering again inside the empty white bag before riffling through a briefcase filled with colored organizers.

"I told Myrtice nine-thirty," she said, pouring herself another cup of coffee. It was difficult to be alone with Duk-Soo. Conversation did not come naturally, and were it not for the coffee, his earnestness and desire to please would have overpowered her will to stay awake. She still did not quite understand how anyone could get a PhD in tourism, but every time she expressed an interest, he would drone on in such detail about how tourism was really a fascinating array of cross-disciplinary studies—ranging from sociology and religious studies to anthropology and linguistics—that she would have to fight off an urge to scream. Aside from his pronouncements on tourism—and politics, which she never liked to discuss, maybe because it reminded her of Mayor Binwanger—Duk-Soo seemed to hold no views of his own. This morning, while waiting for Myrtice, she had tried to get him to make up his mind what sort of frozen pizza he liked best, plain or the type with French bread, but he kept hedging his bet, as if there were a right and a wrong answer. She now returned to the question, hoping it would offer some distraction.

"They are both very delicious. You are perhaps planning to serve us some for lunch today?"

"No, Duk-Soo, this is a purely hypothetical question. I want you to learn how to give a straight answer. It's very important; you can't go through life equivocating. Now tell me, speak straight from the heart, *your* heart: plain or French bread?"

"Plain?"

"Why do you put a question mark after it? Say, 'plain.'"

"Plain."

Eventually, after casting futilely about for livelier topics of conversation, and having genetic engineering and igloos meet the same dull fate as pizza, Mrs. Coco was rescued by the sound of voices in the driveway.

"Bring me back some jumbo eggs, the brown kind!" Mrs. Fitt, Myrtice's mother-in-law, called out after depositing Myrtice in front of the house. Mrs. Fitt drove a long, fancy Oldsmobile with an "I love the J.C. Penney catalog" bumper sticker.

"Eggs," Myrtice grumbled as Mrs. Coco held open the front door. "As if I don't have enough on my mind as it is. Hello, Duk-Soo."

Duk-Soo and Mrs. Coco had already tuned up on the back porch, where the rusted screen was so overrun with cross vine and honeysuckle that even on sunny days a lamp was needed in order to see properly. It was damp out here, but cooler than in the living room, which was too large for an air-conditioner, at Louisiana Power and Light rates. The Cocos had an air-conditioner in the master bedroom, and that was it.

"So George Henry's in a snit," Myrtice said after Mrs. Coco informed her that he wasn't showing up to rehearse. "Well, I can't see as I blame the boy."

"If you don't mind, Myrtice, let's stick to business," Mrs. Coco said, peering at the mirror taped to the inside of her cello case. Her foundation was dried and caked. Well, that does it, she thought; no more bargain makeup from that roadside stand by the snake ranch. She would go to Holmes at the mall for some Estée Lauder.

The Borodin was difficult, and Duk-Soo kept on coming in a measure early, at letter C. Mrs. Coco's white blouse was soon dark under the arms, while Myrtice, chewing a sugarless gum in time to the beat, her charm bracelet rattling as she bowed, somehow managed to stay cool as a cucumber. Unable to bear the rattle or Duk-Soo's mistakes, Mrs. Coco stepped outside for a moment, ostensibly to check and see if her husband had put the coals out properly last night on the barbecue pit. Hidden by a chinaberry, she drew a single cigarette from her pocket, the first she had smoked in over five years. The pleasure was immense, too immense, really; she had hoped in the back of her mind that she might be repulsed by the taste, as hypnotherapy had suggested. It was all George Henry's fault, this relapse. If he didn't insist on trampling upon all her hard-earned beliefs, making a mockery of everything she held sacred, she was sure she wouldn't be such a bundle of nerves.

"Y'all want to know something?" she said when she returned to the porch, having popped a Sominex into her mouth for good measure. "I just don't think we're ready for the Borodin yet. Let's do the Boccherini instead."

"No, Ethyl Mae," Myrtice said. "This is a good chance to try it out in front of an audience. After all, they're all retarded. They won't know the difference."

"Not retarded," Duk-Soo said, leaning over to check his hair in the cello case mirror. "Norris State Hospital is primarily for autistic and emotionally disturbed juveniles. It is situated on twelve and a half acres of wooded property, a former sugar cane plantation belonging at one time, if I'm not mistaken, to the Freydaux family."

"You've been reading up on this," Myrtice said.

"I always like to know where I'm going," he said, arranging a silver lock. Glancing suspiciously at the mirror, Mrs. Coco noticed with a slight tremor of distaste that Duk-Soo, sitting there with his back to her, was indeed looking at her, not his hair. This was not the first time she had felt him staring at her with a look of almost disapproval on his face. She made a mental note to speak to him about it someday when they were alone, because it was really quite rude and made her feel as if she had crumbs or something on her face.

"I don't intend to break down in front of *any* audience, disturbed or not," Mrs. Coco said, wondering if it was the caked foundation Duk-Soo had been staring at; or maybe there *was* a Danish crumb on her chin. "We'll play the Boccherini."

"All right," Myrtice said, yanking off a loose hair on her bow, "have it your way. But I bet if George Henry were here—"

"Well, he isn't."

Myrtice ran her bow over a cake of rosin wrapped in blue velvet. "Yes, he isn't—all because you believe in the Pope."

"I don't know what the Pope has to do with it. It's *me* who doesn't believe in second marriages."

"Like Larry's, right?"

"Right. I don't believe in his, either."

"Well, hon, no one's asking you to believe in them. All George Henry wants is for his mom to bring her bod and set it down in a pew for a few minutes. He's not asking for a big reception or anything like his brother got."

Outside the quartet Mrs. Coco and Myrtice hardly socialized at all, so it was disturbing to have her poking her nose where it didn't belong. Myrtice had attached herself to a group of country-club ladies who had maids and gave luncheons that were written up in the paper. Aside from the Rosary Altar Society, a self-imposed duty, Mrs. Coco had no need of such social entanglements to complicate her life. What with raising six children and practicing the cello and improving her mind with the Great Books, she simply hadn't the time to cultivate any of the shallow relationships that Myrtice seemed so proud of.

"Oh, I just remembered," Myrtice said. "Can I use your phone?"

Mrs. Coco didn't bother to reply as Myrtice rested her viola on the wicker chair. Suffering from some sort of minor kidney ailment, Myrtice made use of a whole repertoire of euphemisms to excuse herself in company. "Can I use your phone?" was an old war-horse, almost as popular as "I need a breath of fresh air." While she was gone, Mrs. Coco brought out a plate of week-old Rice Krispies marshmallow squares which she couldn't bring herself to throw out.

"Please," she urged when Duk-Soo held up a broad hand in front of the plate.

"I can't, really."

"Come on, you need to keep up your strength."

With a dim smile the Korean reached for the smallest square.

Ten minutes later, when Myrtice still hadn't appeared, Mrs. Coco decided to investigate. Company was only allowed on the first floor, where Mrs. Coco had managed, on a very limited budget, to subdue the too-large, dank, Victorian space with a semblance of taste and refinement, relying mainly on furniture that Mr. Coco had been awarded when he sued his wife's brother and sister for tampering with their father's will. Large as it was, the Coco home was actually only half a house. The original building, a boarding-house for workers in a nonpareil factory, had been sawn in half to make room for the Bessie Building next door, the largest office building in Tula Springs, noted specially for its marble camels' hitching posts. The camels, imported by an enterprising young Yankee who thought they might be just the right sort of beast for Louisiana's climate, had hauled a few bricks for a construction company before expiring of disease and homesickness shortly after the Bessie Building was finished in 1922. Other stores and offices had grown up around the Bessie Building, completely surrounding the Coco house, which remained the only private residence in the business district, except for a few apartments above the Sonny Boy Bargain Store.

Straightening a nylon Navaho rug whose colors picked up the yellows and orange of a print of New England woods in autumn, Mrs. Coco rapped on the door of the bathroom situated beneath a handsome black oak staircase that led into a wall—this was where the house was sawn—and then peeked inside and saw the closet was empty. With an "oh" of irritation she hurried up a second, narrower staircase to the floor where none of the colors were coordinated. The worst room, the one Larry and George Henry had shared, was adorned by a charred mattress on Larry's wagon-wheel bed. This was meant to remind Larry, when he visited with whoever happened to be his wife at the moment, of the day he had returned stone-cold sober from high-school graduation and called his father a Dago while George Henry was upstairs sneaking a cigarette. Since it wasn't Larry who was responsible for the fire—George Henry had hidden the cigarette under his blanket when Helen Ann burst into the room— Mrs. Coco didn't quite understand the logic behind all this; but Mr. Coco, not exactly renowned in the household for his rationality, insisted that the charred mattress stay. Poking her head into the room, Mrs. Coco checked to see that the old *Boys' Life* magazines covered the charred spot, which Mr. Coco didn't want any sheets or blankets hiding.

Myrtice was eventually discovered, but only after Mrs. Coco had wandered through Helen Ann's old room (a candy wrapper on the floor: so Mr. Coco was sneaking candy again, after he had promised . . .); Lucy's gloomy den, bare except for a magazine photo of Susan Sontag; Sam's octagonal room—he was in Banff now, studying weaving . . . she must finish her letter to him warning him not to try salmon fishing (a documentary about grizzlies the night before had worried her, especially since Sam was so trusting of anything that was natural); and Nancy's old room, where she found a whole pile of candy wrappers in a flowered wastebasket— ten, no, eleven! She carried these as evidence into the master bedroom, where Myrtice was perched on the edge of the new Craftmatic Adjustable Bed, which Mrs. Coco could not look at without seeing red.

"I'm waiting for the Citizens Patrol to call me back," Myrtice said, putting down the book she had been leafing through.

"There's a phone downstairs, you know." Up until now Mrs. Coco had succeeded in keeping Myrtice from inspecting the upstairs; fortunately she had vacuumed yesterday.

"It's personal. I didn't want to be disturbed, Ethyl Mae."

"Is anything the matter?"

"I'd rather not discuss it," Myrtice replied, fingering the ivory brooch on the flat side of her chest. The previous year Myrtice had undergone a radical mastectomy, which nearly resulted in her and Mrs. Coco's becoming friends. The day before the operation Mrs. Coco had held her in her arms while Myrtice wept. But after the operation Myrtice seemed to go out of her way to deny this intimacy, working extra hard at being vapid and aloof. Seeing her now, though, looking a little helpless and demoralized on that idiotic, extravagant contraption of a bed, Mrs. Coco felt a pang of regret. Maybe she had been too hard on her. Who knew what the woman might be going through?

"I'll be downstairs," Mrs. Coco said, frowning at the battered book Myrtice had been glancing at, *29 Ways to Have Wholesome Fun With Your Son*. Mr. Coco had brought it down from the attic the other day, although why he wanted to remind himself of all the fights occasioned by that volume—Larry used to cry when his father made him play one of the tedious games suggested by the PhD author to improve posture and coordination—was beyond her.

Downstairs Mrs. Coco couldn't resist picking up the hall extension when the phone rang. After all, she reasoned as she gingerly lifted the receiver, it was her house; it might be a call for her.

". . . and another thing," she heard Myrtice say to the Citizens Patrol, "I don't want you touching those tuna croquettes. They're for my DAR steering committee, you understand?"

"I'm not wearing no wig, DAR or no DAR," said the voice on the other end of the line. It was Myrtice's mother-in-law, not the Citizens Patrol. Being a practical woman, Mrs. Fitt, a sufferer from scalp itch, got a crewcut once a month at the Tiger Unisex, where she was the only female customer.

"Now Mrs. Fitt," Myrtice said, her voice trembling, "I was on my hands and knees waxing last night, and I'm not going to have you ruin everything by—"

Her curiosity satisfied, Mrs. Coco cradled the receiver and headed back to the porch. Poor Myrtice, her life was so boring she had to pretend she was involved with the law. And when she came downstairs, she was sure to act mysterious and vague, Mrs. Coco told herself. The poor woman.

Charity demanded that Mrs. Coco keep her mouth shut about the Citizens Patrol, and so she managed to do after she and Myrtice had packed themselves and their instruments into Mrs. Coco's eighteen-year-old green Dodge Dart.

"What a funny man," Myrtice commented as they waited for Duk-Soo, who was covering his scooter with a plastic tarp in case it rained. "Weird."

"I think he's nice-looking," Mrs. Coco said, not because she thought much of his looks; she just didn't feel like agreeing with Myrtice.

"The way he goes on about the Russians."

"Well, we can't let them get ahead of us, Myrtice. We need those bombs."

"Oh, I know, the Russians are horrible and all, but still . . . You really think he's nice-looking?" she asked as Duk-Soo trudged past the vegetable garden, which had been ruined by too much rain. Without waiting for a reply Myrtice started in on how people like him gave Republicans a bad name, but Mrs. Coco, irked by politics, tuned her out. Her gaze wandered to the manure Mr. Coco had been forced to buy for the garden, it was such a bargain. Flowering weeds had sprung from the pile he had promised to spread a month ago. In the shed opposite the neon sign for the College of Beauty and Charm next door there were two bushels of rotting Maine potatoes—another bargain he couldn't afford to pass up. Was that man ever going to learn?

"Can you believe— Look at her hair," Myrtice said as the beauty operator who gave Mrs. Coco a ten percent discount walked across the street to put change in the parking meter beside her Cadillac. "Looks like she got her head stuck in a cotton-candy machine."

Mrs. Coco was tempted to say something about Bishop's House of Beauty, which cost twice as much as the beauty college, although you wouldn't know it from looking at those blotches in Myrtice's hair. Highlights, Myrtice called them.

"Oh, Lord." Myrtice sighed, her eyes glazing from a stifled yawn. "I wish that slowpoke would hurry up."

Behind the Korean, who continued to trudge toward the car with a look of grim determination, the widow's walk on the old boardinghouse seemed to list slightly as a fault cracked the cloud-laden, stone-gray sky; for a moment Duk-Soo and the house had shadows, but then the sky closed.

"By the way, did you ever reach the Citizens Patrol?" Mrs. Coco heard herself say. Well, she had *tried* to keep quiet.

"No, dear, I didn't," Myrtice said as Duk-Soo climbed into the back seat. "There seemed to be some sort of strange interference on the line. I hope you can get it fixed."

3
❁

Surprisingly small and homey-looking for a public institution, Norris State Hospital was tucked into a bend of the Mississippi, whose swollen, churning waters, higher this spring than ever before, were hidden from view by a grassy levee, upon which a lone grayish cow wandered ghostlike in a steady drizzle. Huddled beneath an oak in the asphalt-covered playground, Myrtice, George Henry, and Duk-Soo, who had unfolded a rain hat to protect his hair, watched warily as a burly girl laid into a tire swing with a spatula. "Bad, bad, bad!" the unfortunate girl screamed as Mrs. Coco gazed down on the scene from the second floor of the plantation house where the hospital administrators had their offices. She was annoyed with her colleagues for acting so childish, gaping like that at the poor girl instead of going over and getting her out of the rain. After all, this wasn't the first institution they had played in. As a strict Catholic, Mrs. Coco felt compelled to tithe the Pro Arts's services to nursing homes and hospitals, especially when paying engagements were scarce. It was a good opportunity for them to keep in shape before an audience while offering themselves to God. Of course, George Henry and Myrtice claimed they weren't playing for God, they were playing for themselves, but Mrs.

Coco, with a Levite's indifference to what the sacrificial oxen might think about the matter, offered them up anyway.

"Come here, Ray Jr., come here, boy."

Dr. Jewel, Program Director at Norris, coaxed the teen-ager over to his desk and then collared the boy's thick neck with a pale freckled arm. Ray Jr. yelped with delight as the doctor administered noogies to the boy's cropped head. Turning from the window, Mrs. Coco adjusted the scapular beneath her blouse while trying to smile at the doctor's rather juvenile behavior.

"You gonna be a good boy, Ray Jr.?" the doctor said in a whiny voice. "You gonna be a good boy, son?"

Ray Jr. was a husky lad, much bigger than the doctor, but he let himself be manhandled like a puppy in a child's clumsy arms. Dr. Jewel gave Mrs. Coco a wink, obliging her to smile back at him again. Two-toned, with orange side-burns topped by gray wiry hair, the doctor had rubbed her the wrong way ever since he had introduced the Pro Arts Quartet this morning in the dining hall as the Professional Arts Quartet, which was famous for having played in every single parish in the state—a blatant falsehood, since if he had bothered to ask her and not Myrtice, Mrs. Coco would have informed him that they had appeared so far in only seven parishes. Then he went on to tell the children that the quartet only played music by very, very famous composers who had statues made of them, and if anyone in the au-dience felt any hostility, he or she was free to spend the next hour in the Animal Lounge.

"Give me five, Ray Jr."

Ray Jr. and Dr. Jewel exchanged complicated hand slaps; then the doctor's eyes narrowed, and his freckled face, mapped now by tense boundary lines, took on a distant look. Without a word Ray Jr. got up off his lap and latched on to a steam pipe behind the desk.

"This good lady here is fixing to take you out to lunch, Ray

Jr. Now you know she's an artist, boy, a real artist. You always wanted to meet up with a real artist, right?"

"Yes, sir. I want to learn how to paint babies."

Dr. Jewel contemplated the terrarium on his desk, where a box turtle languished beneath a yellowed fern. "Listen up, Ray Jr. She's not that kind of artist. She's the kind that plays things, so don't bother her none about painting babies, understand?"

"Sir, yes, sir."

"You do what she tells you. She's the boss, Miss Coca's the boss. That's your sergeant there, Ray Jr. You don't mess with the sergeant."

Mrs. Coco was about to say that it really wasn't necessary to think of her as a sergeant, when Dr. Jewel gave her a stern look.

"Dismissed," he barked. Somewhat taken aback, Mrs. Coco clutched her purse and headed for the door.

"Private Ray Jr., dismissed," Dr. Jewel said, frowning at her. "Sergeant Coca, remain please."

"It's very fine of you to offer to take Ray Jr. out," he said after the boy had left the room. "His daddy wasn't able to come get him this Easter 'cause he got parasites. I like to see Ray Jr. get out as much as possible. Merrit and me, that's my wife, we took him to that new Santa Land they got up the river, and then there's this old Jew down the road visits him twice a week. Sometimes they go to the movies if there's a calm picture playing, but they don't make too many of them nowadays."

"What do you mean by parasites?"

The doctor picked up a pen and began doodling on the turtle's back. "Real fine of you to let the boy try out your cello after the concert, Miss Coca. A lot of folks would be more fussy about their instrument." With his middle finger he pushed his smoked aviator glasses up his bony nose. "Course you know I'm breaking all sorts of rules and regulations letting you take him out. The Big Cheese wouldn't like it," he added, jerking his thumb in the direction of the Executive Director's office.

"Well, if you think I shouldn't, then maybe . . ." She felt she should remind him that it was he, not herself, who had suggested taking Ray Jr. out to lunch. She had gone along with the idea only because she hated to disappoint the boy, who seemed excited by the prospect. But before she brought up this point, she was anxious to clear up another matter: "Now, Dr. Jewel, was it the father or the boy who got para—"

"Let the Big Cheese scream," he said, slamming his hand down on the desk; the turtle's tail retracted. "To me what counts is people—first, number one, people, and to hell with all your goddam petty rules and regulations. Christ, far as I'm concerned, they could shut down this whole shiteating place tomorrow a.m. and I wouldn't give a rat's ass. Think I couldn't get another job like that?" He snapped his fingers.

"Perhaps it would be better," she said, glancing nervously out the window at her colleagues, who were now watching the live oak get spanked, "it might be better if I came back another time for Ray Jr. What do you think?"

"Good, drop him off at Annex B when you're through," he said, rummaging in his desk drawer. "And here," he added, handing her a white pill, "make sure he takes this after lunch."

"Doctor, I don't know if I should . . ." She regarded the pill in her hand. "Perhaps it'd be better if you administered it now."

"Oh, it's nothing," he said, jerking himself out of his chair. "Just a little Mellaril to help him relax. Hey, you!" he barked, poking his head out the door.

A tiny girl in a starched pink dress continued to clump down the hall in cowboy boots, following a dazed-looking college-age boy.

"Get that helmet on, kid," Dr. Jewel said.

The boy, who had a button pinned to his T-shirt ("Sigma Chi Cares"), turned and crammed a football helmet over the girl's curly white hair, while Ray Jr., who had been standing at attention beside a fire extinguisher, looked anxiously at the cello case Mrs. Coco carried out of the office.

Myrtice was already installed in the front seat of the Dart, so Mrs. Coco put Ray Jr. in back with Duk-Soo. It had taken them a few minutes to get to the car since Ray Jr. had to stop off in his room to change into his eating-out shirt, a baggy olive affair with golfers on it. As Myrtice glued on her fingernails, which she couldn't wear when she played, she told Mrs. Coco that George Henry had driven on to the ferry landing, where he said there was a restaurant that had terrific lamb chops.

"Ray Jr., you remember everybody, right?" Mrs. Coco said as she pulled out onto the road that paralleled the levee. "This is Mrs. Fitt . . ."

"We've met," Myrtice said, blowing on an oyster-pink nail.

"And beside you is the man who plays second violin. Mr. Yoon, maybe you'd like to take off your hat?"

"Huh?" Duk-Soo felt his head and, discovering the see-through rain hat, untied it with haste.

"And please don't sit on the maps."

Mrs. Coco drove slowly, fearing that one of the cows grazing on the levee might suddenly decide to jump out in front of them. Glancing in the rearview mirror, she saw Ray Jr. hunched against the door and requested that he sit up straight since the lock might be defective. Then she asked Myrtice to give him one of the TravelWipes in the glove compartment so he could refresh his hands and face (what *did* that doctor mean by parasites?), but the lock on the glove compartment was jammed, and Myrtice couldn't open it.

They drove in silence for a few miles while Myrtice sulked

and blew on her nails and Duk-Soo muttered over his bibliography. Mrs. Coco could understand Myrtice's behavior—she had her nose out of joint because they had to have lunch with a schizophrenic—but Duk-Soo, well, she was surprised at him. She thought he, unlike certain small-minded individuals, would make some effort to put the boy at ease.

"Look, isn't that a pretty tree?" she said, craning her neck around to smile at the boy.

"Yes, ma'am," he said as they passed a moss-laden pecan.

"I swear, Ethyl Mae," Myrtice grumbled, "you got to go two miles an hour?"

"You know Mr. Banks, the man who delivers the dry cleaning? He told me his cousin was driving through Idaho and a deer jumped out and came through the windshield and its legs sliced his wife's head clean off, just like a guillotine."

"I just saw Mrs. Banks the other day at the Piggly Wiggly."

"The cousin's wife, not Mr. Banks's wife. You've got to realize, Myrtice, everything becomes razor-sharp at sixty miles an hour." She felt a tap on her shoulder. "What?"

"They's following us," Ray Jr. whispered in her ear. "Oh, my God, they's following us."

In the rearview mirror Mrs. Coco glimpsed the pickup that had been tailgating them. "Sit back, Ray Jr.," she said as she stuck her hand out the window and signaled for the truck to pass. When the pickup pulled into the left lane, she noticed that a horse trailer was attached to it, and figuring that it would never make it around her with that load, she pressed down on the gas to get ahead again. Ray Jr. moaned softly as the truck blasted them from the barrel of a shiny horn mounted on the hood.

"Do you think this rain will ever end, Mr. Yoon?" Mrs. Coco asked, ignoring the vulgar honks. She was more concerned about the Mississippi, swollen by unrelenting spring rains to record-breaking heights. Tula Creek, which fed into the Mississippi, had twice overflowed its banks in April, forcing some of Tula Springs' citizens to sleep on Red Cross cots in the high-school gym. Luckily North Gladiola, where the Cocos lived, was high enough to escape the worst of the flooding. There had been some unacceptable water levels in their yard, though, because Mrs. Coco had come out one morning to get the paper and discovered in a small puddle near her Jerusalem cherry a dead armadillo, drowned, no doubt, even though the puddle wasn't that deep.

"Mr. Yoon?"

Duk-Soo looked up from the yellow notecards that covered his lap and half the back seat. "Pardon me?" He adjusted the paisley scarf which he claimed was a Gucci, but which Myrtice, who owned the only real Gucci in Tula Springs, insisted was a fraud. "No, it will stop sometime. How do you do?" he added with a nod toward Ray Jr. before returning to his cards.

Failing to draw Duk-Soo away from his bibliography so that he could entertain the boy, Mrs. Coco took the burden on her own shoulders. "What you heard this morning, Ray Jr., was a composition by a man named Wolfgang Amadeus Mozart, M-O-Z-A-R-T, who lived hundreds of years ago at a time when musicians were lumped into the same class with servants. Mozart was a certifiable genius, Ray Jr., yet he, like his friend Haydn, H-A-Y-D-N, no E, was expected to sit down at the servants' table with the maids and dishwashers and—"

"We know, we know," Myrtice put in. "You already said all this in your speech this morning."

"Anything worth saying is worth saying twice."

"Speed up," Myrtice said, pressing her foot to the floor, "we're going past the lepers."

"Hansen's disease," Duk-Soo said without looking up from his cards. "I believe that is the preferred nomenclature. A student of mine wrote her term paper on Carville. I awarded her a B plus."

Slowing down a little to gaze at the vast, genial grounds of the National Hansen's Disease Center, complete with golf course and a softball diamond, all empty now except for a lone cat patrolling the fence, Mrs. Coco experienced a small thrill of Biblical horror. For a moment, while the pickup tried again to pass, she became absorbed in imagining a new holy card popular with uniformed schoolchildren. On the card was a woman in white straddling a cello while lepers, their faces rapt with a strange beauty, crowded close for a touch. "Oh, girl," she softly chided herself, wondering how she could be so juvenile.

"Hurry," Myrtice said.

Mrs. Coco obliged, leaving behind the pickup, which once again had failed to pass.

"Oh, my God, my God," Ray Jr. murmured as the honking blasted them again.

Perched on top of the levee, they looked below for George Henry's Toyota, and when they didn't see it, Myrtice began to wonder aloud if they were at the right landing. Perhaps George Henry had meant the one at White Castle? Duk-Soo said there was no restaurant at White Castle. Myrtice, glancing disdainfully at the Red Top Café a few yards from the ferry dock, said there didn't seem to be any restaurant here, either, while Mrs. Coco worried about the steep incline down the levee on the oystershell road. What if the brakes failed? They would plow straight into the line of cars waiting for the ferry to arrive. While the three of them all talked at once, Ray Jr. stuck his head out the window to get a better view of the ferry, which had begun its return journey by cutting diagonally across the swift current.

"Well, you can't sit here all day," Myrtice said when the

cars behind them began to honk. Pulling out her parking brake a click or two, Mrs. Coco began the descent.

They found a space beneath a diseased cottonwood, far enough away from the dock where the cars would load and unload. Unlocking the trunk (they did not want to leave the instruments there because of the heat and thieves, which were everywhere nowadays), Mrs. Coco started to worry about germs—did they wash the dishes properly at the Red Top?—and about George Henry—could he have had an accident along the way?—and continued to worry as she lugged the cello inside the dimly lit café, a Quonset hut with portholes instead of windows.

"Did I lock up the car?" she asked, collapsing into a chair beneath a porthole Myrtice was trying to crank open. Duk-Soo, absorbed in the menu, did not reply. Aside from two old men seated near a pool table with a gash in it, there were no other customers for the nine- or ten-year-old behind the cash register to keep an eye on. Clad in a grimy purple tank top, the sunburned child—Mrs. Coco wasn't sure if it was a boy or a girl—stared dully into the gloom while working a toothpick.

"What do you suppose happened to him?" Mrs. Coco asked, wiping the Formica table with a TravelWipe.

"Oh, pooh," Myrtice said, sticking out her tongue at the porthole, which wouldn't budge.

"Duk-Soo," Mrs. Coco said, taking the greasy menu from him, "what do you suppose happened to—"

"Isn't that him out by the river?" Myrtice said, settling into a chair with a lurid swordfish painted on its back. "Now where's the waitress? I'm starved."

"George Henry? What's he doing out there?"

"Not him. The psycho."

"Oh, Lord." Mrs. Coco knew she had forgotten something; it was Ray Jr. Sidling by her cello case, which stood upright on its own, she hurried outside past a long line of cars to the dock where Ray Jr., his golf shirt ballooning in the breeze, stood stiff as a scarecrow, one arm raised in an arrested gesture of some sort. When Mrs. Coco approached, a mottled gull perched on a piling spread its wings and without a flap let the wind carry it away.

"The air," Ray Jr. exclaimed, his dark blue eyes shining with excitement, "look at the air!"

Anger, as well as the brisk walk, made Mrs. Coco's heart thump fast and hard. That darn doctor had no business trusting a patient with people like Myrtice and herself. Here Myrtice had been staring right at the boy all this time—who knows what he might have been contemplating?—and she hadn't said anything until the last minute. With a sick feeling Mrs. Coco looked down at the café au lait water, where a branch covered with desiccated leaves and toilet paper lurched upriver in a contrary side current.

"Hon, it's time to eat," she said. Tires roped to the pilings thudded in the wake of a barge heading down to New Orleans.

"I want to know the humidity," he said, staring hard at her. For a moment doubt and fear seemed to get the better of him. It was the same look she had noticed during the concert as he sat in the front row, more frightened than pleased by the music. Several times during the Mozart he had covered his extraordinary eyes—they were such a deep greenish blue—with his hands, like a girl at a horror movie.

"It's Mrs. Coco, heart—remember?" she said, taking his hand.

"Sergeant Coca," he barked, imitating Dr. Jewel almost perfectly. "She's the boss, Ray Jr. Better not mess with the boss."

"Do you like weather?" she asked as they trudged up the hill toward the café. "Is that why you want to know the humidity?" His grip was warm and moist and surprisingly powerful.

"I love it, Sergeant Coca. I've read every book in the library on clouds, and when my daddy comes, he's going to bring me all the books they got on heaven. Oh, look!"

"What?" she asked, a little alarmed.

"Oh, oh," he moaned happily, but all she could see were the bored, restless faces behind the windshields of the cars waiting for the ferry.

Myrtice had ordered a Manhattan on the rocks from the child at the cash register while Mrs. Coco was down by the river, and was already halfway through it when they returned. Ray Jr. wouldn't sit down at the table until Mrs. Coco assured him—by opening it up—that no one was hiding inside her cello case. After that he acted about as normal as one can expect a teenager to act and occupied himself with the pickled pig's foot Mrs. Coco had bought him; prodding and poking it with a half-eaten Slim Jim, he occasionally held it up in front of Duk-Soo, hoping to scare him. Duk-Soo was anxious to order, but the child had told him that they would have to order food from the food waitress, who was out back buying a used shock absorber from this man.

"I'm worried about George Henry," Mrs. Coco said, wondering why lamb chops were not on the menu. "What are you going to have, Myrtice?"

"A BLT."

"This New England clam chowder looks good," Mrs. Coco said, hoping to steer her away from a sandwich. Myrtice always took her sandwiches apart and rearranged them so nothing stuck out; it drove Mrs. Coco nuts.

"I only eat Manhattan-style chowder. And stop worrying about George Henry. If there were an accident, we would have seen it. He's probably just gone on ahead to a filling station or something."

"I wonder what their Wiener schnitzel is like," Duk-Soo mused aloud, waving away the pig's foot in his face.

Mrs. Coco peeked at the mirror in her handbag to check her foundation and noticed the pill the doctor had given her. She was afraid to give it to Ray Jr. and afraid not to, so for the time being she clutched it in her fist.

"Oh, good," Mrs. Coco said as a worn, bedraggled teenager in jeans approached their table. Mrs. Coco had seen her kind before: prematurely aged by years of drudgery on a farm or behind a five-and-dime counter, they were a hopeless lot, oppressed by shiftless, sexist husbands and the inevitable passel of diapered brats. Her heart went out to this poor waitress, and she determined to leave a generous tip even if the service was—as it undoubtedly would be—bad.

"Good afternoon, dear," Mrs. Coco said. "There's four of us for luncheon today. This weather is something, isn't it?"

"God, is it ever," the waitress said, pulling up a swordfish chair. Mrs. Coco stiffened. Why was it that when one gave them an inch, the lower classes invariably took a yard?

"You were thinking about the chowder, weren't you?" Mrs. Coco said to Myrtice, hoping to move things along.

"Where'd you get that drink?" the waitress asked Myrtice, wiping raindrops from her pasty face with veined, mannish-looking hands. "I could sure use something to forget this weather."

"The child over there."

Suddenly the pasty face broke into a vague approximation of a smile. "Well, so we finally meet," she said to Myrtice, "and like it didn't kill you or anything, right? I've heard so much about you, it's like the minute I walked in, I said to myself, that's her, that's just got to be my George Henry's mama."

Mrs. Coco clenched the TravelWipe she was using to clean the silverware. So this was Heidi, the hot-tub salesperson. Thirty-five if she was a day, pockmarked, too tall, and pudgy, to boot, this was the girl George Henry couldn't live without. And Connie, his ex-wife, who looked fresh as a daisy and had doctors and dentists begging her to marry them, Connie wasn't good enough for him.

"Oh, darling," Mrs. Coco said, beaming as hard as she could, "what a nice surprise. George Henry didn't tell me you'd be coming. *I'm* Mrs. Coco, by the way," she said, awkwardly extending her left hand; the right had the pill in it.

"You? But you're so thin," Heidi said. "I never imagined you'd be so thin and young-looking."

In spite of herself Mrs. Coco could not smother the soft, furry pleasure the remark gave her, especially when she saw how stricken Myrtice looked. With all her Scarsdale dieting, Myrtice was still on the plump side.

Unable to bear any compliment not directed at her, Myrtice tried to dilute it with a torrent of happy words: Where did you get that cute little accent? she asked Heidi, and when Heidi informed her she was from Babylon, Long Island, Myrtice said she had been to Long Island once by accident with the DAR. They were trying to get to the Statue of Liberty, but their cabdriver had just come over the day before from Albania and took them to Queens instead, so they had to take a public bus back to Manhattan Island, which is where she bought this scarf she had on, at Gucci's on Fifth Avenue, where they make you feel like dirt for wanting to buy something from them. And did Heidi ever notice how many bicycles in New York had their front wheels stolen right off them? Why would anyone want to steal a wheel?

"Where is George Henry?" Mrs. Coco asked Heidi.

"I don't know. He told me to meet him here."

"My name is Mr. Yoon," Duk-Soo said, extending his hand across the table.

"I'm sorry," Mrs. Coco said. "Mr. Yoon is our second violin, and that's . . . Ray Jr., enough. Put that foot down, heart."

A hoarse blast from the ferry alerted the two grizzled men on the other side of the café; they got up and left. Mrs. Coco, finding no more compliments coming her way from Heidi of Babylon, wished she, too, had an excuse to get up and leave. The meal ahead promised to be such a trial, and she really shouldn't drink, not with all the driving left.

"Go get the food waitress, hon," Myrtice said to Duk-Soo, while Mrs. Coco surreptitiously popped a Sominex into her mouth to help calm her nerves—only—and she realized this too late, after swallowing it—it wasn't a Sominex that she had been clutching in her fist.

"Why are we the only customers?" Myrtice said. "There should be more people."

"Ethyl Mae, would you like some styrofoam?" Heidi asked. "I got a lot at the store that I just throw out."

"What, dear?"

"Styrofoam."

"Nice, yes." She gave a quick, tense smile, wondering what Ray Jr.'s pill was going to do to her.

"Oh, look," Myrtice said with a little clap of her hands, "Duk-Soo's got the food waitress. We can eat."

4

❃

Two soft-looking young men with identical Fu Manchu mustaches, the campus police, questioned her outside the locked Agricultural Sciences Building and told her to go away, but Mrs. Coco stood her ground. She kept her finger on the bell, hoping George Henry, who was inside servicing a computer in one of the classrooms, would get a move on. She had arranged to meet him here after she finished with her cello lesson in the music building on the other side of the St. Jude campus, next to the lake. The lesson had not gone well. Her teacher, a girl no older than Nancy, Mrs. Coco's youngest daughter, was a marvelous cellist from Indiana University, who insisted that the reason Mrs. Coco didn't seem to be improving was because she was on a plateau. Which was just a polite way of saying, Mrs. Coco suspected, that you can't teach an old dog new tricks. As usual, she had burst into tears over the double-stops in the Dvořák Concerto, which she had been learning for the past twelve years. Meg, her teacher, suggested that perhaps her hands were not large enough for such a demanding piece, but Mrs. Coco was determined not to let anything physical like that defeat her.

The police were still keeping an eye on Mrs. Coco from

their minicruiser when George Henry finally came to the door and let her in. An evil-smelling cigarette dangled from his lower lip as he led her down the hall, her cello gliding on the roller-skate wheels that Mr. Coco had screwed onto the case the night before. He was afraid that his wife was getting a little too muscular from all the lifting and lugging.

"I don't have to tell you why I'm here," she said as he unlocked a door at the end of the hall. It opened onto a stuffy, windowless room not much larger than a closet, in which four computer terminals sat on an ink-smudged table. Taking a bite from a pickle while somehow keeping his cigarette in his mouth, George Henry squatted behind one of the terminals with a flashlight.

"It's childish behavior, not showing up like that. We all thought you had been in a terrible accident. Are you listening to me, Nancy . . . uh, Larry?"

"Try George Henry," the voice came from behind the machine.

"And as if that's not bad enough, sneaking Heidi in like that. Honestly."

"You wouldn't have come if you knew she was going to be there," he said as smoke rose from behind the terminal. "I just wanted to give her a chance with you, that's all."

"Please put out that cigarette, then give me a direct answer. Where were you?"

The broken veins on his nose and cheeks came into view as he stood up with a groan, like an old man. "I was home, Ma, I went back home. You want to know why—I'll tell you why. Because I thought when you asked me to lunch, it'd be just you and me. I didn't know you were going to ask Myrtice and Duck Soup along, too. Hell, I've got nothing to say to them. And then you just had to drag along that poor sick kid, didn't you? I mean like what's the use of trying to talk when you've surrounded yourself with—"

"George Henry, I didn't ask that boy out to lunch. It was the doctor."

"Ma, I was there," he said, aiming the flashlight at her. "I was there when you asked him."

"No, sug, really, how can you forget? I let him play my cello a little after the concert, remember, because he wanted to see what it felt like. And then the doctor came up, Dr. Jewel, and he started talking about how bright Ray Jr. was and—"

"And you said you'd like to take him out to lunch."

"No, no, I didn't say anything. I mean if I did say something, it was probably something like wouldn't it be nice to have lunch someday—someday. I was being polite and hypothetical."

"And the doctor said he wasn't sure if it was such a good idea and the kid got all excited and then you said—"

"Now stop it, stop playing with my mind. I'm sick and tired of having words put in my mouth."

"Believe me, Ma," he said wearily, "I don't have to put any in. You say enough on your own. Like maybe you'd like to explain this sudden great love of the Jewish race I heard about. Heidi says you spent most of lunch telling everyone how much you admire Jews."

Pretending that his cigarette smoke made her start coughing, Mrs. Coco was able to camouflage a violent blush. Ray Jr.'s pill had made her a little more relaxed and garrulous than a Sominex would have. Discovering that Heidi was Jewish, something George Henry had never bothered to mention before, Mrs. Coco was determined to make it perfectly clear at lunch that she didn't have one iota of prejudice in her bones, that this had nothing whatsoever to do with any objection she might have to the marriage. She had always respected the Jewish race, she let Heidi know, and her only regret in life was that she herself had not been born

Jewish. Recalling all this now, Mrs. Coco had to admit to herself that she had gone overboard.

"Oh, darling, please do put out that cigarette."

"Were you drunk?" he asked, squashing the cigarette in wax paper. "Heidi thought you were plastered at lunch, you know."

Although the truth would have been the easiest way out for her—"I accidentally took the wrong pill"—instinct took over: "George Henry, I didn't have a thing to drink, not a thing."

"Yeah, that's what had Heidi confused. She figured you must have been tippling a little before she showed up."

"And I suppose you agreed with her right off. You never thought of getting my side."

"Well, Dad did tell me that you put another dent in the Dart on your way home from the restaurant."

"That stop sign was leaning into the road. I couldn't help hitting it. It was a choice between that and getting rammed from behind."

George Henry regarded her a moment with those pale yellowish eyes which most people would describe as cold. His mother, though, took a more charitable view: they were practical, no-nonsense eyes that, bloodshot or not, could see patterns and connections in a maze of wires and circuits. She could appreciate the value of eyes like that. After all, he was the only one of her children who could afford to live in a decent house with wall-to-wall carpeting and built-in vacuum cleaner outlets. Sam, her youngest son, the weaver in Banff, lived in a log cabin, and Larry, God help him, with those gorgeous long-lashed cow eyes of his, still lived in a trailer park.

"All right, Ma, have it your way. You weren't drunk. You were your normal self."

Somehow this didn't sit well with her. "Well, now, I . . ."

"What? OK, so you adore everyone of the Jewish persuasion. What's the big problem, then? Why can't you accept Heidi?"

Mrs. Coco was trying to prop open the door to get some air. In a room this size her son loomed too large, especially when he was smoking. "George Henry, if you *must* get married, then get married. Just don't expect me to applaud when I see your faith go down the drain."

"Hey, lay off the religioso stuff. I'm talking to you—one on one. Don't drag in the damn Church." There was a hard look in his eyes that reminded her of her husband when he had been thinking too much.

"People used to die for the Church."

"Christ, Ma," he snapped, accidentally knocking his elbow against her cello. It squeaked a few feet across the tiles. "You really are nuts, you know. All I'm asking . . . I mean I'm not asking you to stop believing or anything. You can believe in all the bullshitting popes you want to. Just come to the goddam wedding."

"This language will not do," she said, rolling the cello into the dim, clean-smelling hall.

"You don't come to the wedding, Mae," he said, following her toward the bluish haze of the glass doors, "you don't come and maybe you'll find yourself minus a first violin. What do you think of that, huh?"

It was the first time he had ever called her anything but Ma or Mother; really, his impertinence knew no bounds.

Outside a light shower flickered in the sunny, almost cloudless sky like static on a tv screen. George Henry continued to trail his mother to the car. After hoisting her cello into the back seat, she got in but did not start the engine. Her son was staring off into the lot beside the red-brick building, where two Black Anguses grazed in a catatonic stupor, overwhelmed, it seemed, by the idea of their great bulk.

"Dear," she said out the car window when the silence began to seem a little silly, "those sideburns of yours—they make you look like a filling-station attendant. Now listen. Your father wants to price some hot-water heaters, so we'll be driving into Baton Rouge next week. If you and Heidi would like to have dinner . . ." Mrs. Coco had little hope of talking Heidi out of marrying her son, but she was anxious to demonstrate to the girl that she did not always giggle and slur her words when she was dining out.

George Henry's face brightened. "What's the old man need a hot-water heater for?"

"Oh, sug, you know your father. He gets these notions in his head, and that's that. I swear our old one's perfectly good. The only problem is that we're getting scalding hot water in the commode, thanks to the plumber your father hired, a real bargain—only five dollars an hour. The boy was smoking marijuana all morning, then sprayed Right Guard all over my bathroom to cover it up. Now get in out of the rain. Don't just stand there like a . . ."

George Henry waved as she pulled out of the parking space, but she was too busy steering to wave back.

Before returning to Tula Springs Mrs. Coco wanted to drop off the bowings she had marked in the Borodin for Duk-Soo. His dorm was on the far edge of the campus, where only a few yards away a bayou popular with local wild-boar hunters twisted through cypress and tupelo gum before emptying furtively through a sewer pipe into Lake Pontchartrain. The landscaping around the dorm wasn't finished yet, but once the palms and banana plants were put in, the grounds, according to the St. Jude catalog, would draw the eye of young and old alike. Five different types of brick were used in the building's facade, each representing a different region of the state, and the design was so modern that there wasn't a single window in the entire place.

"Yes, may I assist you?" the dorm mother said as Mrs. Coco's clacking heels echoed off the lobby's cement-block walls. Mrs. Hicks, the dorm mother, was a pretty widow in her mid-fifties with bee-stung lips and a matching Betty Boop voice. The navy blue blouse she wore had a large sailor collar, a motif that was picked up in her tennis shoes, which had little anchors on them.

"Hello, Mrs. Hicks," Mrs. Coco said, reluctant to help her out. She must have visited Duk-Soo a dozen times, and yet the dorm mother never showed the slightest sign of recognition. Mrs. Coco had read somewhere that life, to dogs, was a perpetual wonder because of their dim memories; perhaps this explained why Mrs. Hicks never seemed bored or unhappy at her dismal post.

"You're faculty, right?"

"I'm Mrs. Coco."

"Yes, I know." After a short pause Mrs. Hicks ventured, "You're here to see someone foreign."

"I'm here to see the American citizen Duk-Soo."

"He's in," she said after running an orange fingernail down a chart marked "Ingress and Egress." "He came in at one twenty-three p.m. after dining in the cafeteria. I try to encourage my boys to make frequent use of the cafeteria and to avoid such places as Hardee's and BurgerMat, where you might get free stemware, sure, but what about a well-balanced meal? Tell me honestly, Mrs. Cola, do you think you can get food from all four food groups at a participating Hardee's?"

"Not all four."

"By the way, whether they're naturalized or unnaturalized, Koreans are very sensitive about their names. I consulted with Dr. Waid in our Modern Languages Department, and she advised me to always refer to Mr. Yoon as Mr. Yoon. According to Dr. Waid, no one but a parent or elder sibling, and possibly a professor, may refer to a Korean by his or her first name. Even best friends call each other Mister or Miss This or That." She stood up. "I'll page *Mr. Yoon* for you," she concluded, but before she got to the intercom, she was sidetracked by two boys in gym shorts who had just walked into the lobby. "Mr. Versey, if that's me you're talking about to your friend, I'd appreciate it if you'd speak up. I might like to hear also."

"Then take the dildo out of your ear, mother."

Mrs. Coco wasn't able to follow the rest of the conversation, for she had chosen that moment to slip through a swinging door into the hall. She did not want to talk to Duk-Soo in the lobby, which was the only place women were allowed in the dorm. Walking up a flight of metal stairs, she sidestepped a splattered ice-cream cake and emerged onto the second floor, where Duk-Soo had a room next to the pay phone in the hall.

For the life of her Mrs. Coco would never understand why a man his age would choose to live in such surroundings. Surely he could afford a decent apartment in town, considering all the money he lavished on his videotape equipment. His collection of German Expressionist films had even been mentioned in a footnote in a South African film journal, which he had proudly shown her one day, explaining that there was, of course, no truth to the inference that one of his early Riefenstahl prints, transferred to a VHS format, was pirated.

The door opened a crack, the chain still on, after Mrs. Coco knocked and identified herself. Told to wait a moment, please, she heard several spray cans hiss and then was admitted to the room.

"How nice, how nice," Duk-Soo said while Mrs. Coco eased past the giant tv screen. "Now we go down to the lobby."

"Relax, hon," she said, depositing the Borodin on a desk covered with STP decals. Settling into a plastic lawn chair, she noticed Duk-Soo's roommate in the top bunk.

"Hello, Bruce," she said after he grunted a hi in her general direction. Duk-Soo's roommate was a junior who had had to go through a special interview with Mrs. Hicks so that she could make sure he wasn't prejudiced against Orientals or middle-aged men. Mrs. Coco was acquainted with Bruce's aunt, who was an operator at the beauty college next door to her house in Tula Springs.

"Would you care for some Tang?" Duk-Soo asked.

"No, thanks. Sit, please. I have something very important to— Oh, by the way"—she pointed at the music on the desk—"that's the Borodin with the new bowings. Don't ask Dr. Miller what he thinks of them, either. It's how I want it, understand?"

He nodded, glancing at the door.

"Now, sug," she began, contemplating a varicose vein on her calf, "this has to be handled just right. Dr. Miller is a very busy man, and from what I understand, he has a tendency to be a little on the curt side." Dr. Miller was Duk-Soo's violin teacher at St. Jude. She had decided that it would be better if Duk-Soo sounded him out first before she approached him with a definite offer. With Dr. Miller, a real professional, as first violin in the Pro Arts, she was sure they would have no trouble getting a grant from the Louisiana Council for the Arts, which had refused to fund the quartet so far, and bookings at places other than crawdad rodeos and mental institutions. She was also hopeful that once she had hooked Dr. Miller, it would be an easy matter to persuade his wife, an excellent fiddler, to play second violin in the quartet, a plan Duk-Soo needn't be aware of just now, of course.

"Do you think Dr. Miller might be interested in joining the Pro Arts?"

"But Mrs. Coco," he said, sinking onto the lower bunk, "I have worked so hard. You must not . . ."

"Duk-Soo," she said, shaking her head, "why must you

imagine that everything revolves around you? I'm speaking
of George Henry. He and I had a chat this afternoon, and he
informed me that he wants to quit, so—"

"Oh, terrible," the Korean said, unable to hide his relief.
"Terrible, terrible."

"Yes, terrible. But the show must go on."

"But Dr. Miller is too good for us. I can't—"

"Hon," she cut in, annoyed by the *us*, "I'm not asking for
an opinion. All I want is for you to pave the way for me at
your next lesson. Tell Dr. Miller a few things about me so
that when I call him, it won't be from out of the blue."

A moan from the top bunk caused her to glance up. Bruce,
as she had been informed on her last visit, was practicing for
Talent Night at his German Club, where he was scheduled to
cram his fist into his mouth.

"Perhaps if I talk to George Henry, I can make him change
his mind," Duk-Soo suggested.

"His mind is made up. There's no way he's going to
change it, I guarantee."

"Hey, Slant Eyes," Bruce said, his head drooping over the
side of the bunk, "can I use the Sony tonight? Some guys
from my Marx class want to watch *Friday the Thirteenth Part
Two*."

"I don't believe that is in my collection."

"We're going to rent it."

"Well, Bruce, you must be careful. I don't want you spill-
ing beer on the screen again."

"What time you going out, man?"

"Around eight."

"Can't you go a little sooner?"

"Bruce," Mrs. Coco interjected, "Mr. Yoon will be leaving
at eight, if you don't mind. And I would appreciate it if you
wouldn't practice your fist till I left."

The roommate rolled over to the wall side of the bed.

"Duk-Soo, you have a lesson this afternoon, I believe," she

said. "This would be a good opportunity to slide it into the conversation. Tell Dr. Miller that I play the Dvořák and don't say too much about Myrtice, if you know what I mean. And make sure he understands that we make money."

"We do?"

"Didn't I just give you twenty-five dollars last week?"

"Yes, but you made me give back twenty-seven fifty for sundries and gas."

"Must you always be so negative? Honestly, it's a wonder you ever bother to get out of bed in the morning. Just look at you—worry lines all over your face." She reached out and rapped on his knee. "Wake up, sug, life isn't that horrible. If you want, life can be turned into a wonderful banquet, but it's up to you to make it that way." She was irked to find herself paraphrasing the flap copy of her birthday present, the book she despised so much. "If you always look for the worst to happen," she went on, wishing she could shut up and leave the poor man alone, "it will. You've got to train yourself to look on the bright side, make a conscious effort to *choose* happiness and good fortune and then . . ."

There was a sharp knock on the door.

"Mr. Yoon," Mrs. Hicks said, bursting into the room, or at least trying to burst in; the giant tv near the entrance slowed her down as she squeezed past it.

"It's not my fault," Duk-Soo said, springing to attention. "I asked her to go down to the lobby."

"Mr. Yoon, did you have Welsh rarebit for lunch?" Mrs. Hicks demanded. "Answer immediately, yes or no."

"I'm not sure. What is Welsh rarebit?"

"Stick your finger down your throat."

"Pardon me?"

"I want you to stick your finger down your throat, Mr. Yoon."

He regarded her for a moment, somewhat daunted, it seemed, by the grim look in her eyes. "Do I have to?"

"If you don't know whether you ate rarebit or not, yes, you'll have to. I just heard on the radio that five students have gone into convulsions after eating the rarebit in the cafeteria. They suspect it's PCBs in the cheese. The melted cheese, Mr. Yoon. It could be disastrous unless we act immediately. I have my instructions straight from the infirmary."

Mrs. Coco, who had been listening to all this from the lawn chair, was impressed with Mrs. Hicks's firm control of the situation, like a bubble-headed stewardess suddenly turning into a real woman during a crisis on a plane.

"No, listen," Duk-Soo said as Mrs. Hicks swiped an emery board off the desk. "No, please, I had Salisbury steak, I remember now. No cheese."

"Are you certain, Mr. Yoon? Are you a hundred and ten percent positive?" The emery board hovered near his lips.

"Yes, positive."

"Is there a washroom?" Mrs. Coco said faintly, rising from her chair. She had just remembered what she had eaten in the cafeteria before her cello lesson.

Mrs. Hicks gave her a hard look. "Dear child," she murmured, placing a kind, cool hand on Mrs. Coco's brow.

"Oh, my," Mrs. Coco said, recalling the fate of her French teacher, who had eaten just a single oyster—and she had had three helpings of rarebit, three!

"This way, dear, hurry. Mr. Yoon, you're in the way—move it."

5

❁

The Reconciliation Room at Our Lady of the
Flowers contained a vestigial confessional—a screen and
prie-dieu—for those not quite modern enough to let it all
hang out face to face. Though she was not particularly
ashamed of her sins, Mrs. Coco preferred using the screen,
closing her eyes to shut out the cheery white walls, which,
unlike the shadowy confessional booths, didn't seem very
sacramental to her. The confessionals had been torn out in
the early seventies when Our Lady received a face lift; life-
size, brightly painted statues of Saint Bernard, Saint
Christopher, Saint Anthony, and Saint Francis with a yellow
dog were replaced by twelve modest Stations of the Cross,
semiabstract aluminum modules with Pac-Man-like Roman
soldiers. Instead of the elaborate three-tiered wooden altar
there was now only a simple granite slab, where the priest
said words she could understand. Somehow Latin had made
being a Catholic much easier. In her mind the unintelligible
drone was connected with the early days of her marriage,
when her husband seemed so formidable, his word law. She
had been a passionate convert then, attending Mass at seven
every morning with no makeup whatsoever, waiting patiently for another sign from Saint Francis, whose lips had

once moved when she had been praying alone in the darkened church after her husband had thrown her chicken cacciatore into the fireplace.

On this particular Saturday, Mrs. Coco, by force of habit, showed up for her bimonthly confession; but instead of kneeling behind the screen, she surprised herself by taking a seat in the folding chair facing the new pastor, a Samoan. She was not sure, because his skin was so dark, but it looked as if Father Fua blushed when he saw her, which made her want to get up and retreat to the screen.

"Uh, hello," she said, unable to remember the opening ritual, which she must have said a thousand times before.

"Good day, my child." No one knew how old Father Fua was; he seemed as ageless as a squat South Seas idol. Needless to say, he wasn't very popular with the ladies in the Rosary Altar Society. As Mrs. Wattels, the president, commented, it was a fine state the Church was in when they couldn't even scrape up a plain and simple, dime-a-dozen Irishman. No one could stand Father Fua's tedious homilies, including Mrs. Coco, but she defended him nonetheless. After all, it was only fair that the natives whom we have preached at for so many years should finally have their chance to preach back at us. And besides, it didn't really matter what a priest looked or sounded like. They all had exactly the same powers to loose or bind, whether or not they looked like Harvey Korman, which was what Father Fua's tall, popular predecessor looked like.

"Bless me, Father, for I have sinned," Mrs. Coco said, the formula finally coming to mind. "It has been two weeks since my last confession. I talked uncharitably about my husband to my daughter about three times . . . four. I was ten minutes late for Mass once because I couldn't find a parking space. I talked uncharitably about my daughter five times. I stole five dollars from my husband's wallet three times. I told social white lies so I wouldn't hurt people's feelings about six . . . uh, twenty-six times. I was unkind to a chihuahua about five times. I wasted good food eight times, mainly because of my husband. He's always buying bargains, bushels of things that we can't possibly finish, so I have to throw them out. Last week it was Spanish onions that he bought at a firecracker stand, and the ones on the bottom were already rotten. That's all the sins I can remember, Father."

"You sorry for dese and all other sins you may forget? Why you take money?"

Looking down at the age spots on her hands, she replied, "To pay the man to haul the manure away. My husband bought manure for the garden because it was a bargain, and then he never spread it around."

"Next time you ax him for money."

"Yes, Father."

"Do you contribute to support of Church?"

"Yes, Father."

"For penance say five Our Faders and tree Hail Marys. Now make good Act of Contrition."

When Mrs. Coco finished the prayer, which she muttered quickly, trying not to be confused by the absolution he was muttering at the same time, she surprised herself again by remaining where she was. Father Fua cleared his throat and adjusted an Argyle sock.

"Father, may I . . ."

"More sin?"

She nodded, tears welling up in her eyes. "Father, the other day, about a week ago, I thought I was poisoned . . ." The humiliation of being taken to the washroom by Mrs. Hicks still burned fresh in her mind. There had been no poisoning at the St. Jude cafeteria; the boys in the Jervis C. Mawks Men's Residence Hall had made a special tape cassette for their dorm mother, which they pretended was a ra-

dio broadcast advising emergency procedures involving
fingers and throats.

"You should not eat rotten onions, my child, no matter
how cheap."

"Father, no, it . . ."

"You tell husband bad food is never a bargain. God wants
us to eat quality food. It may cost a few cents more, but it is
very much worth it."

Mrs. Coco patted blindly at her tears with a swatch of slip-
cover fabric from her purse. "No, Father, it was Welsh
rarebit. I thought something terrible was going to happen to
me, I was afraid I might die, and then I realized . . ." She
had such a lump in her throat she could barely get the
words out. "I realized, Father, I'm not sure if I believe in
anything. I mean everything I thought I believed in, Jesus
and Mary and heaven, love, all those things, I suddenly realized they were just words, they didn't mean a thing. Father,
something is wrong with me. I just don't care anymore, I
don't care about anybody or anything. I pretend to, I pretend to all the time, but deep down, I know I don't. I might
as well be dead."

A benign smile softened his broad face, which she realized
was not so ugly after all, at least when he smiled. "Dis very
common with woman your age. You go see family doctor.
He tell you about dis time of life."

"Father," she said, prickling, "I went through that time of
life nearly ten years ago."

"Yes, but the mental part," he said, tapping his receding
hairline, "sometime dis come later, make you very confused.
I see lots of dis, honey, many women your age depressed in
Spokane, Washington. Do not worry. Everything fix up. You
have nice husband and children. You love dem very much.
God commands you to love dem. It is very dangerous to stop
loving, just because you don't happen to feel like it, you're

not in the mood. Always there will be reasons not to love and people who will try and make you stop loving. It's like when dey try to kill the spirit of Christmas, the birth of de King of Love. Dey have been doing dis through the ages. First happens in year sixteen-fifty-three in England. Protestants try to stop Christmas because it is Popist. Women just like you arrested for making plum pudding. Dey make mayor of village climb up a tall pole to take down very nice wreath. Den remember Boston in eighteen-forty-two. Dere was a Catholic bookseller, much revered, who closed his store on Christmas day, and all de Protestants gathered around and asked him, 'What's de matter? Did your aunt die? Did a relative die?' So you see, honey. All dis is nothing new. You must fight to love, fight every day, every minute. Use all your muscles, both fits, 'cause most people are against it. Most people don't want love to work, understand. Dey are afraid of it. Now for penance say twenty Our Faders and ten Hail Marys and five Glory Be's. Go in peace, God bless you. And pray for me, please. I am sinner, too. Remember me."

After confession Mrs. Coco went home and called George Henry to let him know that she and his father would not be able to make it to dinner that night as they had planned. She said his father was not feeling well, he was having one of his dizzy spells, and she thought she might be coming down with the flu and didn't want to risk giving it to Heidi and him. And also, the Skylark was in the garage, and she wasn't sure the Dart could make it all the way to Baton Rouge—the oil pan was leaking. In the middle of the fifth reason George Henry hung up.

Turning on the air-conditioner in the bedroom, she sat down on the edge of the Craftmatic and sorted socks from the beige plastic laundry basket while saying the Our Fathers, Hail Marys, and Glory Be's that she couldn't bring herself to say at Our Lady. Having completed the penance, and the socks, and still not feeling absolved, she set herself down in front of her mother's old sewing machine and began to pump it into action with her feet. "Hail Holy Queen, mother of mercy, our life, our sweetness, and our hope," she droned mechanically as the needle pierced the trousers she was altering for Larry so that he would look decent for his daughter's high school graduation in Lake Charles. "To thee do we cry, poor banished children of Eve. . . . Turn then, most gracious advocate, thine eyes of mercy towards us, and after this our exile, show unto us . . ." Her feet quit pumping the metal grill; the needle rose up and down a few times, then stopped. It was no use. Why was she trying to be forgiven for the one real feeling she had had in a long time? What she had told Father Fua was true; she really did not care about anything or anyone. It was all just words, stupid words, and she had no intention of spending an entire evening saying things she didn't mean to George Henry and that girl friend of his.

Unaware that he was suffering from a dizzy spell, Mr. Coco returned home to find his wife sitting motionless in front of the sewing machine.

"What are you going to wear tonight?" he asked as he contemplated the Johnny Carson jackets in the closet. "Not that brown dress again, I hope. You know, Mae, I saw a very becoming dress in the window at Sissy's, tangerine with pink trim. It had your name written on it." He decided on the Johnny Carson labeled "Darkish Blue" inside; he was color-blind.

"Mae?" he said, noticing now that the sewing machine was still. "You all right?"

"We're not going."

"What?"

"I've already told George Henry we're not going."

Mr. Coco sat down among the sorted socks on the bed and

crossed his long legs. His nose looked a little raw where the doctor had removed a patch of skin cancer not long after his seventy-first birthday, which he had refused to celebrate. "All right, Mae," he said warily, "let's discuss this calmly, reasonably, like two adults. There's no need to fly off the handle."

Mrs. Coco, who hadn't the slightest desire, much less the energy, to fly off the handle, frowned at her husband's obtuseness.

"What we have to do is learn to debate the pros and cons. I can learn something from you, and you can learn something from me. Then we put this information together and come up with a rational decision, something that is in both our best interests. Pretend you're a businessman and this is a business decision."

"Leave me alone, Louis. I'm tired."

With a grandmother's cluck of annoyance he reached for the scrub brush on the night table and, after pulling up a trouser leg, took a few swipes at his bony knee to get the circulation going. "All right, dear," he said, "I can understand why you might be upset. I was a little put out myself, getting the news from a clerk at Powell's."

"What are you talking about?" she said, distracted by a cricket that was hobbling over a VISA bill on her desk. "And what in heaven's name were you doing in Powell's?"

"Mae, you're slipping. Don't you remember, you asked me to see about a graduation present for Amy, so I . . . What? What's the matter?"

Powell's just happened to be the most expensive jeweler this side of the Mississippi. Amy, Larry's seventeen-year-old, who was graduating this month with a C average, could darn well be satisfied with something from Penney's. "Go on."

"Well, anyway, I dropped by at lunch and saw they were having a sale on creamers, so I—"

"Louis, no. You didn't buy Amy a creamer for graduation?"

"Of course not. I was thinking of us." He fiddled with a pair of rolled socks until they came apart, then took another swipe at his thin, almost hairless leg with the brush. "I'm tired of being ashamed of our coffee service. People notice those things."

There was a crack a yard long in the wall next to the staircase, a bleach stain on the Navaho rug where the beauty college's chihuahua had gone to the bathroom, a broken rail in the side porch, and yet it was the creamer people were noticing. Mrs. Coco got up and swatted the cricket with a *Catholic Commentator*. "Go on."

"I'm not going on unless you promise to be reasonable."

"I'm reasonable. Talk."

He fiddled with another sock. "Well, the girl who sold me the creamer—"

"It's going back."

"What? The girl thought I was buying it for George Henry. She said Connie told her—you know Connie works at Powell's now."

Of course Mrs. Coco knew she worked at Powell's. What a ridiculous thing to say to her. He knew darn well how much Connie meant to her. As a matter of fact, George Henry's ex-wife felt more like a real daughter to her than any of her own children. Genes really meant so little when you came right down to it. Take Helen Ann, for instance, Mrs. Coco's oldest girl—could any two people be more different in outlook than she and Helen Ann? There she was, practically forty, and instead of doing some hard thinking about how she was going to manage in her old age without a husband, Helen Ann, a widow, was behaving like a girl right out of college, giving horseback riding lessons in some godforsaken town in Australia—Wollongong. Then there was Lucy, selling pralines and trick sunglasses in the French Quarter while trying to be a poet. Mrs. Coco had read one of Lucy's poems in a magazine that had a cow eating a horse on the cover; she hadn't understood anything in the poem except the four-letter words. Nancy, the youngest, was at least working in a practical field, nutrition, which could be put to good use someday if she wanted. But no, Nancy had her heart set on working in a women's penitentiary as soon as she got out of Columbia Teachers College. It was enough to make any mother want to throw in the towel.

"Louis, would you get on with it," she said, back at the sewing machine, her feet pumping deliberately up and down.

"Dear, I am. You know Connie lives out in Rise with a girl friend. They have sheep, I think."

"Goats."

"Anyway, that's how she heard about it, in the Rise paper. And she told the clerk who sold me the creamer."

"Told her what?"

"I thought you were just talking with George Henry?"

"Louis."

"The wedding, dear. Didn't he tell you? He's gone ahead and got married."

The needle came to a sudden halt. "What?"

"The clerk told me Connie sent him and Heidi a creamer as a wedding present."

"I don't believe it. How could he be married? How? I was just on the phone with him, and he didn't say a word about it!"

A faint smile softened Mr. Coco's slightly horsey, handsome face. "Let's face it, Mae. You and George Henry aren't exactly the AT&T of communication. It seems obvious to me he wanted to wait and tell us in person tonight at dinner. That's why I think it's our duty to go."

Noticing that Larry's trousers had slipped to the floor, Mrs. Coco picked them up, which gave her an excuse to groan. "No, I don't believe it. I just can't. I'm going to phone him right this minute."

"Mae, I don't want you talking to him in this frame of mind. You'll only upset him. Facts are facts—there's some things in life you just got to learn to accept."

Getting off the bed, he reached into his pocket. "Take a look. Connie brought this into Powell's, and the clerk let me take it home for our scrapbook."

It was a clipping from the Rise *Vindicator*, which she needed her glasses to read. The glasses were in a sewing box next to a half-empty pack of cigarettes that she hoped her husband wouldn't notice when she opened the lid.

"Take it easy, Mae," he said when the lid slammed shut. "You know, I bet we're the only family in Tula Springs without a scrapbook. Most women like to keep scrapbooks. I don't understand—you're always throwing the children's things out so you'll have clean closets. . . . Oh, well."

"Nuptials Celebrated Amid Hosts of Wildflowers," she read while trying to block out her husband's ridiculous chatter. "In an unique ceremony Rachel 'Heidi' Green of Babylon Long Island (NY State) was united in holy matrimony to George Henry Coco of Baton Rouge amidst host of local wildflowers chosen by the bride's sister, Mrs. Hunter Ludlum, teacher of remedial English at L.S.U. The bride, a local franchiser for California Hot Tubs at 12178 Choctaw Drive, wore a pale tulle . . ." The words blurred together on the page as a sharp pain, like a sword, pierced her side. "Well, good," she said. "I'm glad."

Mr. Coco, who had been hovering over her, settled onto the edge of a chaise longue with "GH + PW" carved on its wooden scroll. "Now remember, Mae, before you say or do anything, remember it was you yourself who told him to go ahead and get married without you."

"I told you I'm glad," she said as a vivid image of her good scissors plunging into her husband's side flitted through her head. "Would you please . . ." she added, frowning at the bare leg embroidered with red and blue veins.

"The newlyweds will honeymoon at the Ramada Inn in Ozone," she read while he rolled down his trouser leg, "where they plan to tube Warsaw Bayou."

"Now that's the spirit," Mr. Coco said as his wife got up and went to the closet. "It's high time you came to your senses. Darn it all, Mae, all your talk about the Church and divorce, it was really beginning to worry me. It's water under the bridge now. We'll go to Baton Rouge and show Heidi how glad we are to have her a part of the family."

"Worry you, dear?" she said, taking a fawn dress off a hanger.

"Well, yes. I mean in this day and age to make such a fuss over someone getting married again. And George Henry's nearly forty, and Connie couldn't care less."

"I was a bit of a fool, I suppose."

"Helen Ann, you know she called me the other day at work—did I tell you? She had just got through talking with George Henry, and she suggested that maybe I ought to see about getting you some help, professional help. Of course, I never took the idea seriously."

"You mean a psychiatrist?" Mrs. Coco smiled pleasantly while she yanked another dress off its hanger. "Helen Ann, who hasn't a cent to her name and is calling everyone and his dog from twenty thousand miles away like she was at the corner drugstore, she wants you to send *me* to a psychiatrist, *me*?"

"Now, Mae, I wasn't going to mention this to you," he said as she flung another dress onto the chaise longue. "You know how the children are. They've always worried that you might be a little too religious for your own good. But believe me, dear, I stick up for you. I tell them you'll get over it. See, they don't seem to understand that it's harder when you're a convert. I guess it takes a while to get the hang of it, to see what's meant as symbols and metaphors and . . . Hey, what's that for? We're not spending the night, are we? George Henry didn't say anything about spending the night."

Mrs. Coco was tossing the dresses into the Grasshopper suitcase she had won at the grand opening of the mall. "Yes, Louis, it *is* harder to get over when you're a convert—much harder. But, dear, I do think I've succeeded. Are you happy now? Where's my Lady Gillette? How many times have I asked you not to use it?"

Even after she had packed and was downstairs in the kitchen looking for the keys to the Dart, even then Mr. Coco kept the bemused smile on his face, unable to believe that she was actually going home, as she put it, to Mississippi. This was inconceivable, he declared, not after all these years. But Mrs. Coco was not playing games.

"All right, Mae, enough is enough," he said after she had shoved the cello into the back seat of the Dart. A rickety truck overloaded with logs came to a halt in front of the driveway, where traffic was backed up at the intersection. She wondered if she could squeeze past the red flag that hung from the longest pine log.

"I will not have it, you understand," he said, his eyes bleary now with rage. "You cannot leave me."

This rage, though, was only a pale reflection of the anger that used to frighten her so much when she was first married. She saw now that he was basically, when you came right down to it, a small, mean-spirited, very selfish man.

"I can and I will," she answered simply, calmly. She wished someone was there, besides herself, to admire her self-control. "I'm driving straight to Brookhaven, where I intend to spend the rest of my natural-born days among people who love me for what I am." This sentence had been composed in front of the whirring sewing machine; what satisfaction to have it pronounced without a hitch.

"Have you finally gone around the bend?" her husband asked, his face buckled with pain. The side-view mirror twisted under his white knuckles as he glared down at her. "Maybe Helen Ann and the kids are right, maybe you really are sick, Mae."

"Yes, I am sick. Sick and tired of you and your crazy children. I hope I never see any of y'all again, never." Except for Larry, she amended silently to herself. Larry would always be welcome in Brookhaven, and Nancy, of course, if she gave up that fool notion about penitentiaries. She would also like to see Sam, but he thought the entire South was racist and fascist, which is why he lived as far north as he could, way up in Banff.

"You're an unnatural woman, I've always thought so—downright unnatural. You never did like sex, did you?"

It was things like this, things that he would say that had no relation to anything that was going on, that made her lose control. She started the engine, hoping to get away before she ruined her scene. But the log truck was still blocking the driveway, and her husband had followed her to the end.

"Mae," he said hoarsely.

"Get your filthy Dago hands off my mirror!" she cried, and then with a blare of the horn she squeezed past the red flag. It scratched horribly over the Dart's right door like a nail on a blackboard, but she kept going, aiming north through a blur of tears for the state line.

There was something medieval about the child Emmanuel Miller, who, like most children of that era, was dressed and treated like a miniature adult. Emmanuel had been thrust upon the Pro Arts by his father, Dr. Miller, when Duk-Soo informed his teacher that the quartet had an opening. Myrtice was indignant about playing with a twelve-year-old first violin, prodigy or no prodigy, and threatened to quit if someone at least five feet tall didn't replace him. Although Mrs. Coco was impressed with the child's technical abilities—he was not a prodigy, but he was certainly a far sight better than George Henry—she, too, had qualms about appearing in public with someone whose feet didn't reach the floor. On the other hand, she reasoned, there might be some novelty value attached to Emmanuel that could generate publicity. And if she let Emmanuel remain with them, his mother might still be persuaded to play second violin one day.

Because rain was leaking through the porch ceiling, the quartet was forced to practice in the living room, which was damp and stuffy. They tried using a fan, but the noise was too distracting and the breeze blew Myrtice's forty-dollar permanent out of place. Through it all Emmanuel insisted on wearing a tie even though his pinstriped shirt was soaked. With his protruding eyes the child always looked somewhat agitated, and a slight discoloration of the flesh beneath his eyes made him seem perpetually hung over. Mrs. Coco was planning to query Dr. Miller someday about his son's diet.

"Why don't you ask her to come in?" Mrs. Coco suggested when they had finished reading through the first movement of Mozart's K.421. Myrtice's ninety-two-year-old mother-in-law had been parked out in the driveway for the past ten minutes, staring into space.

"I told her, don't come for me till four," Myrtice said. "Her own fault she's got to wait. And anyway, she's got air conditioning."

Mrs. Coco laid her cello on its side. "Well, I suppose we could use some refreshments. How about a nice big glass of Kool-Aid, E.M.?" She did not like calling Emmanuel E.M., but he insisted.

"Make it club soda and you got yourself a deal," he said.

"Iced coffee," Myrtice said, "one lump if it gets here before I faint, two otherwise."

"I would enjoy a Mountain Dew," Duk-Soo said in a hoarse voice, the result of an all-night argument with his roommate about Friedrich Engels.

In the kitchen, which never felt clean, no matter how hard she scrubbed—she needed new Formica counters, no-wax tiles on the floor, and a stainless steel sink like Myrtice had—Mrs. Coco got down a package of red raspberry Jell-O from a cabinet that wouldn't stay shut and stirred the powder into a pitcher of ice water and Sweet 'n Low. From the sink window she could see the rusty hot-water heater her husband had moved outside lying in a patch of whitish grass like one of those two-bit Buster Crabbe spaceships. Mr. Coco had gone ahead and bought a new hot-water heater while his wife was in Mississippi but was keeping the old one, hop-

ing to sell it through an ad in the Tula Springs *Herald*. To-
bacco Road, that's what he was making this place look like,
she had told him this morning, but it had no effect. He had
still not forgiven her for calling him a Dago, even though he
had been civil enough when she had pulled up in the driveway about a week ago. She had lasted only three days in
Mississippi. Quailie, her sister, was the main problem. They
had cried and hugged each other, and then squabbled over a
bottle of wine that Quailie, the good Baptist, wouldn't allow
in her house.

Her brother, Denmark, a widower who lived with Quailie
in the same house they had all grown up in, was as kind and
gallant as ever, letting her share the gin he kept in a rubbing
alcohol bottle, and taking her off almost immediately on a
tour of a water treatment plant. Although he had never finished high school, Denmark had a scientific turn of mind
and wanted to know how everything worked in the community of man. Quailie, who had buried two husbands and was
working on burying a third—he lived in his own apartment
in the attic, reached by a separate outside staircase—became increasingly jealous of the attention her sister was getting from Denmark. As for Mrs. Coco, she was becoming
increasingly annoyed by these very same attentions: neither
the water treatment plant, the fire station, the transformer
at the power plant, nor the capping machine at the Nehi
bottling factory seemed as fascinating to her as they did to
her brother. Whenever she tried to veer the conversation
away from the marvels of a modern animal shelter or the
actual height of the Brookhaven water tower, hoping to get
some indication that he was sorry for not having written or
phoned in so long, that things would be different in the future, Denmark's face would go blank for a moment, and then
he would smile and reel out a few more statistics on sewage
tonnage.

Unlike her brother, Quailie did enjoy discussing more personal matters. At first Mrs. Coco got a charge out of being able to talk so freely about her husband, how his knee-brushing nearly drove her insane; how on the first of every month he would pay the bills while soaking his feet in warm tea, to keep them from sweating; how he had no conception that other people had needs and wants of their own; how he never laughed at her jokes and never got the water hot enough when he did the dishes; and how he smiled so hard at everyone at the store while looking like death warmed over at home. On and on she went, spurred on by Quailie, who had known he was no good from the minute she had first laid eyes on him.

"You always thought I didn't approve of him 'cause he was a Guinea," Quailie said one morning over coffee while Denmark was upstairs preparing to show off the Brookhaven jail to his sister. Quailie was much stouter than her sister and wore a ring on each finger; she claimed she felt naked without them. "I told you once, I told you a thousand times, it isn't the case, ma'am. It's his eyes. They're the coldest set of eyes I ever looked into."

"Louis has very nice eyes," Mrs. Coco replied, resenting the fact that her sister had hit on a truth without waiting for it to be volunteered. His eyes could indeed be cold and flinty; there was rarely any hint of that old spark to make them come alive, except, of course, when they argued about candy bars.

"Furthermore," Quailie went on as she reached over with a jeweled lighter to light another cigarette for her sister, "any man his age interested in a seventeen-year-old, there's just got to be something wrong somewhere. I mean he was practically forty when he married you."

"Thirty-one," Mrs. Coco said coldly, her resentment growing as another sore spot that was best left alone was probed. It really wasn't right for a thirty-one-year-old to want to marry a seventeen-year-old, no matter how beautiful and bright she might have been. "There's nothing wrong with that. I was very mature for my age, Quailie."

"I'll grant you that, sugarplum. You always did look old for your age—least that's what Denmark always says. But anyways, there he was, thirty-one, as you say, unattached, no family—"

"He's got plenty of family."

"Honeybunch, you tell me how anyone named Coco can have family and I'll tell you how to stuff a nigra. It just isn't possible."

"I asked you not to say that word in front of me." Mrs. Coco frowned at the lipstick on the rim of her sister's coffee cup. Quailie said something back, but the jelly doughnut in her mouth made it easy for Mrs. Coco to pretend she hadn't understood. "And another thing, Quailie. Last night I kept my mouth shut, but I've been thinking about it. You had no right to say those things you were saying about the Pope. I feel you owe me an apology."

"That wasn't me—that was that magazine," she said, re-tying the sash to her kimono, which was always coming un-done. "Right there in black and white, that R. C. banker hung like a dog from London Bridge. He was probably try-ing to defect to England."

"London Bridge is in Arizona."

"Ethyl Mae, I don't care if London Bridge is on the moon. That Church of yours is run by a dictator. That's what y'all believe in—it all boils down to dictatorship, bowing down in front of some man straight from a Communist country. Lord, child, it's beyond me how someone raised in this house, surrounded by good Democrats . . . which reminds me, before you and Denmark take off for the jailhouse, I'd appreciate a little help around here. These floors don't clean themselves, you know."

Quailie had really let things go to pot—mildew on the bathroom tiles, smudges on every light switch, finger marks wherever you looked. It was truly disgusting, yet Mrs. Coco had no intention of becoming a personal maid for her sister.

"Do you know what I found under my bed when I vacuumed this morning, Quailie? A dead squirrel. I wasn't going to mention it, but really . . ."

"What do you want me to do? I can't keep tabs on all the wildlife in Brookhaven. They want to come into my house to die, they'll come no matter what I say. There's just some things you can't control, Ethyl Mae, and the sooner you learn that, the better."

"What does control have to do with it? I'm talking about a little normal vacuuming every now and then."

"You are a controlling woman, always were, always will be. I could tell you hadn't changed a bit the minute you set foot in this house. There you were, sniffing around with that delicate snoot, just dying to get me on my hands and knees with a bucket of suds. Boy, hon, sometimes I can't help wondering if Louis might not have bit off more than he could chew. You're a handful, all right. Hey, what's the matter? Aren't you going to finish your oatmeal? I made a special trip for that stuff—just for you."

"Quailie, I think . . ."

She never finished the sentence, but her sister was not surprised when, instead of going to jail, Mrs. Coco packed up her Dart and headed home.

E.M. refused a glass of Jell-O—Mrs. Coco had noticed her mistake in the kitchen but, not wanting to waste good food, served it anyway, without, of course, mentioning the mixup—and went back to practicing intimidating snatches from the Brahms and Mendelssohn concertos. Myrtice accepted the ersatz Kool-Aid with a sigh as Mrs. Coco explained that she couldn't bring herself to serve guests anything but fresh coffee, which there wasn't time to make. Duk-Soo found the drink, garnished with mint that grew wild next to the garbage cans, very refreshing.

"Hey, you guys," E.M. said, "let's get rolling. This Mozart's a goddam mess."

"You guys," Myrtice said, winking at Duk-Soo. She liked to poke fun at Emmanuel's accent. He and his family had moved here from Baltimore two years ago, and they still talked like Yankees.

"Just a minute, E.M.," Mrs. Coco said from the door, where she was trying to open an umbrella with one hand while holding a drink in the other. "I want to see if Mrs. Fitt would like some Kool-Aid."

"Oh, leave her be," Myrtice said.

Outside under a canopy of live oak that kept out most of the rain, Mrs. Coco had the feeling of still being indoors; the close, muggy air oppressed her as she rapped on the Oldsmobile's tinted window.

"Mrs. Fitt," Mrs. Coco said, pointing to the glass in her hand. The window glided down with a hum.

Myrtice's mother-in-law was a well-upholstered widow who believed strongly in comfort. When it was hot, she liked to wear shorts and a halter top that barely contained her generous bosom. After the halter tops were outlawed—Myrtice had given them all to the maid—Mrs. Fitt switched to T-shirts, which, together with her crewcut, made her look vaguely punk.

"Some tea, dear?" Mrs. Coco asked.

"Tea?"

"I mean Jell-O," Mrs. Coco said, wondering why she had said tea; she must get a grip on herself.

"Jell-O?"

"Uh, Kool-Aid."

"Just tell Miss Priss in there to get a move on. I haven't got all day." A newscaster on the car radio rattled off something about rockets in Damascus. "Did she trump? Quite frankly, Ethyl Mae, I don't see how you can stand playing with that girl. Drives me nuts, the way she bids."

"Oh, no, Mrs. Fitt. This is just a rehearsal."

"Lord, child, no amount of rehearsing is going to help her bridge any. Just get on with it so I can get home." She reached out for the glass, took a gulp, and handed it back. "What's this nonsense I've been hearing about you, Ethyl Mae?"

Mrs. Coco masked her consternation with a smile. How could anyone have found out that she had tried to leave her husband? Louis himself would never have let the cat out of the bag, that's for sure. "My sister was ill, Mrs. Fitt. That's why I had to—"

"Your sister? Myrtice told me it was you that was sick, upchucked all over that Jap's dorm. Course I never believed it was 'cause you were drunk. I mean I've heard you drink— everyone knows that—but still . . . I told Myrtice, consider the source. That's my rule of thumb in these matters: consider the source. Myrtice heard all this at the beauty parlor, nothing but a bunch of cackling old biddies. I'll be doggone if I ever set foot in one of them again, so help me God."

"Mrs. Fitt, I never . . ." Fury leavened by embarrassment made it impossible to go on. So Bruce LaSteele, Duk-Soo's roommate, had blabbed to his aunt at the beauty college, who had blabbed to her friends at Bishop's House of Beauty until the story had gotten completely out of hand. The truth was, Mrs. Coco had been unable to throw up in the washroom, not with Mrs. Hicks standing over her, urging her on. After a feeble effort at sticking a finger down her throat, she had told Mrs. Hicks to drive her immediately to the hospital, where she could get proper medical attention. As they were coming out of the washroom, they found Bruce convulsed on the floor of the hall, surrounded by his pea-brained friends, all of them laughing hysterically. It was a vile scene that she had tried hard to forget.

"Don't you worry none," Mrs. Fitt said, patting her on the arm. "I'm on your side, Ethyl Mae."

"There ought to be a law," Mrs. Coco said, moving out of patting range. A sudden honk made her cringe.

"Hi, Ma," George Henry called out as he pulled into the driveway.

Mrs. Coco waved feebly to her son. The first thing she had discovered when she got back from Mississippi was that George Henry was not married after all. As was the custom, Heidi had filled out in advance several forms provided by the local papers describing the ceremony, and had mailed them in. When the wedding was postponed, she had notified everyone but the Rise paper, which was what Connie had read. Perhaps this was a Freudian slip, Heidi wanting to make sure that Connie got no ideas. In any case, George Henry was still of a mind that there would be no wedding without his mother.

"Sug, what are you doing here?" she asked, pecking him dutifully on the jaw as he got out of the car. He was looking downright fat, and his eyes were bloodshot.

"Myrtice told me there was a rehearsal. I had to sub for a P.E. class, that's why I'm late." He took the glass from her hand and emptied it in a few vulgar gulps. "What the hell?" he said, staring at the glass.

"But you quit, George Henry. Don't you remember? You quit."

"What?"

"Hey, you," the old woman said, "you're blocking me. Move that heap, buddy."

"Ma, I never said—"

"Now look, don't start with me again. I distinctly heard

you say—remember, we were in the home ec building at St. Jude—"

"I've never been in the home ec building."

"You were fixing the computers and you told me you were quitting."

"Look, for one thing, it was the Aggie Building. And I never said I was quitting. I said I *might* quit if you didn't come to the wedding. *If.* As far as I'm concerned, you're coming."

"We've been over this; I don't have the energy to—"

The Oldsmobile honked.

George Henry went back to his car while his mother walked slowly to the house, brooding over Myrtice. She had some nerve calling George Henry up and telling him about this rehearsal, let alone gossiping about her being drunk in the dorm. If only women could be physical with one another in a socially acceptable way: Myrtice deserved a good sock on the jaw.

"She's taking a piss," E.M. said when Mrs. Coco asked her whereabouts.

"She's in the washroom," Mrs. Coco corrected.

"So what'd you ask me for? Now look here, Donald," the child went on. He was standing beside Duk-Soo, who was sitting with his violin poised under his chin. "Elbow down and get this around." E.M. pried the Korean's beefy hand into position. "That's it, man. Now take a good look, that's how we hold our hand. And for Christ's sake, get those nails cut. HEY, MYRTLE!" he bellowed. "Come on already!"

"That will do," Mrs. Coco said, picking up her cello. "And his name is Mr. Yoon."

"Get out of here," E.M. said with an impertinent smirk.

"Have you any nail clippers?" Duk-Soo asked.

"Oh, please, not now," she said, glancing nervously at the front door.

"What's this deal we're playing for tomorrow?" E.M.

asked, pulling a handkerchief from the pocket of his Bermuda shorts, which hung well below his knees.

"The Bottle Bazaar," Duk-Soo said. "We're supposed to report to the gymnasium at two-fifteen, the Tula Springs High gymnasium."

"Oh, God," E.M. groaned, mopping his brow. Beneath his jaw, where the violin rested, was a patch of rough purple skin, which Mrs. Coco stared at from time to time.

"Then at five-thirty," Duk-Soo went on, his gaze having wandered to Mrs. Coco, "we assemble at Dick's China Nights."

"Would someone mind telling me what the fuck a bottle bazaar is?"

"Emmanuel," Mrs. Coco said, interrupting her facial exercises, silent screams that prevented double chins, "in this house we do not—"

The honking outside had become too much for her. She laid her cello on its side so she could see what all the fuss was about. The last thing she needed now was for the beauty college operators next door to call the Citizens Patrol with yet another complaint against her. Already she was on record with the CP—which, by the way, she refused to subscribe to—for Canine Cruelty, the charge appearing in the Personal section of the *Herald* Classifieds. Of course, she had not deliberately splattered the beauty college's chihuahua with hot bacon grease; all she had meant to do was scare it away from her Navaho rug with the skillet. In any case, it was a vicious little beast and had tried to bite her. She had no idea how it kept sneaking into her house, unless there was a hole somewhere.

"Mrs. Fitt, please," Mrs. Coco said, rapping on the Oldsmobile's window as the horn continued to blare. George Henry's car was still blocking the drive, but he was nowhere in sight.

"Did you see where my son went?" Mrs. Coco asked as the window eased down.

"I don't care where he went to," the old woman said. "I want this drive cleared."

The rain was heavier now, breaking through the canopy of oak leaves and pelleting the modern perm of ringlets Mrs. Coco had let herself be talked into by her sister in Brookhaven, along with a blond rinse, the first time she had ever used coloring on her hair. Fearing that her gray might return, she hurried back to the front door, where her way was blocked by George Henry. He had apparently used the side entrance to get in.

"Who's that little twerp in there?" he asked as she requested him to move out of the way. His eyes, like everyone else's ever since she had returned from Mississippi, kept gravitating to her hair—everyone's, that is, but her husband's. He didn't seem to notice any difference at all.

"The young man in there is our new first violin. Now please let me in."

"I can't believe it," he said, staying put. "You let this kid take *my* place? It's a joke, a fucking joke."

"You want a joke?" she said, hoping anger would clear a path through the general muddle she felt herself in. "I'll give you a joke: it's certain clowns who do things only halfway. They say they want to be in the quartet, but do they ever practice? They say they want to get married, then change their minds and get divorced. And as if that's not bad enough, they don't even have the integrity to stay divorced properly. No, they even get divorced halfway and go back to getting married. Now I want to tell you something, George Henry. You go in there and look under that boy's chin. Go on, look."

"You're nuts, Ma."

"There's a scar there. I want you to take a good look at it. That boy's only twelve years old and already he's got a scar from practicing. Four hours a day, George Henry, four hours each and every day."

"Sure, fags can practice four hours a day. They don't have anything better to do."

Mrs. Coco had only meant to clear a way past him, but somehow the back of her wrist connected with his too-red, drunkard's nose.

"Oh, look what you've done now!" she moaned, cradling her wounded wrist as blood dribbled down his chin.

"Hey, Charlie," the old woman called as Mrs. Coco slammed the door on him, "I'm going to count to three."

7

❊

Dick's China Nights was the most expensive restaurant in Tula Springs, offering a variety of Mandarin and Polynesian specialties, along with a full selection of French and traditional American dishes, including diet hot dogs. Mr. Qumquist, who managed Dick's as well as the BurgerMat, had read in a trade magazine that classical music stimulated the vagus nerve, so in the hopes of making people hungrier, he decided to give the Pro Arts a try. A little worn out from their engagement at the Bottle Bazaar that afternoon, the quartet dined gratis on chop suey with the busboys in the kitchen before setting up in the main room. Mrs. Coco, who had refused to comply with the request to wear something Chinese, tried to get her mind off the plastic chopsticks Myrtice had jammed into her ridiculous geisha bun.

After playing their first selection, "Wiener Blut," Mrs. Coco excused herself and hurried off to the ladies' room, where she snuck a cigarette and a Sominex. Since returning from Mississippi she had continued to suffer from homesickness, only now she didn't know what or where the home was that she was sick for. Mississippi seemed as bad, if not worse than, Louisiana. Furthermore, the Rosary Altar Society Bake

Sale, which she was chairman of, was coming up next week, and it depressed her that she would have to stand outside Our Lady all day selling cakes for a God she wasn't sure she believed in. The trouble was, the more she thought about this God she had been praying to for so long, the more distinct His features became; to her dismay she discovered that He bore a striking resemblance to Mayor Binwanger, with a little of her husband's flinty eyes and thin, disapproving mouth thrown in for good measure. Of course, she realized this was absurd, but when she tried to banish this image, there was nothing but a vague, beardlike cloud to take its place.

As if all this wasn't bad enough, the buzz had returned in her cello, causing E.M. to give her several stern looks. There were no two ways about it: that boy was getting too big for his britches. Imagine, him telling her at the Bottle Bazaar that she was flat, and saying it loud enough for Mrs. Ulands, the president of the PTA, to hear.

"Young man, don't you ever talk to me in that tone of voice again, understand?" she had told him after Mrs. Ulands had returned to the booth where the PTA was raffling off a five-gallon jar of homemade French dressing.

"You *were*."

"I don't care if I was playing backwards. It's not your business to correct me."

"I thought this quartet was a democracy."

"When you reach voting age, it'll be a democracy. For now, you can do as you're told."

"*Jawohl!*" he said, thrusting out his arm.

"I'm going to faint if I don't get something to eat," Myrtice put in, just as they were about to play. "E.M., be a dear and go get me some of those sugar cookies. Here's a dollar."

When Mrs. Coco confiscated the dollar—Myrtice owed her far more for gas, after all—Myrtice hooked the scroll of her viola to the stand and then, after rearranging her Gucci, slid from her chair to the floor of the gym. What Mrs. Coco could not help admiring, despite the ruckus it had caused, was that Myrtice had somehow managed to fall into an actual, medically sound faint, as Dr. McFlug, who was buying a jar of shiners at a nearby booth, was willing to attest to.

Peering at her face in the ladies' room mirror, Mrs. Coco was surprised to see how well she looked. If only she had Myrtice's ability to make herself legitimately ill—a touch of the flu, perhaps—how lovely it would be to curl up on the divan in the sewing room, playing again and again the record that invariably brought tears to her eyes, the last act of *Manon Lescaut*. Could anything be more wonderful than Des Grieux's almost saintly love for the faithless little flirt? What man nowadays would have the courage to follow his beloved to the end of the world, to ruin, utter despair, caring nothing for his own self?

Returning from the lavatory, she had to make a detour behind a pillar to avoid running into the ubiquitous mayor, who was being seated by the hostess, a nice-looking young lady with one shoulder higher than the other. Whether this was a deformity or simply a case of bad posture worried Mrs. Coco until she caught sight of a broad back that made her veer again. It was Father Fua, dining alone beside an abstract sculpture on loan from the St. Jude Student Collection. She hadn't been back to confession since her last humiliating encounter with him, when he had made her feel like such a fool for admitting how hollow her life seemed. If her own husband didn't understand what she was going through, what in the world ever made her think a Samoan would, a male Samoan at that? Really, there was something askew in the world when women were forced to confess to men, of all people. There was so much that was simply beyond them.

"Don't look now," Myrtice whispered when Mrs. Coco finally regained her seat, "but guess who just came in."

Looking across the almost empty room—oh, why couldn't Father Fua eat in the rectory, where he belonged?—she saw the hostess leading a familiar face to Mayor Binwanger's table, a handsome young man smartly turned out in a blazer and tan trousers.

"I know him," she mused aloud, trying to place him.

"You should—it's your son," Myrtice said.

"What?"

Myrtice pointed in the other direction, at the red-padded doors where George Henry and Heidi were standing, waiting to be seated.

"Did you tell him we were going to be here?"

"Ethyl Mae, I resent you asking me that," she replied truthfully.

"I fainted," Myrtice said to George Henry after the quartet had played the Largo from *Xerxes*. George Henry and Heidi had taken a table right next to the players. "I fainted at the Bottle Bazaar this afternoon."

"You're too hard on yourself," he said, careful to avoid looking at his mother. "Gotta start eating more, Myrtice. You'll waste away to nothing. Well, if it isn't . . . are you *the* Emmanuel Miller?"

Unabashed, the child gazed at him for a moment through half-closed eyes, then turned to Mrs. Coco to suggest a new bowing. She listened while snatching glances at the table. Heidi, a dreamy smile drifting in and out of focus on her pale, curious face—it looked strangely bloated, almost waterlogged—had dressed for the occasion in gray overalls of some sort, adorned by a shawl made up, it seemed, of shredded feather dusters. All the fancy plumage was relegated to the male of the species, who was decked out in a pink jacket, bowtie, and yellow trousers. He was also sporting a moustache, which seemed odd; how could he have grown one so fast? Or did he have one the last time she had seen him? It was hard to keep track. George Henry was forever either growing one or shaving one off, never content.

"Is that the one you punched out?" E.M. whispered to Mrs. Coco, loud enough for George Henry to hear.

"I feel so . . . I don't know, happy," Heidi observed to no one in particular as the waiter placed a menu in front of her. "There's just so many good things to eat. And look, George Henry, look at all the different nationalities," she added, gesturing toward the Pro Arts. "I feel like this is sort of like, you know, the entire world, all mankind and all come together in this one little place. Oh, love, you're going to have to help me. I can't make up my mind, it's like everything, I want everything."

"How about some General Mee's chicken?" George Henry suggested.

"Do I have time to go to the gentlemen's room?" Duk-Soo inquired.

"No," Mrs. Coco said. "We've got to play now. I don't know why you always have to wait till the last minute. There was plenty of time before."

"Hey, Duk—go," George Henry said from his table. "Just stand up and go."

"What's the matter?" Heidi asked, looking up from her menu.

"Duk-Soo's mother won't let him go potty," George Henry said.

Mrs. Coco stoically regarded her music, refusing to be baited, while the Korean, a blank expression on his somewhat red face, assiduously rosined his bow.

"You gotta go, then go!"

"Love," Heidi said, patting George Henry's cheek, "not so loud."

"Goddamn it, he's just going to sit there. Can you believe it? He's just going to sit there. It's disgusting."

"Don't say that. Everything's beautiful, can't you see? All

your friends here to make pretty noises in the air for you so you'll have nice thoughts and all. Now relax."

When they began playing the Andante from K.421, they found themselves in competition with gunshots and tire squeals escaping through the gold-flecked fiberboard that separated the restaurant from the Leon Cinema. Mrs. Coco did not know if she would make it through the Mozart, much less the entire evening. Usually she felt slightly ashamed at what the Pro Arts did to the music of the great masters, but now the music itself seemed insipid, meaningless. The smoke from George Henry's cigarettes, his rude laughter, the Grasshoppers he ordered one after the other, was almost more than she could endure.

At his corner table Father Fua examined the check the waitress had just brought, then hoisted himself up with a glazed, disoriented look. Mrs. Coco followed him with her eyes, urging him out, as he scooped a handful of mints at the cash register. She was counting a rest in the Mozart while the other three played. When she came in again, Father Fua was gone. But there was no sense of relief. She still had no energy for a vibrato, and the horsehairs just whispered over the aluminum strings, two of which, the D and G, would have to be changed soon, and they were so expensive.

While making an effort to concentrate on the music, she had the unpleasant feeling that Duk-Soo was staring at her again. Turning her head sharply to catch him unawares— she simply must have a talk with him about this—she found him innocently engaged in his part. Still, she could not rid herself of the feeling. Looking over at George Henry and Heidi, she saw they were too absorbed in each other now to be aware of anyone else. Heidi was sticking the tip of her shawl in George Henry's Grasshopper, which made both of them giggle like schoolgirls. What a clever wife she would make, Mrs. Coco thought.

Glancing uneasily about the room, Mrs. Coco's eyes suddenly connected with an extraordinary pair of eyes full of pain—or was it bewilderment? Taken aback for a moment, she didn't know what to think until the Mozart jarred her memory. Why, of course, the young man who had looked so familiar when he had walked into the restaurant—it was his eyes that had been staring at her—this was none other than Rob Jr. But what in heaven's name was he doing with Mayor Binwanger? No, it was Ray—Ray Jr.

"For Christ's sake, play!" E.M. whispered, recalling Mrs. Coco to the music, which she realized now she was simply listening to, not performing. The mayor had said something that made his schizophrenic companion smile, and with that smile the pain the music described had suddenly become vivid to her, almost too vivid. Finding her place, or what she thought was her place, she joined in with a full vibrato, the bow digging in with newfound strength.

"I swear," Myrtice grumbled at the twentieth-century dissonance, which made everyone, even Heidi, wince.

E tu scruta il mister dell'orizzonte e cerca, cerca, monte—o casolar

—*Manon Lescaut*

8

The house in Ozone was not right on the lake, but it was close enough for Duk-Soo to enjoy the lake breeze, which at first he mistook for a prowler as it rattled the japonica against his bedroom window. At 4:45 a.m. the Mr. Coffee on his night table would automatically switch on so that at five, when he awoke, he could drink a cup without having to get out of bed. At 5:15 he would be at his desk in the bedroom, agonizing over the chapter in his dissertation—"*Das Unheimliche*: A Mediated Reply to the Existential Dilemma of the Tourist"—that his adviser was making him rewrite.

At seven Ray Jr., who had been instructed not to talk loud, would forget and talk loud to himself while making breakfast, forcing Duk-Soo to rap on the stucco wall with whatever was handy, usually a stapler. Aside from the talking, Ray Jr. was, generally speaking, a satisfactory housekeeper, specializing in sinks, which were kept so immaculate that Duk-Soo felt guilty using them. When Duk-Soo returned from school in the evenings, there would always be an interesting meal waiting for him, one that Ray Jr. had invented out of his own head. He wasn't able to follow any of the recipes in the *cuisine minceur* cookbook Duk-Soo had given him, since it turned out that Ray Jr. couldn't read. But Duk-Soo had nothing to complain about, except that sometimes Ray Jr. went overboard with the vanilla extract, which he liked to put in everything, including the A.1. sauce.

At eight Ray Jr. would unlock the bicycle stowed behind the japonica and bring it out front, ready for Duk-Soo to mount. Even at this hour it was already hot, and as they headed east along Lake Pontchartrain, Ray Jr., running shirtless and barefoot beside the bike, would bark playfully like a drill sergeant whenever the Korean strayed into a patch of oak shade to catch his breath. The ten-speed bike he had bought from a campus policeman would often slip its gears, making Duk-Soo, perched in pain upon the rock-hard saddle, veer and almost lose his balance. He would have preferred riding his motor scooter to St. Jude, two miles up the road, but Ray Jr. insisted that if he didn't run, he should at least pedal.

During the day, while Duk-Soo immured himself in his reserved carrel in the library, emerging only to oversee a freshman study group in anthropology or to meet with his adviser or once a week to take a violin lesson, Ray Jr. would put in five hours at Bee Bee's, a laundromat where he folded clothes and ran errands. In the afternoons he lifted weights under the persimmon and drew crayon pictures of wrestling monsters and volcanoes. When there was no longer any room on the walls in Duk-Soo's bedroom for his artwork, Ray Jr. started composing songs, which he sang into the Korean's cassette recorder as a special surprise. Duk-Soo used the recorder to help organize his thoughts about Freud's essay on *das Unheimliche*, the uncanny, and was indeed surprised when Ray Jr.'s raw, nasal voice broke in to sing about the station wagon he was hoping to get for his birthday.

Besides the caseworker from the Parish Mental Health Center in Ozone, their only other regular visitor was Dr.

Jewel, who had resigned his position at Norris State and was now on the faculty at St. Jude. It was Dr. Jewel who had suggested to Duk-Soo that he might enjoy living with Ray Jr., an idea that Duk-Soo had at first politely, but firmly, turned down. Although Duk-Soo enjoyed the boy's company, he did not feel himself qualified to tend a schizophrenic, despite the skill with which he had handled the situation at Dick's China Nights back in May when Mayor Binwanger had jabbed the boy, his cousin, with a fork during dinner. Ray Jr. had burst into tears and run into the men's room, where Duk-Soo, prompted by Mrs. Coco, had gone to see if he could be of any assistance. It turned out that Ray Jr. had been stabbed because he had said *ain't* too many times; the mayor was trying to teach him good grammar. Comforting the boy as best he could, Duk-Soo felt so sorry for him that he promised to come visit him again at Norris State.

One visit led to another, and soon they were on familiar enough terms for Dr. Jewel to allow the boy to leave the hospital premises in order to watch Emil Jannings on Duk-Soo's giant screen in the men's residence hall. Dr. Jewel was concerned that, unless he could place Ray Jr. somewhere soon, Dr. Lily Oustelet, the Executive Director at the badly overcrowded Norris State facilities, would have Ray Jr. transferred on his nineteenth birthday to the adult institution in Florence, where, Dr. Jewel assured Duk-Soo, anyone who wasn't insane to begin with was sure to become so. As it was, Dr. Jewel himself didn't believe Ray Jr. was really schizophrenic. His theory was that Ray Jr. suffered from a severe form of dyslexia that had produced, as secondary symptoms, certain emotional and socialization aberrancies. This, coupled with a predisposition to hyperactive behavior, a mild paranoia, and an imaginative use of language, had fooled Dr. Oustelet into sticking a schizophrenic label on the boy. The main point was, however, that Ray Jr.'s father, a sometime pro wrestler and full-time methadone addict, could not be counted on to provide a proper home for the boy, whose mother had been shot and killed during a holdup of the Sunoco station she managed. And neither could Ray Jr.'s cousin, Mayor Binwanger, since he was really only a second cousin and the mayor had all he could handle with a wife and four kids, plus two sets of grandparents dependent on him. There were no friends to take Ray Jr. in, the halfway house had a six- to eight-month waiting list, and, of course, Ray Jr. couldn't be expected to live alone.

Though these arguments were persuasive, Duk-Soo still would never have brought himself to take that final step of moving in with Ray Jr. were it not for the Spanish-style house in Ozone that Dr. Jewel offered him in June, rent-free. The house, once owned by a swindler who had fled the country, was the property of the state and would eventually be auctioned off in a sheriff's sale to the highest bidder. In the meantime Dr. Jewel had enough pull with certain high-level officials to keep the property off the auction block until Duk-Soo got his PhD the following spring.

Were Duk-Soo not in dire financial straits, plagued by a collection agency from the Video Ranch and, now that the summer session had begun, unable to stay in the subsidized dormitory because of a silly, bureaucratic edict, he would have looked askance at moving into a swindler's house with a schizophrenic. But it seemed as if there was no other way out for him. Even if he could afford an apartment of his own—which he couldn't—he found the idea of living alone unbearable. And neither could he stand the thought of moving back in with Bruce LaSteele in the fall. He had never forgiven Bruce or the boys in Jervis C. Mawks for their shocking behavior in regard to Mrs. Coco and the Welsh rarebit. So Duk-Soo accepted Dr. Jewel's offer, consoling himself with the thought that it would only be a temporary arrangement, just a few months until the day came when he would finally have earned the name Dr. Yoon.

Despite having freely given his consent, Duk-Soo couldn't help feeling during the first week that he had been rail-roaded into a living arrangement he basically didn't approve of. Accompanying his resentment was a free-floating anxiety that made him bolt his bedroom door at night, uncertain what the pseudo-schizophrenic—Dr. Jewel's term—curled up in a pup tent in the living room might do at night. As an added precaution, after Ray Jr. finished the supper dishes, Duk-Soo always snuck the sharper kitchen knives into his desk drawer.

By early July, though, Duk-Soo had stopped feeling homesick for Jervis C. Mawks and actually looked forward to meeting Ray Jr. outside the library for the ride home along the lake. Ray Jr. seemed genuinely eager to hear about Duk-Soo's day and would pester him with questions about what it was like at St. Jude. Fearful at first that too much small talk might somehow sap the energy for dissertation-type thinking, and worried, too, that the young people's slang he sometimes tried to use was not correct, Duk-Soo was not very garrulous in the beginning. But after a while Ray Jr.'s bad grammar and rather unusual idiomatic phrases made Duk-Soo less self-conscious about his own English, which Bruce LaSteele would mock at the drop of a cap. Although Duk-Soo had lived in the U.S. since he was sixteen, his anxious parents had drilled him unmercifully in German, French, and Italian, so that he ended up relatively fluent in five languages but felt at home in none. It was a relief, then, to find someone who would listen uncritically to his gripes about the way Dr. Miller kept him waiting a half hour for his violin lesson or how Myrtice Fitt's perfume gave him stomach cramps. Myrtice stories turned out to be Ray Jr.'s favorites, and often, before falling asleep, he would beg Duk-Soo to tell him a Myrtice, like the time Mrs. Coco accidentally spilled coffee on Myrtice's Gucci scarf, or the time E.M. put gum on her charms to keep the bracelet from jangling.

"Oh, Dr. Jewel, Dr. Jewel," Ray Jr.'s voice rang out on the new cassette tape deck his second cousin the mayor had given him for his birthday. Duk-Soo was sitting on a lawn chair contemplating the evening sky while Ray Jr. herded fire ants down the persimmon into a dirt corral where they were put to death. "Dr. Jewel he is a wise and greatly man, the smartest in all the land, says he to Mr. Yoon, who's big as Mrs. Moon, I need me some crazies, I need me some crazies, how's I to feed the chillun, I need me some crazies."

"Very nice," Duk-Soo said as the poem seemed to end.

"Hush up, sir. It ain't done yet."

Two blocks away cars hissing over the sticky asphalt of the lakeshore drive sounded like real honest-to-goodness waves, not the tepid bathtub waves the shallow lake afforded. Duk-Soo sprayed more 6–12 on his face and into the air, hoping to discourage the mosquitoes that bred so happily in the swampy pools beyond the yard, where the undergrowth was formidable enough to prevent the ill-mannered neighborhood children from taking a shortcut to the Matterhorn, a giant water slide that had risen triumphant over every zoning ordinance in the book. Sitting with his back to the garish snowcapped peak, Duk-Soo, who suffered greatly from the heat and did not venture out into the yard often, asked Ray Jr. to adjust the fan so that it was aimed right at him. And watch out, he added as the boy stumbled over the extension cord that snaked across the carefully mown crabgrass into the kitchen window.

"C-A-T," Duk-Soo said presently while Ray Jr. smoothed the station-wagon photos that adorned the trunk of the persimmon. Although both Dr. Jewel and the caseworker had advised against it, Duk-Soo was determined to teach the boy how to read. The Dr. Seuss book in his lap was a week overdue, and they had still not finished going through it.

"C-A-T," he repeated, reaching for his snifter of Courvoisier.

"See a what—where?"

"Ray Jr."

"I ain't reading none of that baby stuff." He sighted over an imaginary rifle and blasted away at an egret that had arisen from the swamp like, Duk-Soo mused, savoring a sip of the cognac, a Kantian Idea, pure and luminous.

"I done read everything they wrote about the clouds," Ray Jr. added, swatting himself on the neck.

"Why don't you put your shirt on? They'll eat you alive."

Years of lifting weights had packed solid, well-defined muscle onto Ray Jr.'s sturdy frame, but Duk-Soo, taller, heavier, and well-versed in the art of jujitsu, was not in the least intimidated. In his dreams he had already given the boy two sound thrashings.

"I ain't putting on no shirt, Mr. Yoon. There's too much heat."

"It's too hot," Duk-Soo corrected with a distracted look, reaching again for the snifter. He needed the Courvoisier— his only real luxury in life—to help dull his anxiety about the chapter he had to rewrite, in which he hoped to demonstrate how Freud's equation of *heimlich* (homely; secret) with its opposite, *unheimlich* (uncanny), was integrally related to tourism. Particularly annoying this evening was a phrase he wished to use—"*eines aus dem natürlichen Sein aufgestiegenen Spieles*"—but he had forgotten to note the source on his index card. Was it Frenkel-Brunswik or Funck-Brentano? He must find the source this evening before going to bed so he could tie the phrase in with the comment Myrtice had made when the quartet returned from an engagement in Ruston. Myrtice had been looking forward to seeing what north Louisiana looked like—she had never been there before—but when the group finally arrived in the town, she claimed it looked just like Tula Springs. This in turn reminded Duk-Soo of a remark that E.M. had made a few days earlier. E.M. didn't understand what the big deal was about the Mason-Dixon line—he and Myrtice had been arguing about it—since everything south of it looked the same as everything north. Duk-Soo called this phenomenon, where the unfamiliar place turns out to look familiar (Freud's *unheimlich* effect), *Reisetäuschung*, a neologism that his adviser, Dr. Barnes, claimed was meaningless, but let him use, nonetheless, after an impassioned verbal defense by the doctoral candidate.

"H-A-T," Duk-Soo said while Ray Jr. tried to zero in on a lone firefly. There was something else Myrtice had mentioned that might prove useful. She had been complaining that everything was named after everything else, towns and rivers in Louisiana named after towns and rivers in Mississippi, streets in Tula Springs called Texas or Utah or Wyoming, Florida Boulevard in Baton Rouge, Warsaw Bayou in Mandeville, Babylon in Long Island—the list was endless. Duk-Soo pondered this phenomenon. An existential dilemma was posed: if everywhere was dependent for its identity, its sign, on somewhere it was not, then one ended up with no actual "here" at all, only a perilous semantic obfuscation of "there." And even when one seemed to be dealing with a "here" and not a "there," a nebulous cloud of ambiguity descended on the meaning. Take North Gladiola, for instance. It was in the southern half of Tula Springs, and furthermore, there existed no South Gladiola, no Gladiola even. What did *North* in this case signify? And why *Gladiola*? The street was not a flower, not even a metaphorical flower, being as it was in the heart of the business district. Was it named after another North Gladiola by a homesick settler from Virginia or Illinois, thus making North Gladiola not a "here," after all, but a "there"? Of course, Duk-Soo was aware that hidden in the name was a Latin sword (*gladius*) and coincidentally, an Italian god (*Dio*), but he very much doubted that the namer himself was aware of this; so this was no clue to its meaning.

"What's wrong?"

Duk-Soo felt a hand upon his silver hair. Although Dr. Jewel and Ray Jr. were always punching and hugging and shoving during the psychiatrist's visits, Duk-Soo, a firm believer in respectful distances between people, removed the hand from his hair.

"I am distressed that you will not even try to learn to read. This is not acceptable."

"I done told you, I can."

Duk-Soo studied the boy's face for a moment, wondering what it could be that made such handsome features—a firm jawline, striking greenish eyes, a rosy complexion almost as fine as a girl's—seem somehow wrong, unfinished. An important element was missing, some basic selfishness that would knit the face together into a more familiar, less disturbing sight.

"I never seen no one so unhappy. It hurts my feelings, Mr. Yoon."

"Me? I am happy."

In the dusk that softened the painful blue of the Matterhorn, bullbats swooped neither near nor far, like illusions in a badly-lit 3-D movie.

"Are the Communists making you sad?" Ray Jr. asked, squatting beside the lawn chair.

The week before, Duk-Soo, having indulged in more cognac than he was accustomed to, had told Ray Jr. about a friend who had been kidnapped by the Communists. This metaphorical tale, embellished with an occasional fillip of truth, helped give vent to certain feelings that were making life so difficult for Duk-Soo. Of course, he could not tell Ray Jr., or anyone for that matter, the truth, which was that he, Duk-Soo Yoon, was married to a Communist. The idea that he, who had always believed so fervently in free enterprise, who loathed and detested labor unions and the creeping socialism of Ralph Nader's seat belts, could wind up like this, the literal husband of a Communist, was simply too much. Often he had nightmares that Dr. Barnes and the Dean of Humanities had found out the truth about him, and he would babble himself awake trying to explain.

But was there any use explaining? The cold facts remained the same. He had met his wife, Mi-Wha, at Luna Beach Christian College in Long Beach, California, where, after making an intense study of the Old Testament, he became a confirmed atheist. When they both decided to transfer to Berkeley, Mi-Wha got involved with a group protesting General Chung Hee Park's military regime in South Korea. This newfound activism worried and upset Duk-Soo, and soon the newlyweds were engaged in bitter political arguments at home. Mi-Wha insisted that she was not a Communist, that she was simply interested in freedom for all Koreans. Later she admitted she might possibly become a Communist if it meant that Korea would be free and united. To her it was an impossible state of affairs to permit an arbitrary line drawn by foreigners—the 38th Parallel—to divide a country that had not known political division for over a thousand years. To her there was no North or South: only Korea. Soon Mi-Wha would not speak English at home, only Korean, and she criticized her husband mercilessly for letting people call him by his first name. It was a mark of gross disrespect, she insisted. Had he no honor? Was he simply going to be a sham American for the rest of his days?

In 1967 Mi-Wha's brother was arrested in Seoul for subversive activities. Hearing reports of his torture, Mi-Wha made up her mind: although she loved her husband, loved him enough to want to save him and restore his true identity as a Korean, she realized she loved her country more and left the U.S. Duk-Soo never really recovered from the separation. In 1971 he made a trip to Seoul, spending his entire savings and what little he had inherited when his parents died, but all he learned was that someone—a friend of a cousin of a great-aunt living in Queens—had seen someone resembling his wife walking through the streets of Yonsan, a town near the Chinese border. Since then Duk-Soo had drifted from one graduate program to another, trying his best to avoid fellow Koreans, and succeeding best here in south Louisiana.

"You want to go to Calcutta?" Ray Jr. asked. In the dusk fireflies roamed like electrons, leaving traces of where they were not any longer. From time to time Ray Jr., incapable of sitting still, would lunge at one.

"Calcutta?"

"Where your friend is. You and me could get us some guns and blast their heads off, them Communists. And if we run out of bullets, I got this knife that could tear their goddam guts out. We'll save your friend."

Duk-Soo remembered now that his friend had been abducted to Calcutta by the Communists. "No, Ray Jr., I'm afraid it's too late. You see, once the Communists get you, they have a way of making you believe they're right, especially if you have been foolish and ignored the proper pursuits of a housewife in favor of study groups run by illiterate subversives."

"Can men do that in Calcutta?"

"Do what?"

"Be housewives? I want to be one, too."

"No, you don't," Duk-Soo said sternly.

"Look—a rat."

Feeling something flutter over his ankle, Duk-Soo kicked out spastically with a little cry while Ray Jr.—having tricked him again—hugged himself with delight.

"I got you, Mr. Yoon! I got you!"

Feeling a little wobbly as he stood up, Duk-Soo squinted at the Matterhorn, wishing it would go away. "Enough foolishness. I must get to work. Don't leave your weights scattered around like this—they'll destroy the grass. And tomorrow—are you listening to me? look at me when I talk—tomorrow I don't want any loud talk in the kitchen. How many times do I have to tell you, I'm working very hard. Now let's have a good-night salute."

"No."

"Private Ray Jr."

Remaining on the ground, Ray Jr. gave a sloppy salute with the wrong hand while Duk-Soo turned off the fan and carried it back into the house.

At three a.m. Duk-Soo arose from a bed of tangled sheets and made a beeline for his desk, where he searched in the dark for the index card with the Funck-Brentano source notes. All he had to do was identify the quotation, and the chapter would be finished—but why was this card so long and sharp? Suddenly it occurred to him that he was barking beside the wrong tree. It was Huizinga, not Funck-Brentano, and Huizinga was in the kitchen, in the third cupboard to the right, behind the Clabber Girl Baking Powder.

Urgently rattling the doorknob, Duk-Soo attempted to leave the bedroom. It wasn't fair; the answer was waiting for him in the kitchen, and they wouldn't let him out. Well, he hadn't studied the art of jujitsu for nothing. Composing himself with a deep breath, he suddenly lashed out with a cry at the door, which somehow managed to twist his shoulder behind his back. The pain, intense as any he could remember, woke him up.

"Quiet, quiet," Duk-Soo said, hobbling into the living room after unbolting the bedroom door. Ray Jr., his cropped head poking through the netting in the pup tent, shrieked again.

"Don't kill me, Mr. Yoon—please don't kill me!"

Groping in the dark for a light switch, Duk-Soo noticed he was clutching a butcher knife, not a file card, in his hand.

With a quick instinctive move he hid the knife behind his back as he turned on the ceiling light, a bare bulb.

"No, go away," the boy whimpered from inside the tent that Duk-Soo allowed him to sleep in, even though it was a big bother to set up and take down every day. Ray Jr. liked to pretend he was outside.

Slipping the knife beneath a chair cushion before Ray Jr. could see it, Duk-Soo got on his hands and knees and lifted up the mosquito netting. "Wake up," he said, vaguely aware that the boy, cowering in the corner, *was* awake. "You're having a nightmare," he added lamely.

"Go away! I hate you!"

"Look here, young man," he said, half in, half out of the tent, "let's stop all nonsense. I was just going for warm milk in the kitchen and . . . the door got stuck. I'm sorry if you have become frightened." He reached out tentatively, as one would to a large, strange dog, to placate it.

"Ow!" Duk-Soo exclaimed, yanking his hand away from the teeth. "Come out of there, young man!"

"Not unless you promise not to kill me."

"Nonsense," Duk-Soo said. But this was not good enough for Ray Jr., and Duk-Soo had to promise, his hand on his heart, not to kill him.

"You scare me so bad," Ray Jr. said after crawling out of the tent and choosing, as luck would have it, the chair with the concealed knife to sit upon. In the light of the ceiling bulb his half-naked body looked yellow, dull, and terribly mortal. "Sometimes I don't want to be here anymore. Sometimes I want to run away when I see your face all cloudy. . . . Don't, stop it."

Duk-Soo tried to make his face less cloudy. "You must not be frightened by me."

"You lock the door every night—that scares me. You're planning something, I know."

"It's the video equipment. I told you, it is very expensive. What if a thief got it?"

"No, it's you. You're writing something to the Communists. They got your friend, and now you want them to come get me."

Duk-Soo went red all over. Why had he ever mentioned Communists to the boy? What if he started talking about Communists to Dr. Jewel, and Dr. Jewel got suspicious? If anybody on the faculty began to investigate his background, he was sure he would lose his assistantship.

"Ah, Ray Jr.," he said, smiling broadly. "I have a big surprise for you. If you're good."

"A station wagon? I knew it, I just knew I'd get one. I want one with a seat that you pull up in back."

"Well, we'll think about that. This is a very nice surprise, though. It's something you've always wanted. If you're good tonight—and if you promise never to say the word *Communist*, never ever—"

"Can I say *Calcutta?*"

"Just don't say *Communist*. It's a bad word, it's wrong."

After talking for a few more minutes he was able to bribe Ray Jr. back into the tent. Then Duk-Soo returned to his room, where he slept fitfully until the smell of coffee brewing signaled the approach of another round—and Duk-Soo felt so groggy—with Funck-Brentano.

9

❁

"Take that watch off, please," Myrtice said after Duk-Soo's new digital watch chimed the half hour with the love theme from *Dr. Zhivago*. Duk-Soo had only made it to page six of the thirty-one-page instruction booklet that came with the watch; he did not understand why, when he had touched none of the buttons, the alarm persisted in signaling every half hour. There was nothing to be done about it but remove the watch for the time being, which he would have done if Myrtice hadn't sounded so impertinent. Now he felt compelled to keep it on his wrist.

During the summer the Pro Arts had swollen from a quartet into a quintet, George Henry having agreed to rejoin the group, though now playing, temporarily, second viola since E.M., who had been on the verge of quitting, refused to step down as first violin when he heard George Henry was returning. Mrs. Coco and her son had called a truce until Heidi graduated from the drug abuse program she had recently enrolled in. About a month ago Heidi had been caught taking heroin in a girl friend's hot tub—the girl friend's girl friend, who was also in the tub, turned out to be a cop—but since it was the first time she had ever used it and since she hadn't been involved in selling it, the judge let

Heidi off by making her sign up for a new program run by a Baton Rouge hospital. The idea was that the students weren't allowed out of the hospital for two months and were forbidden to receive any visitors except during group therapy, which Mrs. Coco, whose presence was requested, refused to attend. Duk-Soo had heard the whole story from Myrtice, who had gone to one of the group sessions to give her impression of what George Henry's mother was like so the counselors could get a well-rounded view of Heidi's drug problem. Of course, Mrs. Coco didn't know Myrtice had been such a good friend to her son, Myrtice being a firm believer that when it came to Christian charity, the right hand should not know what the left was up to. And she made Duk-Soo swear he wouldn't breathe a word to Mrs. Coco.

"Aw, shit," George Henry said in the middle of the first movement of the Brahms F major Quintet, which they were rehearsing that evening on the back porch of the Cocos' house. "Y'all stop."

E.M. was the last to quit playing. "Now what?" the boy asked, knocking together his wing-tip shoes in a nervous jitter.

"This piece is too hard for us," George Henry said, picking up a cigarette from the ashtray his mother and he were sharing. He had promised Heidi to give up smoking while she was in the program, so he was forced to cadge cigarettes from his mother, who had given up smoking in secret. "Besides," he went on, "who's going to want to listen to Brahms at a goddam beauty pageant? I mean come on, give me a break."

This would be the third time the Pro Arts played for the Miss Tula Springs Pageant, but the first time they played anything classical and hard. Previously they had stuck to show tunes and a cello solo arrangement of "Here She Comes."

"George Henry," his mother said patiently, "did it ever occur to you that we might have a certain responsibility in this town? It's our job to raise the level of culture, not to play down to what people think they want. So maybe a few folks will squirm during the Brahms—good, let them squirm."

Out of the corner of his eye Duk-Soo saw, or rather felt, Myrtice's eyes upon him. He tried to look nonchalantly at Mrs. Coco, as if she were just another woman like Myrtice or Mrs. Hicks, hoping that the truth, as he feared, was not written all over his face. Did Myrtice suspect anything? Did George Henry, E.M.? Sometimes Myrtice made sly comments that upset Duk-Soo, yet they were always comments that could be interpreted two ways. Trying to keep his love for Mrs. Coco a secret was a wearing business. For a year he had managed to keep it hidden even from himself. Wasn't it bad enough that he was hopelessly in love with his wife?— he would never forget the night they had parted, the bitterness, the tears, the ecstatic lovemaking—but then to compound the error by falling in love with yet another woman, and this after vowing to have nothing to do with women ever again . . . Was it any wonder he had been afraid to admit this new love to himself—until just recently, when his loneliness in the Spanish house seemed more acute than ever? He used to ponder why he made himself practice when he hated the violin so much. Well, at least he knew why now.

Once or twice the thought had crossed his mind that perhaps the best course for him to take would be to go cold turkey and quit the Pro Arts. After all, what did he hope to gain with this love? She was a married woman with six children. But he simply didn't have the willpower to stop seeing her. Lurking in the back of his mind was a vague, undeveloped thought that if he could just get some sign from her, however mute and obscure, some sign that she, too, suffered with a forbidden love for him, this secret knowledge would be enough in itself to sustain him. Realistically speaking, he had to admit that he was a striking figure of a man, who had fended off more women than he had succumbed to. Wasn't there some hope, then, that Mrs. Coco found him not altogether unappealing? And he was younger, too, by a good eight years. That should count for something.

"Everyone who wants Duk-Soo to take off his watch raise their hand," Myrtice said after another half hour had chimed. E.M.'s, George Henry's, Myrtice's—everyone's hand but Mrs. Coco's went up.

"Please take it off," Mrs. Coco said drily, dashing his hopes. Surely, if she loved him, she would have voted for him. But then again, that might have been too obvious a sign and made the others suspicious.

In the living room, where Duk-Soo planned to leave his watch on the hat tree near the door so he wouldn't forget it, he paused a moment, overcome by a strange, frustrated longing for the Coco home, almost a kind of nostalgia, as if the house were even now a thing of the past. He could never spend enough time in it. Every piece of furniture, every scuff mark on the oak-block floor, every rather tacky picture held for him a special meaning, particularly the staircase that led nowhere. Although he was not allowed on the second floor, curiosity had overcome him at a previous rehearsal, and he had examined the rooms stealthily, committing them to memory as best he could.

Brooding over the vote on his watch, Duk-Soo suddenly kneeled before the Queen Anne chair Mrs. Coco was so fond of and buried his head in the cushion, hoping to memorize the smell, which would nourish him when he had to leave.

"George Henry—that you?"

Duk-Soo stiffened, then turned. On the other side of the dimly lit room Mr. Coco sat puffing on a pipe.

"George Henry, what are you doing there?" Mr. Coco regarded him a moment, his dry, narrow face thorny with doubt and preoccupation.

Keeping his distance—the old man obviously couldn't see without his glasses—Duk-Soo hoped to ease out of the room as George Henry, muttering indistinctly. "I, uh . . ."

"Never mind—just do me a favor, boy. If I say 'Early Bird,' tell me the first thing that comes to mind. Quick now, don't think."

"Uh . . ."

"Come on, Early Bird."

"Uh, helicopter," Duk-Soo ventured, disguising his voice as best he could.

"You're not George Henry. Who are you?"

"Uh, sir, I'm . . ."

"Oh, never mind. Now try this—McNair's."

"Fine clothing and apparel," Duk-Soo said, still disguising his voice.

"Hmm." Smoke puffed from the briar as Duk-Soo headed for the door.

"By the way," the voice within the bluish cloud said, "tell that Chink in there his friend wants to see him. He's out front, I believe."

Passing through the kitchen on his way out the back door, Duk-Soo frowned at the remains of a rutabaga pie Mrs. Coco had attempted to serve the quintet. Mr. Coco had put him in an ill humor, which was churned by the qualms he had about letting Ray Jr. accompany him to the rehearsal this evening. When Mrs. Coco had first heard that Duk-Soo had taken Ray Jr. under his wing, she had been thrilled by such a tremendous display of Christian charity. The thrill, though, quickly turned to puzzlement when Duk-Soo informed her that he was not a Christian, he was an existentialist. From then on she had prodded Duk-Soo with annoying questions about Ray Jr., questions that were difficult to answer since Dr. Jewel had advised him to keep quiet about his, the doctor's, involvement—Dr. Jewel did not want to embarrass the sheriff in any way—and simply to say that he, Duk-Soo, was paying the rent on the Spanish house. This, of course, made it hard to explain why he was living with Ray Jr., other than that he felt sorry for him, which was indeed partly true. Mrs. Coco, however, had some notion that existentialists were not supposed to feel sorry for people—wasn't there a book where an existentialist shot someone for no reason at all to prove his philosophy?—so Duk-Soo was forced to remind her that it was the Christians who proved the truth of their religion by killing millions of people for no reason at all. Which made Mrs. Coco ask if he had ever heard of an existentialist nursing home or an existentialist orphanage.

As a result of these uncomfortable discussions Duk-Soo thought it best that Ray Jr. keep his distance from Mrs. Coco, who had once or twice dropped by the house in Ozone to chat with the boy. Aside from a station wagon Ray Jr.'s other big dream in life was to be allowed to accept one of Mrs. Coco's invitations to come see her at home. Why the boy should find this prospect so fascinating Duk-Soo would never know. He had promised him ten free slides on the Matterhorn, but Ray Jr. would rather see what the inside of Mrs. Coco's house was like, and what E.M. looked like in real life. So after Duk-Soo, eager to get the boy back in his tent on that nightmare night, had promised a surprise, he had little choice but to let him come to rehearsal. Actually it seemed a safe enough proposition since Mrs. Coco would be involved with the quintet. Afterwards Duk-Soo planned to whisk him back to Ozone as quickly as possible.

Ray Jr. was sitting on the curb in front of the house, peering up and down North Gladiola with a pair of binoculars Mr. Coco had let him play with. There wasn't much to see at night other than a few neon signs—the beauty college's, a package liquor store's, and at the intersection a Kansas Fried Chicken's—but Ray Jr. was glued to those glasses as if he were watching the Sugar Bowl. Squinting across the street where the binoculars were aimed, Duk-Soo tried to make out what was so fascinating. All he saw, though, above the Tiger Unisex was Merle Photography Studio, unlit, the blinds down, with a few portraits of brides and graduates displayed in the windows.

"Why don't you give those back to Mr. Coco," Duk-Soo said when a passing motorist looked alarmed by the scrutiny he was being subjected to.

"Mr. Yoon—oh, man, you're here," Ray Jr. said, carelessly dropping the glasses to the sidewalk, which was cracked by the thigh-thick roots of a live oak. "Guess what happened to me? I done got bit!"

"Be careful with these," Duk-Soo said, stooping for the glasses.

"You got to come see, Mr. Yoon!"

"Didn't I tell you not to bother me during rehearsal? Where did you get bit?"

Duk-Soo examined the ankle Ray Jr. bared, and when he didn't see anything—there was maybe a small scratch—told him to pull up his sock.

"It was a rat," Ray Jr. said, tugging at Duk-Soo's hand. "Come look, man—I done killed it."

"Now listen," Duk-Soo said, wrenching free his hand. "I've had enough of your joshing. We are through with rat tricks."

"No—I swear, this is true, cross my heart and hope to die. Come on!"

Faint leaf shadows washed over Ray Jr. as he crouched beneath a live oak in the Cocos' front yard. Duk-Soo, slightly blue from the streetlamp he stood beneath, remained on the sidewalk, his hands on his hips. From the back porch Brahms, rich, mellow, and surprisingly in tune, bathed the deserted business district with an incongruous tenderness that made the *North* in the tilted street sign seem harsher, more desolate and barren. Duk-Soo felt his throat constrict as he followed the cello's line—oh, she sounded marvelous, they all did!—through the complex design. From a distance the piece, which he had found tiresome and difficult when playing, suddenly made sense.

"Come on, man!" Ray Jr. cried out, gesturing frantically.

His heart softened, Duk-Soo decided to let the boy have his fun with him. Walking into the yard, he could see Ray Jr. prodding something with a stick.

"Look at this rat, Mr. Yoon. It's the hugest rat you ever seen, I swear. It come after me, like to bit my leg off, but I got him good."

Repulsed and yet fascinated—Duk-Soo loathed rats beyond measure—he took a tentative step or two toward the boy. At first it was hard to tell just how big the rat was, but when Ray Jr. maneuvered it with two sticks into the direct light of the streetlamp, Duk-Soo couldn't help exclaiming, not over its size, which was indeed quite large, but over its shape.

"Oh, shits!" Duk-Soo said, trying to look away from the chihuahua's limp head. "You crazy idiot! Oh, goodness gracious, Ray Jr., what are we going to do now?" Duk-Soo wandered in a circle, holding his head, moaning. If Mrs. Coco found out they had killed her dog—no, this was unthinkable. "Stop crying, Ray Jr. No crying allowed."

"You hurt my feelings. I done killed it for you. I didn't want it to scare you none."

"Bad, bad," he said, shaking the boy by his broad shoulders. "Do not kill for me, understand? Oh, God, I must get back to rehearsal. You listen to instructions and obey. Private Ray Jr., attention!"

"Sir, yes, sir." He wiped his hand over his runny nose before saluting back.

"Get a shovel in that shed over there. Now see those bushes?" He pointed out a clump of lagustrums near the sidewalk, out of the lamplight. "Bury it in there, make sure it's covered up good. Put lots of leaves and stuff—"

"Can I make a cross?"

"For Christ sake, no! You make it very natural so they can't see anything buried there. We must not let anyone know what happened, or you'll be put in jail. Now stop crying. If anyone asks, you just say you saw him run away . . . uh, no, no. Don't say anything. Let me do all the talking. You are not allowed to say anything. Now forward, march. And be quiet. And if anyone comes out, stop and hide everything . . . and remember, you're a criminal, a bad criminal."

"Mr. Yoon, don't go, sir. Stay here and help me. I'm scared. I didn't know it was against the law to kill a rat."

"Quiet," Duk-Soo said distractedly, his mind awhirl with forebodings as he hurried back inside. "Oh, goodness gracious. God help me."

"That's it!" Myrtice said with a stamp of her foot. "I'm going home."

Outside the screened-in porch the bug lamp crackled as it fried a large curious moth. Duk-Soo, all eyes upon him, stared down at the watch he had forgotten to remove, which had just sent out another half hour signal in the middle of the Brahms.

"Y'all know I can't stand *Dr. Zhivago*," Myrtice said, straightening a turquoise necklace the size of a breastplate, "and you let him torture me with that Commie song."

Duk-Soo's ears got very red. "Forgive me, but Lara was not a Communist. Now look, I'm taking it off, see."

"Myrtice, we've still got a lot of work to do," Mrs. Coco said when Duk-Soo returned from the living room, where he had peeked out the front window to check on the progress of the burial. Fortunately Mr. Coco had retired upstairs to bed; but Duk-Soo was disturbed that Ray Jr. wasn't in the yard. Surely he couldn't have finished already? Maybe he was searching for a better place to dig. . . .

"I just don't understand how y'all manage to make this

piece sound so depressing," Mrs. Coco went on, her face glistening with perspiration. "This is the Spring Quintet—don't you understand what it's all about? Brahms used to spend hours each day tramping happily through the meadows— this is a meadow in full bloom, you see. I want you to sound intoxicated with the scent of wildflowers, the black-eyed Susans and scudding clouds, the breeze rippling through the Queen Anne's lace. George Henry, you make it sound like you're walking through a parking lot."

George Henry took a swig of the Miller High Life that his mother let him keep beside his chair; she had used to forbid alcohol during rehearsals, but because of the strain he was under, she had relented. "I'm still not used to the alto clef," he said.

"E.M., honey, are you rushing a tiny bit, do you think? Oh, please stop that."

E.M. was upside down in his chair, his head where his feet should be, making gurgling noises. Sometimes when he was tired, he would revert to childhood, with a vengeance.

Mrs. Coco sighed. "Whenever the notes get difficult, E.M., you—and everyone else for that matter—start rushing and play loud. Why? Why must you do that?" She drew on her cigarette. "And Duk-Soo, is it asking too much for a smile every now and then? You look like all this is sheer torture. Don't you see, if *you* don't look like you're enjoying yourself, then how do you expect the audience to? Now why don't we listen again to what we should be sounding like."

She switched on a tape of the Juilliard playing the quintet, which was what Duk-Soo had heard when he was standing out front with Ray Jr. He wondered now how he could have been so dumb, especially since he had heard his own part being played.

Smiling whenever he felt Mrs. Coco's eyes upon him, Duk-Soo managed to get through the rest of the rehearsal without betraying too much anxiety. When it finally came time to pack up, he wandered distractedly from window to window, looking for some sign of the boy. Then, just as he was about to go out the front door to hunt him down, Mrs. Coco called him into the kitchen and told him her plan.

"I don't think it is a very good idea," he said after listening patiently. She wanted him and Ray Jr. to spend the night.

"Why? I simply refuse to let you two drive back to Ozone at this hour on that ridiculous scooter. I know there'll be a terrible accident—everyone's drunk on Saturday night."

"We'll drive back with Dr. Miller. He can put the scooter in the trunk."

"Sug, where have you been? E.M. left five minutes ago with a little boyfriend. He's spending the night in town. And Myrtice is long gone. Besides, she wouldn't drive you all that way. Honestly, the idea—two big people on that scooter. I can't imagine what came over you—dragging that poor boy here for rehearsal when there's nothing for him to do. Where is he, by the way?"

"I better go look."

"George Henry is spending the night. Do you think I'd let him drive back to Baton Rouge? Now come on, Duk-Soo. I don't want to have two deaths on my conscience."

Without replying Duk-Soo wandered out the kitchen door. His first instinct had been to get out of Tula Springs as fast as possible, but the more Mrs. Coco talked, the more uncertain he became. With her blue crystalline eyes fastened on him, he was stirred to the very depths of his soul. Was she trying to communicate something to him behind those banal words? Why was she so intent on his staying? Was this the opportunity of a lifetime—and was he going to walk away from it because of an unfortunate dog that she hadn't even noticed was gone? Of course, there was Ray Jr. But he could be put to bed right away. . . .

"Oh, Duk-Soo, hon?"

His heart pounding, he turned and saw her exquisite lithe

figure—oh, how was it possible for a woman her age to be so perfect!—framed in the yellow light of the kitchen door.

"Would you mind taking this garbage out for me?" she said, setting a plastic bag down. "Make sure you close the cover *good*."

Well, that settles it, he thought as he lugged the bag to the green cans. You don't ask someone you're in love with to take out the garbage. What a fool he was to think for one minute she might have been. But then again, you don't ask a guest to take out the garbage, either. When you came right down to it, there was something intimate about the request—it was the sort of thing you could only ask a member of the family or someone . . .

"Oh, no," he moaned after lifting the lid of the garbage can. Nestled in a bed of eggshells and coffee grounds, its head obscured by a bulletin from Our Lady of the Flowers, the chihuahua rested peacefully in its very inappropriate grave.

"Please no, I don't see this."

"Duk-Soo," Mrs. Coco's voice rang out brightly from the kitchen window, "come on back. Ray Jr.'s here in the house. I'm heating up the rutabaga pie for him. You come have some too, hon. I don't want it going to waste. . . . Now listen, Ray Jr. Decide what you want before you open the fridge. Don't just stand there staring like that. Duk-Soo!"

"I'm coming."

"What? What are you doing out there?"

"I'm coming! Just a minute, please."

"That's vinegar, Ray Jr.—you don't want that. Oh, where is that man anyway? Duk-Soo!"

10

❁

"Kings were what they had in the old days, before people knew what was good for them. Today we elect presidents. There's a president who's in charge of the whole United States—think how powerful he is. Now try to imagine a president of the whole world—think how much bigger he would be. And now—you've seen all the stars outside— well, Ray Jr., just shut your eyes and think what it would be like to have a president of all those stars, every single star in the sky. That's what Jesus Christ Our Savior is like."

Perched on the edge of the Queen Anne chair, a single pole lamp beaming down on the boy's robe she wore—whenever possible she bought her own clothes in the boys' departments, which were so much cheaper—Mrs. Coco spoke in a hushed voice, almost a whisper, as if she were afraid that Duk-Soo, upstairs in Lucy's room, might somehow overhear and try to throw in his two-cents' worth. She had never really had any time alone with Ray Jr., and she was determined to make the most of these few moments by planting the seeds of Christianity and democracy in this poor boy's soul. There was just no telling what an existentialist from a dictatorship might be imparting to him, not just by talk, but by subtle gestures, unthinking acts. Ray Jr. needed a decent chance in life, and Mrs. Coco had made up her mind that she was going to give it to him. Of course, the fact that her own religious beliefs were in a state of disarray did not quell her missionary zeal. She still had enough sound morals and ethics left over to last her a lifetime.

"How much does Jesus Christ Our Savior weigh?" he asked. Sprawled on the Navaho carpet in a pair of Mr. Coco's no-iron pajamas, which had to be pinned back at the sleeves and legs, Ray Jr. picked at his home-barbered hair, cropped as close, if not as evenly, as a prisoner's.

"Let's try to concentrate on one thing at a time," she said. It was so important that the boy learn the right way to think about Jesus. She herself was feeling increasingly skeptical about everything she had been taught, ideas that she had accepted without really examining what they were all about. Going back to the Bible, studying it as carefully as the Modern Library Freud she had bought to help her understand her husband, she found herself appalled at what was staring her right in the face. One of the most offensive passages, an almost personal affront to her, was in Luke: "But which of you is there, having a servant plowing or tending sheep, who will say to him on his return from the field, 'Come at once and recline at table!' But will he not say to him, 'Prepare my supper, and gird thyself and serve me till I have eaten and drunk; and afterwards thou thyself shalt eat and drink'? Does he thank that servant for doing what he commanded him?" That in a nutshell was what forty years of marriage to Mr. Coco amounted to, she girding herself day in, day out, without so much as a simple "thank you, ma'am."

"Who gets to vote?" Ray Jr. asked as he peered through the wrong end of the binoculars at the chair that needed new slipcovers, the teak coffee table that she wouldn't let anyone put anything on, and a rhea that Lucy, the middle daughter, had made out of bobby pins in her Girl Scout days. "Do all the devils and sheeps get to vote?"

"Vote, dear? No, heart, no one votes, really."

She was trying to teach Ray Jr., and in the meantime convince herself, that the real message of Jesus had nothing to do with kings and servants and everything else that was an insult to a good Democrat. But now that he had brought up sheep, she found herself questioning the general slant of the Bible's more bucolic metaphors. When you got right down to it, a shepherd tending his flock was not such a benign image. After all, *why* was he tending them? Because eventually one day, in his own good time, he was going to fleece some and butcher the rest. Aside from that, Mrs. Coco didn't appreciate being compared to a sheep, green pastures or no green pastures. As Connie, George Henry's ex, had pointed out when Mrs. Coco visited her goat farm, sheep were basically dirty, dumb, and nasty, while goats, who got such a raw deal in the Bible, turned out in real life to be surprisingly delicate and clean, especially those lovely slender brown Nubians.

"Then how does He get elected?" Ray Jr. asked. "It's no fair if they's no voting."

"Hon, you don't understand," Mrs. Coco said vaguely, her mind suddenly veering from goats to George Henry. It was the best thing in the world that could have happened to him, Heidi being caught red-handed like that. On the day she was incarcerated, George Henry and his mother had had a tearful reconciliation, both trying to take all the blame for the discord between them, with Mrs. Coco, to her chagrin, finally succeeding. Now that he had no one to go home to, he spent more time in Tula Springs and was actually beginning to sound quite good on the viola, which had more room for his thick fingers. Her current plan was to take George Henry shopping with her tomorrow, first to McNair's to buy some

of the underwear that was on sale, then to Powell's to return
the Waterford vase Mr. Coco had purchased for the living
room. There she hoped Connie would wait on her; the rest
was in God's hands.

"I done voted once for this man that was fixing to kill me."

"What do you mean, dear? No one wants to kill you."

"He hit me with this thing, like to broke my head."

"Who? Dr. Jewel? Did he ever hit you, Ray Jr.?"

"Can't. It's against the law."

"How about Mr. Yoon—does he ever hit you? Heart, don't
do that." He was peering at her through the binoculars.

"Why not?"

"It's not polite. Here." She took the binoculars from him.
"Is Mr. Yoon ever mean to you? Don't be scared, you can tell
me." She was beginning to wonder just what sort of guardian Duk-Soo was; the whole arrangement with Ray Jr.
seemed so odd to her.

"I ain't scared of nothing—not even the jailhouse. Y'all
can put me in Calcutta, and I'll just bust out so hard and hit
all the crazy idiots."

After a pause, during which she thought hard, Mrs. Coco
asked, "Do you like Mr. Yoon? Is he nice to you?"

"I'm nice to him all the time. I saved him from the rats,
and you know what he does, he takes all the knives and puts
them in his drawer 'cause he wants to kill me someday. He
thinks I'm a Communist. That's why we don't hug none."

Mrs. Coco blanched. It had never occurred to her before
. . . yet Duk-Soo wasn't married; there had to be some reason why he wasn't. "Does Mr. Yoon ever bother you? Does he
try to hug you? Ray Jr., sit still. This is important."

"Does Jesus Christ Our Savior like rats?"

Perplexed by his responses, Mrs. Coco thought back to the
Monarch Notes she had bought to help her get through
Freud, and concluded that Ray Jr., like most schizophrenics,
must be using something akin to poetic license to convey his

meaning. Offhand the only poem she could think of that had knives and rodents in it was the one with the line "She cut off their tails with a carving knife." Could this be what he was trying to say, that he was afraid of what Freud claimed all men feared? She couldn't remember the exact word for it now.

"Ray Jr., do you ever pet this rat or . . . play with it sometimes?"

"Ooooo! I hate it! It's ugly, horrible."

Good, she thought. He has the beginnings of a proper moral attitude. "Tell me this, sug, do you ever let anyone else play with it? You know that's very bad. Jesus doesn't like that."

"He don't?"

"Hm?" Mrs. Coco said, pondering Communism ("red"? "angry"?) and its connection with Calcutta ("black hole" perhaps; "the womb"?).

"He don't like rats?"

"No, He doesn't like you to touch them, understand. You must learn to keep your hands nice and pure so you'll— Louis, is that you?"

She thought she had heard a sound in the kitchen. Her husband often wandered about at night, checking to see that the doors and windows were locked.

"Come in here, Louis. I want to reiterate something to you."

Materializing out of the darkened kitchen doorway, Duk-Soo stepped hesitantly into the shadows of the far side of the living room.

"What are you doing in there?" Mrs. Coco demanded. "I thought you were in bed."

Duk-Soo swatted abstractedly at Ray Jr., who had scooted on hands and knees across the floor and latched on to his leg with a playful growl. "Uh, I was wondering," he said, looking at the roll of toilet paper in his hand, "do you mind if I keep the wrapping from this ScotTissue? There's a sweep-stakes for a fantasy vacation to Bermuda, and I thought it might be useful for my dissertation if I— Enough, Ray Jr. It's time to fall asleep now. Come." With a sharp yank on his arm Duk-Soo brought the boy to his feet.

"Ow—that hurt!" Ray Jr. said, dealing out a rabbit punch to the Korean's thick neck.

Duk-Soo winced and gave the arm another yank.

"Ow!"

"That's enough," Mrs. Coco said crossly. The idea.

"He needs much sleep," Duk-Soo said while attempting a fatherly pat on the boy's head. "He starts to talk crazy when overtaxed. I'm told by the psychiatric authorities to ignore such tired talk."

"I wonder what the psychiatric authorities have to say about loitering in dark kitchens," Mrs. Coco said as she headed upstairs. "I suppose they would advise us to ignore that, too."

"Pardon me?" Duk-Soo said, not far behind. "Don't schlep your feet, Ray Jr."

Propped up in his old wagon-wheel bed, George Henry was solving the Word Jumble in the Baton Rouge *Advocate* when Mrs. Coco entered with Ray Jr. and Duk-Soo in tow. The first order of business was to get the charred mattress on the vacant twin bed turned over so that the clean sheets she had brought with her would not get smudged. Mrs. Coco accomplished this with the help of Ray Jr. while Duk-Soo wondered aloud why they had to disturb George Henry, who had thrown the paper on the floor and snapped his pencil in half.

"There's a wrinkle," Ray Jr. said after Mrs. Coco had finished putting on the clean sheets and coaxed him into the bed next to her son's.

She smoothed the blanket.

"By my foot." Ray Jr. pointed so she could get that wrinkle, too.

"Ma, I thought you were going to put him with Duk-Soo," George Henry said. "What's he doing in here?"

"I don't mind sleeping with him. Let him sleep with me," Duk-Soo said sullenly from the built-in desk where he was filling out the sweepstake entry on the toilet-paper wrapper.

"Oh, George Henry, please don't confuse the issue," she said, trying not to think about Ray Jr.'s rat. "It's better if Ray Jr. is near a bathroom."

"Can I sleep with him if I get scared?" Ray Jr. asked.

"No," Duk-Soo said, "you leave Mr. Coco alone, understand?"

"By the way," Mrs. Coco said, "you and I are going shopping tomorrow, George Henry—my treat. I want to get you some decent underwear."

"Ma."

"Those boxer shorts you wear are too baggy. You'll look better and feel better in underpants—trust me. White underpants. I don't think men should wear colors."

"Can I ask a question?" Ray Jr. said.

"No," Duk-Soo said from the door. "No talking. Time for sleep."

"Good night, Ray Jr.," Mrs. Coco said. "Night, George Henry. Be nice."

Two years ago Mr. Coco had been given a choice between the new bed that vibrated and gave off heat, and his wife. When he refused to return the Craftmatic, Mrs. Coco arranged a pallet for herself in the third-floor turret, which was called the sewing room, even though she now did all her sewing in the bedroom below. The pine floor of the turret was bare, almost white with hands-and-knees scrubbing, and bare also were the five walls, except for a single crucifix awarded her by the Rosary Altar Society for her carrot-prune brownies. In a perfectly good plastic bookshelf that she had salvaged from the trash outside the Tiger Unisex—it was amazing what people would throw away—was a dwindling supply of Great Books (Mr. Coco had once brought Aristotle on a picnic with the children, and somehow it had ended up in Tula Creek) as well as the newly purchased volume of Freud and the dog-eared Monarch Notes.

On the bottom shelf, propped against a greenish Victrola, was a Douay Bible, *The Phenomenon of Man*, an outdated missal, Bruckner's third, eighth, and ninth symphonies, Albanese singing *Manon Lescaut*, and Messiaen's *Quatuor pour la fin du temps*, a record she found cold and repellent but which she was trying hard to like since the composer was as devout a Catholic as Bruckner and had written the quartet in a German POW camp. If only she were able to appreciate Messiaen—pure music, refined to the bare bone, so unlike Puccini's highly caloric confection of emotion, which she hoped one day to have the strength to renounce—then she thought she might somehow come closer to understanding that equally cold and repellent last book of Scripture, which made Heaven seem so dour, vengeful, and Lord, all that glass, what a nightmare it would be to keep it clean.

While mulling over the problem of Ray Jr.—she was determined to get to the bottom of his relationship with Duk-Soo, which was beginning to sound more and more discordant, with strange, unsavory overtones—she sat at a student desk and wrote a polite letter to Helen Ann in Australia, an angry one to Nancy in New York for spending fifty dollars on an acupuncturist (for a common cold!), and what she hoped was a fair, objective letter to her son in Banff, who had solicited a forty-dollar contribution for Friends of the Earth.

"Dear Sam," it began after she had crumpled the sheet with "Dearest Sam":

It's not because I don't consider myself a Friend of the Earth that I'm not enclosing a contribution. Rather, I feel first and foremost that it is everyone's premiere duty to be a Friend of the Family. I think everyone in this family pretends they are loaded with money and actually go out of their way to pick up the tab off strangers' tables, which is what your father did last week at the China Nights—he insisted on buying a round of drinks for a table of Lions or Elks or some such nonsense. Not satisfied with that, he felt compelled to go out the next day and buy a Waterford!! vase for the living room. This is the same guy who collects all the used wrapping paper on Christmas morning and tries to smooth it out so it can be used again: you figure him out. Anyway, he's sulking now because I'm taking the vase back tomorrow.

Dr. Jewel was at St. Jude now; perhaps at her next lesson she could drop in, casually, under some pretext or other, at the Psychology Department, to inquire about Duk-Soo.

Helen Ann has taken it into her head to quit giving riding lessons so she can farm crickets—practically forty years old and she's farming crickets. I asked the mailman what crickets were used for, besides eating clothes, and he thought some people like to put them in cages. Lucy got a poem published in something called *Tri-Quarterly*, which I asked her not to send me since there's only so much filth a mother can pretend to be proud of. (You remember the last magazine she was published in—those drawings.) Larry has finally got himself a job. He's selling guns now in Lake Charles, which makes me almost wish he were back on unemployment. Amy, you know, will be going to Southwestern in September, but this summer she's working in a car wash. My granddaughter in a car wash—I ask you, Sam, what's this family coming to?

Love,
Mom.

Before sealing the letters Mrs. Coco reread the one to

Helen Ann, wincing at her own hypocrisy. She was still fuming at her daughter for suggesting behind her back that she needed to see a psychiatrist, yet she had not brought any of this up in the letter. Ever since Helen Ann had removed herself to Australia after that disgraceful affair with the mayor, Mrs. Coco had leaned over backwards to make this oldest daughter feel that she was always welcome home again anytime she felt like it, that everything was, of course, forgiven. So what if Helen Ann had made it impossible for her mother to ever hold her head up in the community again? It was just one of many Crosses she was destined to bear. And yet not once in all these years had a single discouraging word slipped from Mrs. Coco's pen, no reprimands, no I-told-you-so's. Needless to say, this epistolary hypocrisy was one-sided; her children preferred to pour out every imagined grievance and injustice on the telephone, whether they were in New Orleans or Banff or Wollongong, usually at prime-time rates. How nice it would be to receive a letter from one of them, a sweet, simple letter telling her that everything was fine, everyone missed her and wished she were there. They might be surprised at how much good it would do them, for Mrs. Coco had a theory about hypocrisy: if you kept pretending long enough and hard enough, your good humor eventually took on a reality of its own and ceased being hypocritical. In a sense this was precisely what the saints did—*willed*, in the face of every sort of suffering and distraction, their good humor, thus making hypocrisy, in a way, the root of all good.

"P.S.," she added on the back of a sealed and stamped envelope that contained a letter to Lucy she had written a week ago at the dentist's office and forgotten to mail, "I just remembered why the boys and I used to fight over Clorox." Lucy wanted to include a reference to Clorox in a poem, but she was muddled about why it had made her mother so angry. "Larry and George Henry used to pour it on the car tires so they could leave big black marks on the Old Jeff Davis Highway. I could have throttled them. Love, M."

Sometime before dawn she entered the gravitational field of a superheated planet not on the regular tourist path. Mrs. Coco wondered why, when it was so hard to breathe, they had included it on the Economy Size Bonus Tour of Leo and its environs.

"Oh, oh," she muttered as gorgeous, lush, green clouds enveloped her. Yes, of course, this was why—its famous clouds.

It was only when she was fully awake, an hour or so later, that she recalled the dream and realized it had been Louis, not gravity, pressing against her. Had he indeed crept into bed with her, furtively, like an overgrown child, and then just as furtively disappeared? The thought was so disturbing that even though she was still very tired, she could not fall back asleep. Obviously he must have been only half-awake, as he usually was when he went to check the windows and doors. Senility was creeping up on him, but she'd be dog-gone if she was going to let it creep all the way up into her sewing room. After forty years of absolutely no privacy, she certainly deserved a sanctuary and would defend it to her last breath: Louis was due for a talk.

When she got to the bedroom, she was denied the pleasure of waking him from a sound sleep, for he was up already—which was really not that unusual for him, seeing as how he rarely slept more than three or four hours at a stretch—reading that book again, *29 Ways to Have Wholesome Fun With Your Son.* Before she had a chance to say anything, he started telling her that he was thinking of writing a book on the same subject, one that couldn't help becoming a best seller. He had already sent off a letter of inquiry to three top publishers, informing them that he would be willing to collaborate with the author of *29 Ways* if the gentleman was receptive to modern, updated ideas about fun and was still alive.

Such self-absorption almost took her breath away. She marveled how he could just sit there—the Craftmatic was in a chair position—without expressing the slightest curiosity about what she might be doing up at this hour.

Too angry to speak, she got a coat from the closet and threw it on over her nightdress.

"Where are you going?" he finally asked in an offhand manner.

"Nowhere," she said, resolved to teach him a good lesson.

Caged in the aerial atop the Bessie Building, a dim Venus was fading into the dawn, which had not yet penetrated the brick canyon of the backyard, where Mrs. Coco struggled with the hot-water heater, intent on getting it out of there once and for all, even though her husband, who still had hopes of selling it, had forbidden her many times to touch it. So, if he didn't want to listen to her, she wouldn't listen to him. Tit for tat.

Rolling the heater onto its side, Mrs. Coco flattened everything in her path, including a crawdad chimney and a zinnia, before she got to the driveway, where she rested a moment, hands on hips, while staring in mild disbelief at Duk-Soo, who was spading the lagustrums in her front yard.

"I couldn't sleep" was his reply after she had crossed the lawn to find out just what the heck was going on.

She stood there, waiting for what would come next out of this man's mouth. Flattened on one side and tufted on the other, his uncombed silver hair gave him a storkish look that made his voice, hoarse and croaking, seem somehow appropriate.

"I often garden whenever I can't sleep. It helps relax my nerves."

She nodded uncertainly. Since when had he become such a horticulturist, him with his crabgrass lawn?

"I wished to aerate these . . . things."

As he backed off from her, taking time to examine a leaf here, a bud there on his way toward the house, Mrs. Coco spent a moment assessing the damage to her "things." Seeing that he hadn't had time to do much harm—there were the beginnings of a small hole, that was all—she went to intercept him before he got away. Might as well get some help from him, she thought. That heater was pretty heavy, after all.

"Duk-Soo, could you give a hand with this?" she asked, tapping the hot-water heater with a pink mule. "I'd like to get it in the car."

Pulling George Henry's keys out of the pocket of her house smock, she went to the trunk of the Toyota and jammed in the ignition key, which Duk-Soo had to yank out for her. Mrs. Coco had only driven her son's Toyota twice, once with his permission, once without, and neither time had she had the slightest difficulty. She would have used her Dart except that she was afraid the trunk wasn't big enough. And besides, George Henry had left the keys on top of the microwave; he ought to be more organized.

"All right," she said once the trunk was open, "if we can just lift this in." Duk-Soo picked up the heater. "Hon, don't bend your knees like that," she said as his face darkened under the awkward load. She pointed to the trunk. "In there. Careful, you'll give yourself a hernia."

"Put that down!"

Half-squatting, the heater hugged to his belly, Duk-Soo seemed to visibly cringe while Mr. Coco, his face a mask of petty, Old Testament wrath, peered down on them from a second-story window.

"Duk-Soo," Mrs. Coco commanded as the heater touched the drive, "pick that up."

"He said to put it down."

"Ignore him."

"Put that down, I say!"

"Duk-Soo!" She gave him a little shove, and the heater plopped into the trunk.

"Do you think we should be doing this?" Duk-Soo, who had been pressed into service, asked as the car rocked over the divider in the driveway, which had a separate lane for the right and left tires. "Where are we going?"

"To the dump."

Coming to a stop at the intersection, Mrs. Coco told Duk-Soo that no, she would not pull over so he could read what the plaque on the Kansas Fried Chicken place said. The whole town had suddenly taken it into its head to become historical, screwing up plaques on every building that looked run-down and in need of a coat of paint. They even wanted to stick a plaque outside her home, making it an official point of interest for the tourists, but Mrs. Coco had put her foot down. "All this hullabaloo," she said as the light turned green, "and I have yet to see a single tourist come through Tula Springs."

"My hair," Duk-Soo said, catching a pale glimpse of himself in the window. He pressed down on a cowlick.

"This I will never understand," Mrs. Coco said after they had driven for ten minutes or so. The town had given way to empty pastures, woods, and truck-farming plots with thin, man-high stalks of okra that swayed like seaweed in a wash of purplish dawn air. In the midst of all this rose a formidable-looking electrified fence that surrounded a development of palatial new homes, each, according to Myrtice, costing at least two or three hundred thousand. "Putting up a fence like that—they ought to have their heads examined."

"We live in a very perilous age," Duk-Soo said.

"Sure it's perilous when your children might be electrocuted making mud pies. This is the work of that Citizens Patrol, you know. They're the ones convinced these people they need to be penned in like convicts. And you know what else they're doing? In the paper yesterday the CP was actually encouraging everyone to go out and buy a gun to protect their home."

"It's in the Constitution."

"Yes, I know. Every child has a right to blow his brains out accidentally with Daddy's gun. You'd die defending it, wouldn't you?" She glanced over at him, trying to decipher the look he was giving her. Was it anger, fear? Well, one thing she knew, this staring must stop. She would speak to him about it, once they had gotten rid of the heater.

"Accidents happen in the bathtub, too," he said. "I don't think you realize how crazy people are nowadays, how unstable the general population is becoming."

"Believe me, I do. Every time I see the mayor and that CP of his, I— Oh, Lord!" She braked suddenly, causing Duk-Soo to lurch forward.

"Doggone it," she said, starting up again with a jerk, "the trunk just flew open. I thought for a moment someone was running into us, but it was just the rope come loose. Must have been that bump we went over."

"Maybe I better tie the trunk down again so you can see in back."

"No, that's all right. I don't want to stop on the highway— too dangerous."

As they rattled over a cattle guard at the turnoff for the dump, Mrs. Coco frowned at a row of bulldozers, cranes, and some sort of bony, no-nonsense road-building machine, big as a prehistoric skeleton: all this just so people could get to the dump a little faster. The caretaker's hut was dark, so she wouldn't have to haggle with him about her expired sticker, or rather, no sticker at all—this was George Henry's car, she suddenly remembered. As she pulled up as close to the dump as possible, an acrid smell of smoldering tires brought tears to her eyes.

"Just toss the heater anywhere," she said as Duk-Soo

reached around to the back seat for the plastic garbage bag he had stuck there when they had gotten into the car. "What are you doing? What is that, anyway?" She had asked him earlier, but forgotten what he had said.

"Leaves and things, that's all," he muttered.

"What in the world did you— Oh, go on, hurry."

While he hurled his bag into the mounds of half-burnt tv dinner cartons, naked dolls, beer cans, mattresses—was it really necessary to throw it so far like that? . . . honestly, that man—Mrs. Coco went back to the trunk and discovered that it no longer held the hot-water heater.

"It must have fallen out when the trunk came open," she commented to Duk-Soo, who was panting from the exertion of heaving the bag. "What did you bring those leaves along for, anyway? And what do you mean by leaves? Was that my good mulch? I don't want you fooling with my mulch anymore, understand? If your nerves are bothering you, you can tear up your own lawn from now on."

They stood there a moment staring across the dump. On the other side the sun, still low, brassy and diffuse, made a few gangly adolescent pines seem to waver insubstantially like the reception one might get on a cheap, yard-sale tv set.

"Ethyl Mae, when you asked me to spend the night . . ."

Startled by the "Ethyl Mae," Mrs. Coco glanced over at him and again saw the look that had puzzled her in the car. But now it suddenly occurred to her what it must mean.

"I know I must sound a little crazy about the trash and all," she said, trying not to panic. She simply must not allow him to go on. "But you know the leaves and twigs and stuff, with the new trash service we have in town, why, you can't just throw them out front like you used to. There's all these new rules and regulations, no limbs over three feet, the men won't pick them up. And the leaves have to be practically gift-wrapped, tied up in plastic bags, and they won't lift anything over eight pounds, I believe, or is it twelve?—the men, that is, they won't. In any case, that's why I had to bring the heater out here myself and—"

"Ethyl Mae, please listen. I must—"

"No, Mr. Yoon, don't, I beg you, don't say—"

". . . how I feel about you, so very very—"

"Stop, don't!" she said, too frightened to meet his eyes, choosing instead to focus on the gulls that had strayed far from any water to pick at the discarded bones and rotting flesh. "Please get in the car, Mr. Yoon. It's time we left."

As they were driving past the bulldozers again, she cast about for something to say that would break the silence. Of course, if she had any sense at all, she would inform him here and now that his services with the Pro Arts were no longer required. The nerve of this man to think for even one second that she, probably the most devoutly married Catholic in Tula Springs, would even begin to entertain any such . . . Why, he ought to be horsewhipped. Yet at the same time that these angry thoughts bustled in and out of her somewhat rattled mind, she was entertaining a second set that were more reluctant to depart, try as she might to get rid of them. These were flattering, smooth-talking thoughts that reminded her that not every woman her age had won such devotion from a man. Unable to deny the exhilarating sense of guilt-edged power this gave her, she asked herself if it wasn't true that Duk-Soo had always behaved like a perfect gentleman. Not once had he made any untoward advance— discounting, of course, what had happened a few moments ago, which could be attributed to lack of sleep, perhaps. But surely in the future she would be able to keep him in line. That shouldn't be too difficult to manage with someone who was basically docile and already, in a sense, housebroken.

"Thank you, Mrs. Coco. I think Ray Jr. might like that," he replied when she suggested picking up a bag of doughnuts.

Mrs. Coco—yes, that was much better. "There's a man who sells them out of his trailer, Duk-Soo. Keep your eyes peeled. It's just to your left when we pass this billboard up here."

11

❀

The Fitt home on Newt Drive was distinguished by three trompe l'oeil dormers and the only solar-heated living room in Tula Springs. Seated around spindly card tables in this glass-walled show room, which had almost appeared in *Southern Living* but had been yanked at the last minute to make space for a feature about a converted barge, the DAR ladies ate their luncheon while trying to ignore the preteens in the yard next door, who were entertaining themselves by pretending to be rock stars, squirming and gyrating vulgarly with broom guitars.

"I'm Maud Herbert," a stout older woman said when Mrs. Coco, her plate filled with stuffed vine leaves from the buffet, sat down by her place card. "I'm not a Daughter of the Revolution—I'm just a friend of a Daughter, Mrs. Keely, over there." She pointed out an attractive woman sitting at the table with the only man in the room, Duk-Soo.

"Mrs. Coco," Mrs. Coco said generally to all three women at her table, but the two well-dressed women who had ignored her when she sat down continued, after a nod in her direction, their own hushed, private conversation. It was an odd feeling to recognize almost no one in the room. Tula Springs was such a small town, yet lately every time she

went to the market or downtown to shop, she would begin to
feel like a stranger. In the old days, when the children were
growing up, it had seemed as if she had known everyone.

Only half-listening to Maud Herbert's comments about
how she really couldn't approve of revolutions—that was
the reason she wasn't a member of the DAR, even though
her pedigree was in order—Mrs. Coco pondered the remarks
she would make to the group after the mayor, who had not
arrived yet, had said a few words. Although Myrtice had
been reluctant to invite her, Mrs. Coco had finally prevailed,
convincing her that the Pro Arts would be a worthy cause for
the DAR to get interested in. Feeling inside her handbag, she
made sure that the tape cassette was still there: the talk
would be illustrated with excerpts from their repertoire.

"Do you realize that Dr. Johnson considered the American
Revolution to be immoral?" Maud Herbert asked as she
sampled a piece of *spanakopitta*. Myrtice had chosen a Greek
theme for the luncheon, with each dish on the buffet table
carefully labeled. "Really, I've been so disturbed thinking
about it lately. What did the Colonies prove but that might
makes right? And what about all the oaths Mr. Washington
and Mr. Adams had made, swearing allegiance to God and
country, which meant Great Britain? Every single so-called
patriot broke his word to God. No wonder they had to use
all that fancy language in the Declaration of Independence,
trying to hide their guilt, justify the fact that they had lied."

"But wasn't the king bad?"

"Was he any worse than these freedom-loving patriots
who kept slaves? Oh, please, let's not talk about it—it's too
upsetting. Coco, you say your name is? Any relation to that
darling man who works at McNair's?"

"My husband. He owns it, actually."

"I do wish you had brought him. Really, I can't stand
being in a roomful of women."

"He's on a little minivacation now," Mrs. Coco said, using

the same words she had tried out on the clerks at McNair's this morning to explain the darling man's sudden departure from Tula Springs. He had told her yesterday that unless she brought back the hot-water heater from the dump, he was going to leave her and move in with George Henry in Baton Rouge. Seeing that he was serious, Mrs. Coco had driven back out on the Old Jeff Davis Highway, and while looking on both sides of the road, she had run over a small duck, which made her very angry at her husband; so she had turned back without ever finding the heater.

"I think it's so nice when husbands and wives take separate vacations," Maud Herbert said, while Mrs. Coco plucked a bit of *spanakopitta* that had flown out of Maud Herbert's mouth off her plate. "I'm always suggesting that to Mr. Herbert. He's such a terrible person to travel with—everything's got to be planned out in advance, right down to the smallest detail. He's a lawyer, you know. We were in Moscow last spring, and he got so mad at me I thought, all right that's it, I'm through. You see, I had gone to the Mongolian Embassy. I wanted to see if we could get on a Chinese car on the train to Peking. Oh, those Russian cars are so dreadful, the toilets and such, I absolutely refuse to go number two when we're on them. But the Chinese were supposed to have such nice clean cars, with showers, too, I heard. Anyway, he was so worried I'd get arrested. And I did."

"You were arrested?"

"Quite. The police took me in for causing a disturbance at the train station. This dreadful old woman in socks and high heels—they all dress like that, you know, absolutely no taste—she came up to me and told me to stop putting my finger in my ear. If it had been the first time, fine, I would have let it pass. But it seemed that everywhere I went, these officious old women would come up to me and tell me to stop doing things. Well, I had had enough. I told her right then and there where she could get off, and the next thing

you know I was in custody. Mr. Herbert was furious—not at
them, at me. Anyway, it was an experience."

Vaguely puzzled and amused, Mrs. Coco regarded this in-
nocuous-looking woman a moment before inquiring, "Why
did you put your finger in your ear, Mrs. Herbert?"

"I have a horrid time with altitude, Mrs. Coco, and I still
hadn't recovered from the Russian plane we were in. I think
they keep the pressure down to save money. Oh, rats, it
looks like I'm going to have to try another parsleyed sar-
dine—they're so good."

Finding herself drawn to Maud Herbert, whose unruly
gray hair was adorned by the only hat in the room, a pillbox, Mrs. Coco suffered a small pang of jealousy when she
began to talk just as free and easy to the other two ladies at
their table. Trying to appear indifferent, Mrs. Coco gazed absently toward the glass wall and blushed when her eyes met
those of a gas man who was wandering around the yard
looking for the meter.

"Tell me," Maud Herbert said as they both replenished
their plates at the buffet, "who is that extraordinary man
you were chatting with a few moments ago?"

"Mr. Yoon—he's my second fiddle."

"You must introduce me."

"Look, I've got it on Off," Myrtice said, emerging from her
knotty-pine kitchen with her husband, who had been tying
flies with the maid. Sleek and lean as a whippet, Dr. Fitt
radiated nervous energy as he stooped in front of the deluxe
walnut-cabinet tv, which apparently would not stop playing.

"I called WBRZ, Dewey, and told them to quit transmitting so we could have our meeting," Myrtice said as Maud
Herbert tried to squeeze past her to the Korean. Next to
Myrtice, Maud Herbert, in a shapeless polyester suit as
bland as her broad, unmade-up face, seemed positively
dowdy and at home, while Myrtice, every hair in place, her

eyes darting from one guest to the next, looked as insecure as a gate-crasher.

"Will you get out of my way?" Dr. Fitt snapped at his wife, thus clearing a way for Maud Herbert and Mrs. Coco. Duk-Soo remained seated at the card table he shared with the three women who had gotten up to view the blue-denim bathroom fixtures that had been written up last week in Mrs. Jenks's society column.

"I think I heard your quartet play once," Maud Herbert said after introducing herself and taking a seat, "but I'm not sure. Are you good?"

"Yes, ma'am," Duk-Soo said.

"Well, then it must not have been you."

Mrs. Coco and Duk-Soo exchanged a glance.

"By the way, Mrs. Coco," he said, "aren't George Henry and E.M. coming?"

"Who are they?" Maud Herbert asked.

"The other members of the Pro Arts. No, Duk-Soo, I thought I told you. George Henry can't make it, and E.M. is at the doctor."

"Oh, his lice."

Mrs. Coco frowned, hoping Maud Herbert, momentarily distracted by the domestic spat over the nonstop tv, hadn't heard. E.M. had contracted the lice at a Boy Scout camp, which his mother was suing, not because of the lice, but because of the bees that had attacked him while he was practically naked, in some Indian getup.

"Tell me, Mr. Yoon," Maud Herbert said, filching a marinated black olive from one of the women's plates, "from your perspective, would you say that rebels who overthrow the legitimate, God-appointed government by superior force of arms, by the fact that they are more skilled in wounding and killing their fellow man, would you say that the self-proclaimed republic they set up afterwards is a legitimate one?"

"Most certainly not," he said.

"You're saying, then, that the U.S. is basically illegal?"

"I beg your pardon?"

"Mrs. Herbert, tell me more about your trip to Moscow," Mrs. Coco said, anxious to avoid a political discussion with Duk-Soo.

"Oh, Moscow, how boring. I'm sure Mr. Yoon knows all about Moscow."

"Moscow? I know nothing about Moscow," Duk-Soo said, suddenly getting to his feet. "Nothing."

"Hmm." Maud Herbert tapped a demitasse spoon on her weak chin as the Korean wove past the other tables. "Is he always this difficult?"

Not heeding Mrs. Coco's advice to leave him be, Maud Herbert got up and with a determined look on her face followed him into the kitchen, which meant that Mrs. Coco was left alone with one of the ladies who had returned from viewing the blue-denim fixtures.

"I thought it meant they were made out of jeans or something," the lady said. Much younger than any of the other women here, she was accessorized to perfection, her purse, shoes, scarf, earrings, bracelet, pin, necklace, and ankle chain all complementing one another in a medley of ivory and gold. "Turns out it's just a shade of blue."

Anxious to pave the way for a warm reception to her talk, Mrs. Coco smiled graciously and commented on Myrtice's lovely home.

"Yes, ma'am. I like everything, too, except the Scandinavian rugs."

"Do you live here in town?"

"My husband and I live out on the Old Jeff Davis Highway, the Beáu Arts Estates."

"Oh, that new development with"—*that horrid electric fence*, she almost said—"all those lovely homes."

"Yes, ma'am."

Stealing a glance at her place card—Mrs. Jane Loll, it said—Mrs. Coco pondered how someone so young, hardly much older than her daughter Lucy, could afford to live in one of those expensive homes. And *her* daughters were always telling her that the world had changed, that no one their age led a settled life.

Intrigued by this young lady's poise and grooming, Mrs. Coco was not at all surprised when during the course of their chat Mrs. Loll brought up the name Connie Danbar, George Henry's ex, who turned out to be a good friend of hers.

"So *you're* the mother," Mrs. Loll said, her hazel eyes, which accessorized so well with her outfit, suddenly becoming bright and animated. "I've always thought it was so great that you and Connie stayed friends after the divorce. I just didn't think someone your generation would understand."

"Nonsense. The only thing I'll never understand is my son. Connie is pure delight, Jane dear. May I call you Jane?"

"Of course." While Mrs. Loll went on to say something about Connie's sweet goats, Mrs. Coco's face clouded with the memory of the trip to Powell's yesterday to return the Waterford vase. George Henry and Connie had been more than cordial, actually kissing each other and exchanging little hugs, but nothing had come of it, no plans to get together again, no questions asked, no response to Mrs. Coco's last-minute suggestion that Connie come over for dinner. Instead, as soon as they were outside the store, George Henry had started up again trying to get his mother to attend a group therapy session with Heidi at the hospital in Baton Rouge, which was where he was now.

"Well, if you ask me," Mrs. Loll said after Mrs. Coco made a few disparaging remarks about George Henry, "your son has been a real pillar of niceness. I'd be proud of him if I were you. I was talking about it to a friend of mine, he's a doctor, and he said George Henry had done the right thing."

The idea that her son's affairs were being examined by perfect strangers was a little disconcerting, but Mrs. Coco hid her uneasiness, anxious to hear more.

"You realize, Mrs. Coco, that Connie was willing to try a little therapy on herself. But George Henry didn't think it would do much good."

"It's not her who needed the therapy."

"That's just what Dr. Jewel said."

"Dr. Jewel? Is he your friend?"

"Sort of. See, my sister is married to his brother, and we all get together every now and then mainly because my husband and Dr. Jewel, they both enjoy frying turkeys. Me, I just hate the whole idea. You know how many gallons of peanut oil they used last Thanksgiving? A twenty-pound turkey, whole, they just dumped it into a barrel in the backyard, and I spent the entire morning waiting for my willow to go up in smoke."

"Hon, is this the Dr. Jewel that teaches at St. Jude?" she asked, curious to find out as much as she could about him. She had tried to talk to him after a couple of cello lessons, but so far he had proved to be elusive, always having left the office just five minutes ago, or ten, for an important conference or a faculty meeting.

"He sees people private, too, and I guess he's doing pretty well since you ought to see the house he bought. I tell you, it was the best thing ever happened to him, getting fired from that dumb old hospital."

"Norris State? But I thought he quit."

"Well, he did, if you want to be picky about it. But for the past three years while he was there, his boss was holding some sort of competency hearings on him—a real dragon lady. She was making his life miserable, so he just decided to quit, even though he knew he really shouldn't since that sort of made it look like she was right about him. Anyway, he's making about five times what he made at that stupid place. Oh, here comes Mr. Yoon. He's so nice, isn't he? I think Orientals are so polite."

Looking behind her, Mrs. Coco saw Duk-Soo and Maud Herbert returning from the kitchen, stopping along the way for a few words with Myrtice, who had just placed an afghan over her tv screen so people would stop staring at it.

"You were saying, Jane, about Dr. Jewel?" She was dying to hear more about the competency hearings but didn't want to appear indiscreet.

"Do you know him?"

"Not really, but . . ."

"Well, anyway, Dr. Jewel thinks it's just a phase Connie is going through. I sure hope he's right. I mean personally I don't mind anyone turning gay and all, if that's what they really want. But somehow I just don't think Connie was cut out to be a lesbian. Oh, hello."

Maud Herbert pulled out a chair for Duk-Soo, then sat down beside him. "I told my friend Mrs. Keely I was appropriating her seat so I could talk to this fascinating man," she said to Mrs. Loll. "I bet you don't know what Korea is really called, do you, Mrs. Coco?"

Still wondering if she had heard right with all the chatter going on about her—no, it was impossible, George Henry had never mentioned a word of this to her, and Connie was so stable and normal, she dressed so ladylike—Mrs. Coco nodded absently.

"You do, huh? What, then?"

"Yes, nice."

"You don't know. Shall I tell them, Mr. Yoon? Well, ladies, it's Han Kook. Now think about it—here's this country that is known to its citizens as Han Kook, and yet everyone else in the world calls it Korea. Isn't that positively insulting?

Why, what if everyone went around calling the United States 'Zululand' or something like that—how would we feel?"

"Jane, how about some more vine leaves?" Mrs. Coco asked, anxious to get away so they could talk in private about Connie; surely there had been some mistake. But Mrs. Loll was not interested in the buffet.

"Listen to this," Maud Herbert said, "*kotkese yo kot.* Isn't that lovely—the rhythm, the lilt?"

"*Kotko kese yo,*" Duk-Soo said patiently.

"Yes, *kotko kese yo*—that's what I said, wasn't it? Does anyone know what that means? Shall I tell them, Mr. Yoon? It means, someone honored is walking. Isn't that marvelous? They have a special tense for honored people in Korean. Which reminds me, it doesn't look like our honored mayor is going to show up after all. I just talked to Myrtice, and she said he had to go to New Orleans at the last minute."

"Probably had to collect some bribes," Mrs. Coco heard herself say, coming out of her brown study. Normally she was much more discreet in public about her likes and dislikes, but the mayor—the man who had ruined her daughter's life—was the last person she needed to have mentioned today of all days. Just before coming over to Myrtice's she had been visited by the mayor's brainchild, the Citizens Patrol, who had wasted a good fifteen minutes of her valuable time cross-examining her about the whereabouts of the beauty college's chihuahua. As if she had the slightest notion what had become of it, or even cared.

"Oh, do you think he's doing something illegal?" Maud Herbert asked.

"Him and that CP of his. Why can't we just have a normal police force like every other town? All this private patrol business, I bet you ten to one there's something crooked going on. Someone's making a bundle."

"Well, I must say, those uniforms of theirs always seemed

vaguely Fascist to me. But does the mayor actually own the CP?"

"No, of course not. But I'm sure he's got his finger in the pie somehow or other. Jane, where—Jane, dear?"

"Touchy, isn't she?" Maud Herbert commented after Mrs. Loll, a peculiar expression on her face, left the table. "I don't know why she can't take a little criticism."

"What do you mean?" Mrs. Coco asked with a significant look at Duk-Soo, who was eating too fast and not contributing much to the conversation.

"I suppose she didn't like us discussing her father. She's a bit of a priss, don't you think?"

"Her father? Mayor Binwanger is her father?"

"Why, yes, I thought you knew."

"No, I— Oh, Mrs. Herbert, why didn't you stop me? Why did you let me go on like that?"

"Hello, dear." Maud Herbert waved at Myrtice's mother-in-law, who was on the other side of the slanting solar wall with Glass Plus in one hand and wadded-up newspaper in the other.

"I don't believe in cleaning glass with newspaper," Maud Herbert commented to Duk-Soo. "It leaves little flecks. Did you say something, Mrs. Coco?"

"She said she didn't see how music had anything to do with democracy—that's exactly what Myrtice told me," Mrs. Coco said as she drove Duk-Soo back to North Gladiola, where he had parked his scooter. At the last minute Myrtice had asked her, since the business part of the meeting was canceled because the mayor wasn't coming, would she mind not giving a lecture. Mrs. Coco had tried to act indignant, but she was secretly relieved, especially after all that had happened at the luncheon.

"That woman is a real pill," she went on. "We had a good chance of squeezing some money out of those old biddies.

They would have been glad to contribute to the Pro Arts, I know."

"I think Myrtice was upset because of her tv. And then when Mrs. Fitt started cleaning the solar panels . . ."

"Of course, Duk-Soo, I know it didn't have anything to do with democracy. By the way, what did you make of that girl?"

"Who? The one with—"

"Never mind," she said dully, deciding that, after all, it wouldn't be such a good idea to bring up anything even remotely connected with Connie. But the news stuck in her craw, an undigested lump that made it hard to focus on anything else and would have certainly made it almost impossible to give a coherent speech to those women. The nerve of George Henry not telling her about Connie—if it was true; was it? could it be?—when every Tom, Dick, and Harry in Tula Springs was calmly discussing it over his fried turkey.

Back at North Gladiola, Mrs. Coco debated whether to ask Duk-Soo in for a cup of coffee. It was a little unnerving being alone in that big house without her husband, and besides, she had to admit to herself that there was something comforting about having a person around who adored you—but only, of course, if you could trust that person not to overstep any bounds.

"I suppose I better head back," Duk-Soo said, standing in the front yard, halfway between his scooter and the door.

"Well, I'd ask you in for a cup of coffee . . ." She felt the scapular beneath her blouse.

"That would be agreeable."

Under the oak a catbird toyed with a bluish grub, letting it drop from its beak, then picking it up again, dandling it, while keeping a sharp eye on Mrs. Coco, who had come to a halt only a few feet away.

"No, Duk-Soo, I can't invite you in," she said with a sudden change of mind. She had just recalled what Jane Loll had told her about Dr. Jewel's being fired from the hospital, and this had triggered a whole series of doubts, including misgivings about the propriety of letting Duk-Soo into the house when her husband wasn't home. Why couldn't she just go ahead and fire Duk-Soo? What was wrong with her? "You see," she went on, trying to remain calm, in control, "I'm just a little tired of being lied to all the time. When I ask you about Ray Jr., I expect a reasonably honest reply. I don't want to hear about your existentialism and your tourism. Why is it that everyone insists on pulling the wool over my eyes—you, George Henry, Myrtice? She didn't have the slightest intention of letting me speak today, but she was afraid to tell me the truth until the very last minute."

"That was dreadful, yes. She is a pernicious woman. To think of all the money we might have collected today."

"Please go home. I don't feel like talking. I'm sorry."

As she headed for the house alone, the catbird rose with half a grub into the stultifying North Gladiola afternoon, which, Mrs. Coco thought, would have made even those twentieth-century shepherds, Lucia and her Fatima cohorts, fidgety and listless, indifferent to Communism.

12

Fall never brought much color to Ozone; the water-oak leaves that did die, withered discreetly beside others that managed to hang on, dully, through the winter. Like an amateur's attempt to render sunlight, the specks of orange provided by smell melons in the undergrowth did little to bring the landscape to life; bolder strokes were needed from a cleaner, less murky palette, Duk-Soo idly concluded as he gazed out the bedroom window at the border of his lawn. He was practicing scales, but after three octaves of E, three of F, F sharp, and G, his mind struggling for the detachment of a nun telling her beads, Duk-Soo could still find no peace. As if it weren't bad enough that his adviser had made him throw out the *Unheimliche* chapter—all that work, the agonizing rewriting, for nothing—there was now that phone call from George Henry to worry about. Mrs. Coco and George Henry were not on speaking terms again because he had let Heidi move back into his house after she got out of the hospital, which meant that the Pro Arts, after just having learned to make the Brahms Spring Quintet sound happy, was back to being a quartet.

"Are you and my mother having an affair?" George Henry had asked on the phone earlier that afternoon. Duk-Soo, unprepared for such directness, could not manage a reply at first. The closest he had ever got to telling her what he felt about her was on that day in August at the dump when he had dared call her Ethyl Mae. But the twisted look she had given him, a clear expression of outraged Catholicism, was enough to make him back off. Since then he had never tried to approach her in that manner, contenting himself with whatever crumbs of affection fell his way as a member of the Pro Arts.

"No, most certainly not. I don't know what you're talking about. What do you mean? No, of course not. What a joke."

"OK, OK, I didn't think so. It's just that everywhere I go people are talking about y'all. And then when Dad left home . . ."

"I believe he left because of a misplaced hot-water heater."

"Yeah, I know, but listen, man, the day before yesterday I went back to Tula Springs to get some clothes I forgot, and this dame from the beauty college next door, she comes over to my car and starts telling me stuff about you and Mom in your dorm at St. Jude. I mean like I wouldn't have given her the time of day except that it happened to be stuff that Myrtice had been hinting at— Oh, and then it turns out this dame's nephew was an eyewitness. Now tell me the truth, Duk-Soo, did you have a roommate called Bruce La-something?"

"Well, yes, Bruce LaSteele, but—"

"OK, so I say, fine, you know how it is when people start telling stories, things get out of hand and all. But then Heidi and I went to this party the other night at my ex-wife's place, and this chick tells Heidi that she saw you and Mom stopping for doughnuts at five in the morning on the Old Jeff Davis Highway."

"Oh, that. I was just helping her remove the hot-water heater."

"OK, you want me to buy that, I will. But then what the

hell were you two doing up at five in the morning? I mean why couldn't you take the heater at nine or ten, something a little more normal? And if you did take the heater there, why is it no one can find it? Dad went and looked all over the dump, you know. And furthermore, what were you doing in a Mercedes? You don't have a Mercedes, do you?"

Duk-Soo hesitated, remembering now that Mrs. Coco had made him swear he wouldn't tell George Henry that they had borrowed his Toyota; he was very touchy about the car. "I don't think so."

"You don't think so? Everyone knows Mom's old trash heap, but this chick swore she was in a fancy Mercedes."

"Oh, yes, a friend of mine, Dr. Jewel, he has a Mercedes."

"You mean to say you were in his car? How could you be? You came over on your motor scooter that night—that's why Mom made you stay over—I mean that's why she *says* she wanted you to sleep over."

"It must have been some other time," he said vaguely.

There was a moment's pause. "Look, Duk-Soo, I'm not trying to hassle you or anything. I mean like deep down I really can't believe Mom is doing anything funny. But then I get to thinking how religious she is, and that throws me. It's like I've never met a religious person who wasn't basically nuts. So then I think, who knows, maybe she is having an affair."

"George Henry, *I* know. It is impossible, believe me."

"Are you afraid of my father? Honest, man, you don't have to worry. I promise I won't tell anyone. It's just that I got to know, for my own sake. It's very important. Listen, I'm going to let you in on a little secret."

"Please no, don't."

"You got to promise not to tell Mom. See, Heidi was in Ozone the other day installing a tub for this dude, and she decides to swing by St. Jude on the way home. So she finds your old dorm and—"

"How did—"

"Hey, let me talk. There's this woman, the dorm mother or something, and you know how good Heidi is at being friendly, making people like her. Well, before long Heidi's got her eating out of her hand, the mother's telling her all about how Mom used to break the pariah rules, sneaking into your room all the time. Now listen, Heidi says this mother was too dumb to make up any lies. It all sounded pretty straight to her."

"She didn't like to talk in the lobby, that's why your mother would come to the room. And as for that time she was throwing up, it wasn't because she was drinking."

"Throwing up? You mean what Myrtice told me was true? I didn't believe that for one second."

"No, no, you see, I tried to tell Myrtice there was no alcohol involved."

"But she was throwing up?"

"Your mother? Well, no, not really."

"Then why did you say . . . Listen, Duk-Soo, you got to play straight with me."

The conversation had gone on like this, up and back, one minute George Henry convinced that the whole town was bonkers, the next that his mother was, while Duk-Soo, against his better judgment, continued to protest too much. It was all most distressing and left Duk-Soo feeling drained and useless when he finally hung up.

After three octaves of C sharp minor Duk-Soo rewarded himself with a shot of Courvoisier and ten minutes of Leni Riefenstahl in Dr. Arnold Fanck's 1930 masterpiece, *Stürme über dem Mont Blanc*, on the video recorder. He really could not get over how much Mrs. Coco resembled Miss Riefenstahl; even some of their gestures were exactly the same. It was this striking resemblance that had first attracted him to Mrs. Coco, and that made him turn for solace to the early Riefenstahl films, the ones she herself appeared in before she ruined her name with *Der Triumph des Willens*. As Miss

Riefenstahl, breathtakingly severe in her icy perfection, scaled the peaks in *Stürme* to rescue her lover from the frozen life of the intellect, peaks that were obviously the objective correlatives of Nietzsche's "unuttered truths," Duk-Soo wondered why he had chosen tourism to write about. Why hadn't he ever finished the film thesis begun at the University of Mauna Loa, "German Expressionism—From Mabuse to Lola Lola"?

The ten minutes of *Stürme* had stretched into an hour, one shot of cognac to five, when the doorbell sounded the first five notes of "La Cucaracha."

"Wipe the dismay from your face, Mr. Yoon," Maud Herbert said after he had opened the door. "We've brought you some goodies." She held up a large straw bag on which colored beads spelled out "HAVE A NICE DAY."

"Hello," he said, nodding to Mrs. Coco also, who was standing a little to one side, looking slightly embarrassed and chilled.

"Just the thing after a two-martini lunch," Maud Herbert said after she had admitted herself into the living room, "a proper tea with plenty of biscuits. Ethyl Mae asked me to drive her to her violoncello lesson—her car's in the garage—and to thank me she bought me lunch at that dreadful establishment right down the street from you, dear. So now I'm trying to salvage the day with a proper tea, and you, Mr. Yoon, are my guinea pig. I just know I can count on you to be interesting."

Ushering them past the pup tent to the used convertible sofa that Dr. Jewel had been good enough to provide them with and which Ray Jr. refused to sleep on—in return Duk-Soo refused to help him take down the tent anymore, which was why it stood there in the middle of the room—he told the ladies to make themselves at home while he checked something in the bedroom.

Putting on shoes and socks for the proper tea, and a shirt,

of course—the ladies had caught him bare-chested—Duk-Soo wondered why Mrs. Coco never seemed to go anywhere these days without bringing that woman along. He could not figure Maud Herbert out. She claimed to have been born in Tula Springs, yet she didn't have the slightest trace of a Southern accent; in fact, she even sounded a little English to him. And why was she studying Mandarin? Did that have anything to do with the fact that she had been detained by the KGB in Moscow? What was she doing in Moscow to begin with? But what disturbed him the most was her lack of respect for the U.S. Government, which made her sound like either a Communist or someone a little to the right of George III—he wasn't sure which. All he knew was that he resented her influence over Mrs. Coco and was anxious not to be seen in public too often with someone so politically unorthodox lest his name be linked with hers in any way, shape, or form.

"Ray Jr.? He's out at the laundry, I suppose," Duk-Soo said when he had rejoined Mrs. Coco in the living room, a foulard about his neck. Maud Herbert had gone into the kitchen to get the water boiling.

The truth, though, was that Dr. Jewel had driven Ray Jr. out to the Beáu Arts Estates for dinner with the mayor at Mrs. Loll's; but Duk-Soo would rather not bring up Dr. Jewel, who had become something of an issue between Mrs. Coco and him. She had told him that Dr. Jewel had virtually been fired from Norris State for incompetency, news that was, needless to say, somewhat disconcerting for Duk-Soo to hear. This constant prying of hers was beginning to wear on his nerves: she wanted to know if Dr. Jewel had any specific program for Ray Jr.'s rehabilitation, or was the boy simply expected to work in a laundry for the rest of his life? Twice already she had clashed with Mrs. Phillips, the caseworker from the Parish Mental Health Center, demanding to know why Ray Jr. wasn't being taught to read, an impossible task, of course, as Duk-Soo had tried to tell her many times. Was he a schizophrenic or not? she had badgered Dr. Jewel one day at the house. Why couldn't anyone make up his mind what was wrong with him, and why were they always changing his medication? Did he need medication at all? And why wasn't anyone providing him with proper religious instruction? Why did she have to shoulder this responsibility herself when she barely had enough time to practice her cello?

On top of all this, Mrs. Coco had recently begun to impugn Duk-Soo's manhood, making vague allusions to the possibility of unthinkable relations with Ray Jr. This hurt all the more, mystified him, since he was sure that she must know the way he felt about her. Was this the proper fruit of celibacy, he wondered, with Tula Springs calling him an adulterer and the so-called adulteress calling him a pederast?

"The laundry's closed, Duk-Soo. We just drove by there to see if he'd like an ice-cream cone." The gray back in her hair, Mrs. Coco was looking a little haggard and worn, her blue eyes more prominent now, like the too-expressive eyes of a *Magic Mountain* consumptive. Duk-Soo was concerned about her health. Even though her husband had returned to Tula Springs, Mrs. Coco, having managed the store during his sojourn in Baton Rouge, had continued to work at McNair's while Mr. Coco, according to rumor, stayed at home all day in his pajamas. As a result there had been fewer rehearsals for the Pro Arts, even though much had to be done to get in shape for the Miss Tula Springs Pageant.

"Oh," he said.

"Oh," she mimicked, looking right at him. "It's necessary, isn't it?"

"What's necessary?"

"To lie to me. I'm forced to conclude that it must be some biological necessity that makes everyone lie to me, some pheromone I secrete into the air. The truth is, Ray Jr. has gone out with Dr. Jewel, hasn't he? They're sailing, right? How you can let that man . . . I really think he has a screw loose somewhere. Wife or no wife, I would never trust him alone with Ray Jr."

It was some consolation, a small one, that Dr. Jewel's manhood was also impugned from time to time.

"They're having dinner with Ray Jr.'s second cousin," he said.

"Oh, that damn mayor," she said, lighting a cigarette. "Do you know what he's done now? Careful, Maud. Let me help you."

Balancing a tray with cups and saucers, Brie, grapes, milk, crackers, and coconut-fudge cookies, Maud Herbert stepped nimbly over the tent's guy rope as she came into the living room. "I'm fine. Sit, Ethyl Mae. I know I may look old and feeble, but remember, I'm the same age as you. Can you believe that, Mr. Yoon? We're almost exactly the same age, and I bet I could pass for her mother."

"Oh, stop," Mrs. Coco said, handing around the cups.

"Did you ask Mr. Yoon about next week?" Maud Herbert asked, settling her considerable bulk into the carved bishop's chair that the swindler had left behind, an uncomfortable high-backed chair that Duk-Soo and Ray Jr. never used.

"You mean about the rehearsal? We have a rehearsal Tuesday, don't we?" Duk-Soo said.

"I suppose," Mrs. Coco said, pouring milk into Maud Herbert's tea. "I've been informed, though, that the mayor has hired a country western band for the pageant. The Pro Arts hasn't been invited back—which is fine by me. Such nonsense, girls parading around . . ." She reached over to pluck a strand of dental floss from Maud Herbert's wrinkled frilled collar.

"What are you . . ." Maud Herbert said. "Oh. Now Ethyl

Mae, I don't want you to start backing down. The mayor has absolutely no right to hire a bunch of hillbillies when the Pro Arts has played for the last three years. You're not going to take this lying down, understand? I've already told my husband that he is going to have a good talk with Binwanger. For one thing, I think it's outrageous what he's paying those hillbillies—nine hundred dollars. Think of all the money the pageant could save with the Pro Arts. You got seventy-five last year, right?"

"Fifty," Duk-Soo said.

"I thought you told me seventy-five, Ethyl Mae."

"Seventy-five minus certain expenses," she said, plucking a grape with studied nonchalance. "Well, Duk-Soo, what do you expect? Should I pay for the gas and the posters and the new stand we needed out of my own pocket? I thought I made that clear."

"Well, anyway," Maud Herbert said, "I think if you and Mr. Yoon showed up at my husband's office sometime before your rehearsal, say around eleven . . . It shouldn't take long for Mr. Yoon to give his deposition." She adjusted the cushion on the bishop's chair, whose elaborately carved back framed her frizzy hair in a tangle of snakes and gnomes.

"Deposition?" Duk-Soo asked.

"Maud's husband is a lawyer," Mrs. Coco said.

"I'm supposed to say something about the beauty pageant?"

"No, dear," Maud Herbert said. "This is about the CP." She fidgeted about in the chair again, prompting Mrs. Coco to ask if something was the matter.

"I'm trying to get comfortable."

"Why don't you sit on the sofa?"

"I like this chair."

"The CP?" Duk-Soo asked, dimly apprehensive.

"Yes, Mr. Yoon, the Citizens Patrol has finally gone too far.

Ethyl Mae has decided to take arms—whether 'tis better to suffer the slings and arrows of . . . whatever, or take arms." She set her cup down on the swindler's marble chessboard, inlaid in the coffee table. "Do you realize the CP had the gall to actually dig up her yard? It wasn't bad enough that they subjected her to a degrading cross-examination, wasting her valuable time and causing her considerable mental unrest, but they actually went out—without a warrant, mind you— and devastated her yard."

"Now Maud, it wasn't actually devastated—just one spot I noticed. And we're not really sure it was the CP."

"Who was it, then? Santa Claus?"

"Excuse me," Duk-Soo said, "but why would the CP wish to dig in your yard?"

"Perhaps they were trying to relax their nerves," Mrs. Coco said, frowning at him.

"The dog," Maud Herbert said. "Ethyl Mae is a suspect. You know, of course, that she has a record."

"I wouldn't call it a record," Mrs. Coco said. "I once had my name in the paper, Duk-Soo. I accidentally frightened the chihuahua once, and that idiotic CP charged me with Canine Cruelty. Of course, there was nothing legal about it."

"In any case, my dear, it was enough to put you under suspicion. You see, Mr. Yoon, the beauty college, in the person of a certain Gyrene LaSteele—she's the head beautician—they reported the disappearance of their chihuahua to the CP. Gyrene claimed that Tee-Tee would never have run away from the College of Beauty and Charm; he was devoted to the girls. Now, since Ethyl Mae has lodged several complaints with the college, claiming that Tee-Tee had broken into her house and once allegedly bit her when she tried to restrain him from urinating on her rug, this, of course, being the reason she doused him with hot bacon grease—"

"Lukewarm."

"Please, Ethyl Mae, let me talk."

"You mean that wasn't your chihuahua?" Duk-Soo said.

"Mine? Whatever gave you that idea?"

"Well, I did see it around the house a lot."

"A sniveling pest, Mr. Yoon," Maud Herbert continued. "In any case, Gyrene told the CP that Tee-Tee just wouldn't have run away like that and . . ."

While Maud Herbert went on about the chihuahua, Duk-Soo glanced anxiously in Mrs. Coco's direction, but she seemed absorbed in a study of the coconut-fudge cookies, her face impossible to read. Had she suspected anything when she caught him with the spade in her shrubs that morning back in August? She had stood only a few feet from the plastic garbage bag with the chihuahua in it, the bag he was forced to bring with him in the car since he couldn't just leave it lying around the yard; someone might have come across it. And he didn't want to put it back in the garbage can. She was so particular about what was thrown away; it was possible she might have inspected it. Oh, that Ray Jr.! Not only had he felt it incumbent upon him to murder a chihuahua, but then later that same night . . . Duk-Soo would never forget his horror when, after hours of agonizing in Lucy's bed, he had gotten up and crept to the third floor to see if maybe Mrs. Coco was also unable to sleep—well, she wasn't with her husband. She might have been trying to tell him something, being all alone up there in that turret. It turned out she was able to sleep, snoring rather loudly, as a matter of fact, which was a good thing, for it helped cover the sound of his footsteps as, numb with apprehension, he crossed the moonlit room and pried Ray Jr. from her side. The gall of that boy! He had told Ray Jr. that if he ever mentioned this incident to anyone, anyone at all, he would be locked up in a dark closet for the rest of his life, a room that would be worse than any jail in the world, worse even than Calcutta's.

"Maud, I'm still confused about something," Mrs. Coco

said while Duk-Soo wondered if he should come clean about the chihuahua. But if he did, he would have to admit, in public perhaps, to being an accomplice, throwing the body into the Tula Springs dump, certainly not very seemly behavior for a PhD candidate. No, this was out of the question.

"Yes, dear?"

"If, as you say, it was the CP that dug in my yard, well, Duk-Soo has a point—why? Why must they dig up my yard?"

"Oh, Ethyl Mae, really."

"No, honestly. I don't understand."

"The body, they're looking for the body."

"The body? What body?"

"The body of the dog you allegedly murdered."

"What? Come now, you can't expect me to believe . . . Me? They suspect me of doing away with it? Why, that's absurd."

"Indeed? Then why do you think they've spent so much time questioning you? Do you realize they even came to me?"

"You talked to the CP?"

"I did indeed. When you told me how they had been harassing you, I summoned Mr. Pusey, their Coordinator, to my library. I told Mr. Pusey that I thought the CP's behavior was reprehensible and that you wouldn't stand for it. I asked him what in the world they thought you had done with the chihuahua—murdered it? I mean just because you might have been capable in a fit of rage of pouring hot grease on the animal, it did not necessarily follow that you were capable, even under the extreme psychological duress you've been under recently, of snuffing out the creature's life. Yes, ma'am, I gave them a piece of my mind, you better believe."

"Why Maud, it was you, then—you're the one who put that idea in their head!"

"Nonsense—I simply read their mind. Of course, they still don't admit to digging up your yard. Mr. Pusey says that's an out-and-out lie. None of his men have set foot in your backyard ever, he claims. But I'm not through with him yet. Now as for you, Mr. Yoon, you will promise to see my husband next week when you're in Tula Springs?"

"Pardon me, but I still don't understand what I have to do with any of this." Did they suspect him? Did the guilt show?

"A," she replied, pulling back a stout index finger, "this is not simply a case concerning a dog. It's about B, the whole question of the legality of the CP. You're probably not aware that my husband's office has received several complaints against the CP, mainly from the town's underprivileged citizens. Don't you see, Mr. Yoon, you're just a cog in a much larger wheel. It's not just Ethyl Mae who's been harassed. Poor black women who've let their driver's licenses expire, minor infractions like that, these women have been treated very shabbily. They've been searched for weapons, given breath tests in the middle of the day in front of their children, verbally abused. Would you like to see your mother yelled at, Mr. Yoon, searched for drugs, spread-eagled on a car hood, simply because she parked on the wrong side of the street? It's not a very edifying experience, I can assure you. So you see why Ethyl Mae is brazening this out. And furthermore, we expect to find some interesting financial arrangements between our honored mayor and the cozy little private security force he introduced to Tula Springs. I can't wait until Mr. Herbert gets his hands on that."

"I agree," Duk-Soo said, wishing there was some way he could eject this noxious woman from his living room. "Very terrible for the black women, very unfair. But I still fail to see how I have anything to do with this."

"You will be both a material and a character witness," Maud Herbert said. "In that double capacity you will first tell Mr. Herbert that you have never seen a chihuahua or anything resembling a chihuahua in Ethyl Mae's house, and second, that you think—having been intimate with her for some time—that she would be totally incapable of such cruelty."

"But I *have* seen something resembling a chihuahua there," he protested.

"Tut," she said with a wave of her dimpled hand. "Not recently. In fact, it's better if you say you've never seen it there at all. Juries tend to see things in black and white. Take it from me, Mr. Yoon, I know."

"But Maud, that would be perjury if he said that."

"Ethyl Mae, if I added up all the times I had perjured myself for my friends . . . well, all I can say is that Mr. Yoon would have to be a pretty small-minded man if he could stand by, lily white, and allow those poor welfare mothers to be stripped of their last shred of dignity."

"I would really like to help, Mrs. Herbert, but I just remembered that I have a meeting with my adviser next week. I will have to discuss Malinowski, you know, and there is so much reading I must catch up on."

"Maud, what are you doing?" Mrs. Coco demanded as her friend started squirming about in her chair again.

"Well, no wonder," Maud Herbert said, pulling a butcher knife from beneath the cushion on the bishop's chair. "I knew there was something funny. The Princess and the Pea."

"Good heavens," Mrs. Coco said.

At first Duk-Soo was unable to provide a satisfactory explanation of what the knife, which Maud Herbert had set down on the coffee table, was doing beneath the cushion. Then when he finally remembered how it had gotten there— he had stashed it in the bishop's chair a few months ago on the night Ray Jr. had had a nightmare and thought he was going to kill him—he was still unable to come up with a satisfactory explanation. "Ray Jr. must have been playing Indians," he said. "Red Indians, cowboys and red Indians."

"You allow him to play with knives?" Mrs. Coco asked.

"Well, I can't watch him every minute of the day."

"You know," Maud Herbert said, "I tried to buy a knife once in Moscow. I stood in line for hours, but then a friend of mine, some official there—I can't reveal his position, of course—he put in a word for me, and the next day I went right to the head of the line. It's the only way of doing business in Moscow, isn't it, Mr. Yoon?—with a friend."

"I'm afraid I wouldn't know," he said, coloring. Why did she always have to bring up Moscow? he wondered. Every time he saw her, she had to make some reference to the U.S.S.R.

"You must be more careful," Mrs. Coco was saying. "The idea of letting Ray Jr. play with knives—it's so irresponsible. I'm really ashamed of you, Duk-Soo."

"Enough of knives," Maud Herbert said. "Let's get back to business. The fact of the matter is that Mr. Yoon doesn't like black people. Is that what you're trying to tell us, Mr. Yoon? Because if that's the reason you won't cooperate with us, I wish you'd come right out and say it."

"No, of course not."

"Well, then, what's the problem? Say this, Mr. Yoon, say you'll *consider* helping us. I'm not asking you to definitely show up next week—just tell us you'll consider coming."

"I'll consider," he said dully.

"Good. Now, moving right along, we'll skip to the social part of the tea. Did you hear, Ethyl Mae, Myrtice finally found out why her tv wouldn't turn off at the DAR meeting? It was because of her anniversary."

"Really? Duk-Soo, why don't you lock up your knives so he can't get at them?"

"Listen to me," Maud Herbert said. "Her husband got so mad at her that he ripped their anniversary card up. It was one of those musical cards that plays a little tune, and it was sitting on top of the tv acting as a transmitter. When he ripped the card up, the tv finally stopped playing. More tea, Mr. Yoon?"

*   *   *

Around eleven that evening Duk-Soo was jolted from his contemplation of Malinowski by a face in his bedroom window—Ray Jr. attempting to be humorous. With a sigh Duk-Soo got up from the desk and, after adjusting his foulard, hurried outside, hoping to catch Dr. Jewel before he drove off.

Cicadas, harsh and metallic-sounding, whined like a decrepit generator, one that might be straining to keep the lights of the Matterhorn on, and only partially succeeding with an *M*, an *A*, one *T*, an *R;* the other neon letters, and the slide itself, were in darkness, leaving a somewhat disturbing mound looming over the Spanish house.

"Can we talk?" Duk-Soo said after stumbling across the lawn, waving an arm to flag the car down.

"Hey, hey, hey, it's Yogi Bear," the doctor said, carefully setting down a joint in the ashtray. "Call me tomorrow. My old lady's waiting, got to get home."

"Please," Duk-Soo said, forced to jog as the car kept moving. "It's important."

The halt was sudden, irritable. "Well?"

"Dr. Jewel, I would like to suggest that another home be found for Ray Jr. I have decided to move back into a residence hall on campus."

"Yeah, yeah, we've already—"

"No, I am serious this time. I have an appointment with the Dean of Men tomorrow."

Duk-Soo had not made the appointment yet, but he planned to do it first thing in the morning. The tea that afternoon with Maud Herbert and Mrs. Coco had been the ultimate straw. He could not possibly afford to be exposed in a legal proceeding, not with his doctorate still up in the air. If Ray Jr. became involved, who knew what sort of testimony might fly out of his mouth on the witness stand, strange tales about rats and Communists that were bound to arouse

Maud Herbert's suspicions. And to have his good name mixed up with hers, a woman who bought knives in Russia with the help of high-level functionaries . . .

"You made an appointment with the sheriff, too, I hope," the doctor said. In the dim starless night his swollen sideburns looked like some sort of skin disease.

"Now look, I don't see what the sheriff has to do with me," Duk-Soo said, not quite truthfully. All he knew was that at this moment Maud Herbert was more of a threat than any sheriff.

"You don't, huh? After all the trouble he went to, keeping the house off the auction block and—well, if folks found out about it, it just wouldn't look too good, would it?" He picked up the joint and inhaled. "And what about the boy, huh? What about him? You want to see him locked up in some institution with a bunch of crazy old men?"

"Dr. Jewel, sir, I am simply not qualified for this job. I don't have the proper credentials. And I'm not sure he's getting any better. The other day he started drawing pictures on my bibliography. I can't tolerate such behavior. And he says funny things that make me nervous. He should be living with an expert, someone who understands what a schizophrenic means when he talks."

"How many times do I have to tell you, the kid ain't a schiz." The doctor slammed a freckled hand against the sheepskin-padded steering wheel. "No way. You want to know what his trouble is? It's you. Ray Jr.'s fine, just fine, as long as he's getting his love. That boy knows when he ain't being loved properly. That's what makes him act crazy. I was with him all day, and he didn't say a damn thing to make me worry about him." The engine already running, he turned the keys in the ignition and winced at the grating sound.

"But—"

"A word to the wise, Mr. Yoon," the doctor said, pulling away.

With a southeast wind blowing diagonally across the water, the lake seemed to be flowing as briskly as a river, but Duk-Soo, who had wandered out to a concrete jetty, knew the motion was just on the surface, ending in a few rough slaps against the manmade bank. First there was Mrs. Coco accusing him of loving the boy, now there was the doctor accusing him of not loving him. But how could Dr. Jewel expect him to love Ray Jr.; that was never part of the agreement. And besides, how could anyone love someone who could kill a poor, defenseless dog? Ever since that night Duk-Soo had found it harder and harder to deal with Ray Jr., especially now that Ray Jr. had taken it into his head to start calling him Dad. That was the reason he had drawn little rats on his bibliography, because Duk-Soo had forbidden him to call him Dad. He did not want to be a dad, and if one day he did end up being one, it wouldn't be to a crazy schizophrenic.

As he walked back from the lake to the Spanish house, he was not surprised to see that he was being shadowed by an inept, clumsy spy who tried to hide behind pines that were far too skinny to conceal him. If there was to be no real love in his life, if the women who meant most to him were always going to remain most distant, then at least, Duk-Soo prayed, let him be free of these shadows. He was old enough now—fifty today, and still not Dr. Yoon—to deserve some peace.

13

"What are you doing here? You're supposed to be in Mr. Herbert's office."

A lone customer examining handkerchiefs in McNair's turned to see who was talking so loud. Maud Herbert, shushed by Mrs. Coco, remained standing in the back of the store, her hands on her broad hips, while Mrs. Coco finished lecturing the new clerk, a young man on a St. Jude work-study program that allowed Mrs. Coco to pay him below minimum wage.

"Now look, Squeaky," she went on, "how do you expect anyone to want to buy clothes from you when you come in wearing a Nehru jacket and no socks? Please, tomorrow do me a favor—look at yourself in the mirror before you leave home and think, *Is this what I want to look like?*" She peered around at the swollen tapping foot squeezed into worn liz-ard heels. "All right, Maud, hold your horses."

On the sidewalk in front of the store the two friends' bick-ering had to compete with the noise of traffic. It seemed as if no one in Tula Springs ever walked anywhere, no matter how poor she was.

"If you only knew what it cost me to get Mr. Herbert to see you—and then you don't show up."

Worried that the hem of her new black-and-white striped dress wasn't even, Mrs. Coco replied with a distracted air, "Maud, I told you, if Duk-Soo hasn't the decency to testify in my behalf, then I don't see why I should— Oh, look, that's her . . . No, don't stare, Maud, please."

A petite, doll-like woman, well under five feet, with a windswept Susan Hayward hairdo, gold heels, and tight eggplant slacks, yanked a ticket from her windshield wiper and began to walk busily down the opposite sidewalk, her many quick, tiny steps making her look as if she were moving faster than she actually was.

"Who is that creature?" Maud Herbert asked.

"Gyrene LaSteele, the beauty college operator." Feeling as exposed as the hoofed beasts of the veld, Mrs. Coco instinctively herded her friend into a neighboring cul-de-sac.

"So that's her. Hmmph. To think you let yourself be bullied by that."

"Listen, Maud, if you didn't insist on acting so weird in front of Duk-Soo, he might have come today."

"Weird? Me weird?"

"Telling him you bought a knife in Moscow."

"Well, I did. I needed a paring knife for Mr. Herbert's fruit. He always gets constipated on our vacations."

Mrs. Coco had made the mistake of telling her friend that Duk-Soo frequently advised her not to have anything to do with her, Maud Herbert. When Maud Herbert learned of this, how suspicious he was of her trip to Moscow (probably the most boring trip she had ever taken, she had told Mrs. Coco; the one to Yosemite when Mr. Herbert got lost in the trailer park was so much more entertaining) and the St. Jude Mandarin course she was planning to drop out of (there was too much homework), she seemed delighted. To be suspected of being something other than what she was, was apparently a thrill that did not come her way often, and Maud Herbert was determined to milk it for all it was worth.

Lately, every time they saw Duk-Soo, Mrs. Coco noticed that Maud Herbert made a point of tossing into the conversation an obscure reference or two to Moscow, no doubt hoping that this Korean Bircher would suspect her of unsavory political alliances. It must have made life in Tula Springs so much more interesting for Maud Herbert. Previously her only escape had been English crime novels, which she read by the yard and which explained her predilection for making such a fuss over tea and certain vowels.

"Maud, I've been thinking. It's just not worth it. I don't want to get mixed up with the CP. There's the store now and the Pro Arts—I'm so worried. We're not rehearsing as much as we should."

"Good, that's the spirit. Here everyone in Tula Springs thinks you've done away with Tee-Tee, and you don't have the time to clear your good name. All right then, forget about yourself. But what about those poor black mothers out there who are looking to you for support? Are you going to abandon them? I find it hard to believe you can be that selfish."

Perhaps she did, but although Mrs. Coco sympathized with these women in a vague, Christian way, there was too much on her mind now for her to see any real connection between her problems and theirs. If only she could confide in Maud Herbert and tell her what was really troubling her, the burden she had been forced to shoulder last night. But lately she had felt herself pulling away from Maud Herbert, disappointed that she wasn't turning out to be the great friend she imagined she could have been. The eccentricities that Mrs. Coco had once found charming were beginning to wear thin, and Maud Herbert's refreshing, broad-minded outlook on life was now seeming a little too broad, almost scatterbrained.

"Maud, I must get back to the store."

Detaining her with a hand to the shoulder, Maud Herbert

regarded her with a complacent, pastoral smile. "My dear, I wasn't going to tell you this, but you have forced me to reveal something rather unpleasant. When I was interviewing Mr. Herbert this morning, I found out why the Pro Arts is not being asked to play for the beauty pageant this year. Do you know the real reason?"

"We've been through this before. People just like country western better, let's face it."

"Indeed? Mr. Herbert was given a quite different reason. He found out that the Pageant Committee was anxious to preserve a high moral tone for the contestants."

"What?"

"The Pro Arts was deemed unsuitable for the occasion because of the group's involvement with heroin, adultery, and murder. For that reason the committee has hired Gerald R and His Mean Machine."

Mrs. Coco might be willing to turn the other cheek when it was a question of her own good name or that of the poor women of Tula Springs. But hearing the name of the Pro Arts dragged through the mud was too much—something snapped.

"Oh, hush," Maud Herbert said to a honking cement mixer as she and Mrs. Coco hurried across the street, arm in arm, against the light.

"Angel, I don't understand what all this fuss is about. It's simply a matter of economics. The committee assumes that it will sell more tickets to the pageant with Gerald R as an attraction than with the Pro Arts." Mr. Herbert, a compact man impeccably attired in muted pinstripes and bespoke English shoes, took the calendar of male nudes from his wife's hands and put it back on his desk.

"The Men of St. Jude College?" she said.

"Evidence for a suit we're involved in. Mrs. Coco, you'll

forgive me, I'm terribly busy this afternoon. My associate, Miss Keely, is waiting for me."

Standing by the window of his office, from where she could see laundry flapping in her backyard—good heavens, her slip, the one that needed mending!—Mrs. Coco, who had never realized before how exposed her house was from this vantage point in the Bessie Building, murmured an apology. She should have known that Maud Herbert was stirring things up again by inventing trouble.

"Just one minute, Mr. Herbert," Maud Herbert said, blocking his exit with her more considerable bulk. "So now it's economics. What happened to all that talk about morality I heard just a while ago?"

"Love, it was my receptionist who supplied you with that information. I advise you to take anything Mr. Pickens says with several grains of salt. Large grains."

"Mr. Pickens!" Maud Herbert called out the door. "Where is that man? Stay where you are, Mr. Herbert. I'm not through with you yet. Here," she said, rummaging in her straw bag, "I have something you simply must listen to. It will only take a second."

"*. . . knows they ain't ripe, but that's how I likes to buy 'em. Just set 'em up on your sill, hon, and they turns nice and red.*"

"What is this?" Mr. Herbert inquired, glancing at his watch.

"I got this at the A&P. She didn't know she was being recorded," Maud Herbert said, switching the tape off. "This was a lady who had a run-in with the CP. She's not black like I hoped, but I plan to get some black ones this afternoon. Mr. Herbert, would you mind putting down that phone? This is important. You wouldn't believe how easy it is to get evidence against the CP. But first, before I play the rest of the tape, I'll fill you in on the background. What happened was that Mrs. Ike, that's the lady who's talking, she was walking down the street one day and was accosted by a second party, Henry Ann. Henry Ann wanted to get close so she could read the small print on the first party's T-shirt. Well, Mrs. Ike didn't want Henry Ann reading her T-shirt. She said she'd already had a chance to read it a couple days ago, so the next thing you know there's a little pushing and shoving, and a CP car happens to be patrolling the neighborhood and . . ."

While Maud Herbert attempted to explain to her husband, who was on the phone three times during the explanation, how Mrs. Ike at the A&P was tied in to the Pro Arts's grievance against the pageant committee, Mrs. Coco glanced out the window again and saw Ray Jr. hanging out more laundry. It was good that he was keeping himself occupied, but she was worried that he might be mixing the coloreds with the whites.

Ray Jr. had shown up the night before while she was upstairs in the sewing room trying to make some headway on the double-stops in the Dvořák, a piece she was a little reluctant to play when Mr. Coco, who had endured twelve years of it, was around. Mr. Coco had gone to Lafayette to lend moral support to his granddaughter, who was nervous about judging Chester Whites at a mock livestock show at U.S.L. It seemed that any opportunity he had to get out of the house these days he took.

As Ray Jr. transferred clothespins from his mouth to the line, she pondered what was to be done about him. Duk-Soo and he had had a falling-out of some sort, which was why Ray Jr. had run away from home, hitchhiking part of the way, jogging the rest. When she had called Duk-Soo to find out what had happened, he had not sounded very rational and claimed that as far as he was concerned, the boy could stay in Tula Springs the rest of his natural-born days. Mrs. Coco was at wits' end. Certainly she wasn't going to turn Ray Jr. over to Dr. Jewel or his second cousin, both of whom seemed as unfit as Duk-Soo to care for the boy. Imagine, hiding a butcher knife in a chair and making Ray Jr. sleep in a tent. What could the man mean by such behavior? After calling the rectory at Our Lady and being told that Father Fua was out blessing a mobile home, she thought about getting in touch with Maud Herbert. But some instinct told her it would be best to keep her out of it, so Mrs. Coco ended up soothing Ray Jr., who was quite upset, with the candy bars Mr. Coco had stashed in his toolbox, and letting the boy stay up till all hours watching Zsa Zsa Gabor on Venus.

"Oh, good, you're here," Maud Herbert said as Myrtice walked into the office, followed by E.M., who slunk past Mr. Herbert into a green leather chair. Mrs. Coco was not sure if the bees had anything to do with it, but ever since E.M. had been stung at Boy Scout camp, he had taken a turn for the worse, in both attitude and grooming. Twice he had skipped rehearsal, saying he had to go to the skin doctor, which was a patent lie, since the pimples that had recently blossomed on his face never looked tended to. Like his friend, the Bradley boy, E.M. had acquired a peculiar greased-back hairstyle that reminded Mrs. Coco of the way Larry and George Henry had used to look in high school, except that Larry and George Henry hadn't worn earrings. E.M.'s striped ties had been replaced by a narrow white vinyl tie, his Bermuda shorts by black chinos, which he wore with either a black or maroon shirt, giving him a slightly gangsterish look that didn't quite fit the image Mrs. Coco desired for the Pro Arts, especially since he refused to remove his sunglasses when he played.

"Maud, what are they doing here?" Mrs. Coco said in a low voice while Myrtice exchanged a few words with Mr. Herbert, who was trying hard to smile back at her.

"Well, dear, since Mr. Yoon refused to testify in your behalf, I asked them to. And besides, it's their job, too, that's on the line, don't forget. Myrtice, where did you get those shoes? I've been looking all over town for a pair to go with my puce stretch pants."

"I went to the mall. It's terrible, the service you get nowadays. No one will lift a finger anymore—and she was wearing a shower cap, the girl who was waiting on me."

"Oh, yes, I see it all the time. It's the latest thing for the poor people. They want people to think they work in a hospital."

"What?"

"When she's out of the shoe store, people will think she's a nurse or something. It's prestigious to them."

"But nurses don't wear shower caps."

"Sure they do. They have to keep their hair out of the medicine."

"You were just in the hospital, E.M.," Myrtice said. "Did you see any shower caps?"

Hunched over in the leather chair, the boy continued to gnaw on a hangnail while staring glumly through his sunglasses at one of Mr. Herbert's cactuses.

"Such a joy to be around," Myrtice said.

"Now look," Maud Herbert said, noticing that her husband had escaped. "I'll be right back," she added, marching out of the room in her white pumps, which normally did not go with anything one would wear in the fall, unless, like Maud Herbert, one happened to have on a white summer dress.

"So what's the big deal?" E.M. said. "Who wants to play in a stupid beauty pageant anyway?"

"If I were a little boy," Myrtice said, "I'd give my right arm to be able to see all those pretty girls up close."

"You like pretty girls, Myrtle?"

"E.M.," Mrs. Coco said, "I appreciate your coming—you, too, Myrtice—but really I don't think it's at all necessary for you to be here. I can handle this myself."

"All right," he said, getting up, "but don't expect me to give back the five bucks. I already spent it."

"What five dollars? You don't mean to say—Maud didn't pay you to come?" This was the limit. Maud Herbert had gone too far this time. Mrs. Coco resolved to give her a piece of her mind once they had a moment alone.

"My time is valuable," Myrtice said crossly.

"Of all the . . . Aren't y'all ashamed? I never heard of—"

"I got him, here, look, I got him," Maud Herbert said as she propelled before her a weary-looking man, who was introduced to everyone as Mr. Pickens, the receptionist. Slightly overweight, his shirt pocket bulging with pens, he proceeded to relate for Mrs. Coco's benefit the reasons he had heard why the Pro Arts would not be playing at the pageant. Mrs. Coco blushed as she heard the charges of drug dealing, marital infidelity, drunk and disorderly conduct, and murder repeated in front of E.M., who yawned and started playing with the earring he had unscrewed from his left ear. When pressed for the source of this slander, Mr. Pickens hedged, forcing Maud Herbert to draw herself up and become formidable.

"Maud, please," Mrs. Coco said, wondering how her life had suddenly become so public. "There's no need to fire Mr. Pickens."

"Well, if you got to know," the receptionist said, running a chubby hand through his thinning blond hair, "it was Miss LaSteele—she's the one told me all this, how George Henry Coco's fiancée got arrested and all."

"Gyrene LaSteele?" Maud Herbert said.

"Yes, ma'am, she's the mother of this friend of mine. I was over to their house the other night and Miss LaSteele was drawing up a chart of whose hair went first and all for the pageant—see, she's in charge of the hair and the charm at the thing. Then Burma, that's her daughter, she starts poking me with this bone and Miss LaSteele yells at her 'cause the bone might break and it's the big evidence they got against Miss Coco."

"Bone? What bone?" Maud Herbert demanded.

"The one Mary Ellen dug up in Mrs. Coco's backyard."

"Who is Mary Ellen, Mr. Pickens, and what was she doing in Mrs. Coco's backyard?"

"Mary Ellen just likes to prowl around, you know. I guess she doesn't get enough to eat, the way her ribs stick out and all. I think she belongs to the old black guy that shines shoes at the Tiger Unisex, leastways they seem to hang around together a lot. Anyways, Miss Coco happened to see Mary Ellen sniffing around out back, and then she got to digging, and Miss Coco got real worried that she'd ruin the begonias, so she rushed outside with a stick and—"

"Now look here, Mr. Pickens, I never saw Mary Ellen doing anything," Mrs. Coco said, recovering her presence of mind. For a moment she had been drawn into Mr. Pickens's version, trying to remember if she had ever chased that mangy hound away from her begonias.

"I meant Miss LaSteele, she was the one saw Mary Ellen from the back window of the beauty college while she was doing a rinse on Cat Rogers. That's how Miss LaSteele got the bone. Course when she grabbed it out of Mary Ellen's mouth, she liked to die, 'cause she recognized it right off. The CP has it now. They say it's Tee-Tee's left femur. Would y'all like some coffee or something? We got herb tea."

"No, that will be all, Mr. Pickens," Maud Herbert said solemnly.

"Well, Ethyl Mae," Myrtice said once the receptionist had left the room. "So I was right all along—you did kill that chihuahua."

"Let's not jump to any rash conclusions," Maud Herbert said, eyeing her friend uneasily.

"Oh, really," Mrs. Coco said, "you can't believe anything . . . Why, it's simply too ridiculous . . . I never . . ."

"Look, if I got to say you're innocent now," E.M. said,

screwing his earring back on, "it's going to cost you a good twenty bucks, take it or leave it."

Trying to hide her confusion, for she did not feel very innocent, even though she knew she was—she had to be!— Mrs. Coco turned to the window. She could not help wondering if this was some sort of punishment inflicted on her for questioning her faith. Had she any right, really, to deny the teachings of a two-thousand-year-old Church by telling Ray Jr. that God was not a king or dictator, that He did not really care about thrones and footstools and tiaras? After Zsa Zsa last night Ray Jr. and she had stayed up talking, trying to figure out what it would be like when they died. Ray Jr. told her it would probably be like the time the sun came down and hit him and he had sharp leaves in his toes. Instead of stopping him Mrs. Coco had encouraged him to go on, even though she knew this sort of talk was wrong, that it had nothing to do with the catechism, which was what he should be learning. And did she really have to shampoo his hair in the kitchen sink? Couldn't she have let him do this himself later, when he was alone in the tub?

". . . has the bone . . ."

"But Mr. Pickens will . . ."

". . . left what? We'll have to . . ." she heard Maud Herbert and Myrtice saying at once to each other in urgent whispers behind her back. After another moment her eyes, which had been shut tight, opened, and she prepared to leave the office as calmly and innocently as possible. But before she did, she happened to glance out the window. Struggling with a king-size Craftmatic sheet that swelled and puffed and flapped like some giant bird straining to rise, Ray Jr., but for his bare feet, was completely enveloped in billowing white—the prey, it seemed, of a somewhat reluctant assumption.

Il tempo vola . . . baciami!

—*Manon Lescaut*

14

While Susan Sontag gazed down, unframed, from the wall, Mrs. Coco, her ears pricked for the sound of footsteps on the stairs, read quickly through the pages scattered on her daughter's canopied bed. The still uncompleted untitled poem which Lucy had been working on for the past three years was supposed to be about Fatima, so why in heaven's name did she have to do "research" on the Miss Tula Springs Pageant in order to finish it? Hoping to find some clue and to determine once and for all if the poem was sacrilegious—Lucy refused to admit that it was—Mrs. Coco tried to decipher such lines as:

> O Francisco, Jacinta, what Clorox has streaked
>   the orb above the oak?
> Did O Seculo, did d'Oliveira Santos in Ourém
>   usurp the reign of flowers?
> i am abducted by the State
> and Pius will garb my Mother in rayon.

"Heart, I asked you not to waste gas on just one cup of coffee. Just put your mug right in the microwave," Mrs. Coco said as she came downstairs, still unsatisfied, with her cello.

Of all times for the girl to show up. Lucy had breezed in unannounced the day before, her mother already in a tizzy over all that had to be done before the pageant, not getting a bit of help from Mr. Coco, who had wandered off to Baton Rouge that afternoon to look for a certain kind of Phillips head he couldn't get in town. Of course, Lucy acted as if she were visiting royalty, bestowing a great favor on the household by simply deigning to be there.

The child was waiting in a decrepit hall chair and, to her mother's relief, seemed presentable in a navy pleated jumper (a touch-up with the iron wouldn't hurt), white blouse, knee socks, and patent leather shoes (were these perhaps a little too shiny?). Looking more like seventeen than twenty-six, Lucy was the oldest of the second batch of children Mrs. Coco had produced after a hiatus of eleven years, during which Mr. Coco had halfway convinced her that it was all right if he, the man, practiced birth control. Her conscience reasserting itself with renewed vigor, Mrs. Coco, no longer persuaded by her husband's liberal gloss on right and wrong, had joined the Blue Army, banned the "things" from Mr. Coco's sock drawer, and given birth to Lucy Agnes, Samuel Bonaventura, and Nancy Veronica. It was always during these Counterreformation times that Mrs. Coco was most sensitive about the Church and demanded the strictest allegiance from her satellites, an allegiance that had been mocked at every opportunity, and was being mocked even today, she suddenly realized, by Lucy's attire: the girl looked like she was still in parochial school.

"But Mother, I didn't wash my hair today," Lucy said when Mrs. Coco, who knew it would be useless to complain about the impertinent uniform, complained instead about the hairs in the sink.

"All the hairs were black, so it had to be you. Now finish your coffee. We've got to get going."

"Microwave . . ." she muttered.

"Hurry, will you?"

In the car Lucy, a very vain child who, because she spurned makeup, thought she wasn't, inquired about old boyfriends, eager to hear that this one had sunk into alcoholism, that into divorce, financial ruin, despair, etc. As a matter of fact, two of them were virtual alcoholics, one had been arrested for selling marijuana, and a fourth had been stabbed in the arm by his wife, but Mrs. Coco wasn't going to give her daughter the satisfaction of hearing all this since she suspected Lucy knew anyway.

"He's doing just wonderful, too, heart. As a matter of fact, I saw Lyle in Woolco the other day, and he's got the most darling little girl."

"Oh, Lyle, he used to masturbate all the time in the girls' locker room."

Mrs. Coco looked sharply at her daughter, who was said to bear a striking resemblance to her, physically, at least. "Lucy Agnes."

"What? It's common knowledge. By the way, what's with you and Father? You barely talked to each other at dinner last night."

"Your father and I are perfectly happy. It's just that when you reach our age, sug, you don't feel the need to express it all the time."

The Miss Tula Springs Pageant was being held in the local white elephant, a warehouse-like building that had once been a five-and-dime, then a John Deere showroom, a discount cafeteria for the aged, a pistol range, and a shoe city and was now slated to be reincarnated as a Wild West mall that was supposed to revitalize the downtown area, luring shoppers away from the mall in Mississippi. Mr. Coco had been offered a prime site for McNair's, but Mrs. Coco thought the rent exorbitant and was not impressed with the artist's rendering of satisfied shoppers pausing to admire the hitching posts. After parking beside Mrs. Fitt's Oldsmobile

Mrs. Coco pulled her cello from the back seat while her daughter walked on ahead, pausing a moment at the entrance of the drab, still unconverted building to cross herself in the abrupt, cursory manner of a prizefighter just before the bell.

On her way in Mrs. Coco noticed that the Pro Arts was not even mentioned on the posters outside, while Gerald R and His Mean Machine were given special prominence. With the help of Maud Herbert, who had proved to the CP that the bone in their possession was the left femur, not of a chihuahua, but of a nine-banded armadillo, family Dasypodidae—what a relief it had been when Mrs. Coco, while trying to recall where she had hidden a can of salty black olives from her husband, had suddenly remembered the Jerusalem cherry in her backyard and the drowned armadillo she had buried there last spring during the floods— Mrs. Coco, her reputation patched up with only a few ragged edges showing, had been able to work out a compromise with the Pageant Committee, allowing the Pro Arts to perform during the slide presentation of economic growth in St. Jude Parish, with billing on all posters to be two thirds as large as the Mean Machine's. Now what did she see but no billing at all, a matter she brought up with the first pageant official she ran into once she was inside.

"I wrote it down real careful so the printer would understand," the official replied, an anemic-looking woman who owned the pet-food store. "Then when I give it to Mrs. Loll— she's the one got to OK everything—she X'es out all y'all's names."

Not seeing Mrs. Loll among the people that had already started to seat themselves on the wooden folding chairs, Mrs. Coco showed her pass to a CP guard and went behind the makeshift stage, which consisted of portable platforms borrowed from Tula Springs High. There she suffered a nervous twinge as she watched Lucy, her note pad out, talking to three young women in extremely immodest bathing attire.

"My name's Dora Schlomm and I'm a junior at Mary Queen of Heaven and I desire to work in an architectural-type firm," a top-heavy blonde was saying as Mrs. Coco unpacked her instrument.

"My name's Toinette Quaid and I'm a dramatic arts major at St. Jude State College," a lanky redhead, her behind disgracefully evident, said while Lucy scribbled in a professional sort of way, barely glancing at her pad.

"Do you feel diminished in any way by walking on stage like that?" Lucy inquired.

"Diminished? No, I'm keeping my heels on," the redhead replied a little haughtily. "What paper you say you worked for?"

"She's writing a poem about us," the blonde said.

"Well, all I got to say is you better not rhyme me with *laid*," the redhead said. "That's been done already, and the poet's still recovering."

"Lucy, must you make a nuisance of yourself?" Mrs. Coco said after the girls had gone to have their hair examined. "Go sit down in front. You're not supposed to be back here anyway without a pass."

The slide show, narrated by Mayor Binwanger, came after the National Anthem, which the Mean Machine got to play. As the commercial catfish, masonry, peppers, cucumbers, commercial alligators, tomatoes, okra, crawfish, and lumber mills appeared on the screen, the Pro Arts, relegated to an unelevated spot to the side of the stage, gave an uncertain performance of a Haydn trio, which was supposed to get soft every time the mayor said something. Killing two birds with one stone, Mrs. Coco had finally mustered up the courage to rid the Pro Arts of both a musical and a moral liability by firing Duk-Soo. Intonation had improved one hundred percent with his departure, and so had her self-esteem, which no longer had to contend with the absurd rumors that drifted back to her, such as the one about the secret champagne brunches they were supposed to enjoy in someone's Mercedes. It had been foolish and self-indulgent to permit him to adore her (mutely, of course), a vain attempt on her part, she realized, to turn back the clock, to pretend that she wasn't a grandmother with age spots on her hands and a husband who, if he didn't stop sneaking candy bars, would not be long for this earth.

With Duk-Soo banished and the Dasypodidae bone correctly labeled, the murky guilt that had sapped her energies and left her in a general muddle, a prey to crying jags in the sewing room while listening to *Manon Lescaut*, was gradually dispelled like a morning fog by the sharp rays of Truth. Even her fragile, somewhat brittle faith was restored to something of its former wholeness, like a cherished broken vase that has been mended and set high on a little-used shelf where the cracks wouldn't show. Finally, after all these years, she thought she understood the wisdom of the Church, why for most of her history she had never encouraged her children to roam too freely about the Bible, which could easily shatter the faith of any Catholic who wasn't well versed in the dogmas of the Holy Church. Just look what had happened to her when she started reading the Bible on her own, without a proper guide. First she had been troubled by all the undemocratic masters and servants, then by goats and sheep, until it began to seem that there wasn't a thing in the Gospel that she couldn't take exception to, up to and including Jesus Himself, who greatly upset Mrs. Coco by saying in Matthew, right there in black and white, that He had been sent only to save the Jews, no one else. Having given up trying to improve on Scripture, Mrs. Coco concentrated now on saying the rosary and receiving the sacraments, returning to the more sacramental anonymity of the screen and the prie-dieu in the Reconciliation Room.

After the slide presentation Myrtice and E.M. went and sat in the audience while Mrs. Coco waited backstage for the talent competition, when she would play an abridged version of the first movement of the Samuel Barber Cello Sonata, minus the piano, to accompany a modern dance number. Nervous about the awkward stretches of sixths and tenths in the piece, she found a nook behind a screen and began to practice softly while the girls on the other side primped and hushed one another.

". . . killed it?" a familiar voice was saying on the other side of the screen. "Oww!"

"Hold still, honeybunch. She killed it all right. Armadillos just don't up and die."

Mrs. Coco stopped playing and leaned closer to the screen.

"Well, it could have been old." There was a hissing sound. "Gyrene, don't put any more spray on, please."

"When I get through with you, I want you to go see my daughter, Burma, over there. She'll even out your eyes."

"Someone once told me, or I guess I might have seen it on tv—anyway, they say that armadillos are the only animal that can get leprosy. They use them for experiments over at Carville."

"You mean to say you think the armadillo died of leprosy on Miss Coco's lawn? Look at me—no, don't tilt your head—now smile. Uh-uh, don't crinkle your eyes, relax into the smile. That's better. Remember, a smile's not a smile unless it's fluid."

"Carville's not so far away, Gyrene. And besides, why would Mrs. Coco suddenly decide to kill an armadillo? She's one of my best friends. I just know Mrs. Coco wouldn't hurt a flea."

"If a flea got in her begonias, she'd hurt it all right. The smartest thing you ever did, girl, was to get yourself unhitched from that family. Take it from me, they're all nuts, they're gone. I don't know how that poor Mr. Coco stands it. He's such a doll."

"Mrs. Coco is, too. I just love her. She's been such a good friend."

"How old are you, Connie? Thirty-seven, eight?"

"One, thirty-one."

"Well, you still got a lot of growing up to do."

Connie! What was Connie doing here? Surely she wouldn't have the gall to enter the contest herself? Ever since finding out the real reason why George Henry and she had gotten divorced, Mrs. Coco had avoided Powell's and refused to return any of Connie's phone calls. In defense of himself George Henry had said that the reason he hadn't told his mother about Connie turning gay was that he didn't think she was mature enough to understand—and besides, it was none of her business. But it was very much her business: how many times had she had coffee with Connie and her "friend" at the goat farm, sitting there in the living room with two women who actually loved each other? It was too disgusting to even think about. Mrs. Coco had been forced to throw out the philodendron Connie had given her, even though it was such a lovely plant, giving just the right touch to that ledge next to the bay window.

"Mother, what are you doing?"

With a start Mrs. Coco noticed Lucy by her side. "I'm practicing," she said, moving away from the screen. "What is it, Lucy? What do you want now?"

"I saw George Henry."

"What is he doing here?" Mrs. Coco asked, vaguely concerned about a spot on her hand that didn't resemble the other age spots. Connie was right; Carville wasn't far away, and the armadillo didn't look as if it had drowned. In fact, didn't armadillos walk underwater sometimes? Who had told her that?

"He said . . ." Lucy began as Gyrene herded five boys in

top hat and tails up a stairway lined with glittering okra and catfish that ended in a flimsy moon. "Uh, he wants to know if you'd like him to play. He brought his violin."

"What in heaven's name is he doing here? I didn't ask him to come."

"I guess they came to see Connie compete. Heidi said something about . . . oh, I don't know."

"Heidi's here too, huh? Well, you can just tell your brother his services are not required." The idea, Connie a contestant; and the Pageant Committee was worried about the Pro Arts' morals.

"Y'all played that fancy music so sweet," Gyrene said on her way back from the moon, giving Mrs. Coco a little squeeze on the arm. Her smile was fluid.

"Thank you," Mrs. Coco said before she had time to think.

"Mother, I was just talking to Mayor Binwanger. He told me the teahouse went under."

"Teahouse? What teahouse? And what are you doing talking to that man?"

"He came up to me. I was—"

"Lucy, where's my Barber? Did you take my Barber?"

"Here," her daughter said, picking the music up that Gyrene had accidentally knocked off the stand. "What is the matter with you, Mother? Why can't you relax?"

"I don't want you talking to the mayor, understand?" she said, watching Connie being hoisted up on the moon. Thirty-one indeed; she was thirty-nine if she was a day. And look how chunky her thighs were—had she no shame?

"He was telling me about Helen Ann," Lucy said. "She's real depressed because the teahouse went broke. She's decided to give it up."

"I thought she was running a cricket farm."

"Oh, Mother, really. The cricket farm went under ages ago."

"Well," Mrs. Coco said, angry at Helen Ann for keeping

this from her. "Would you mind telling me, Lucy, how the mayor could inform you about a teahouse in Australia that is none of his business?"

"They talk every now and then on the phone, Helen Ann and him. It's sort of sweet, isn't it? Old flames getting gray and all. The mayor says she isn't doing too well—she's depressed and lonely and can't find a boyfriend. You ought to talk to her more often, give her a ring sometime. Our family is so cold—we might as well be WASPs."

Next Wednesday at three-thirty Mrs. Coco was scheduled to testify before the Concerned Citizens Committee Maud Herbert had formed to investigate the CP and its connection with the mayor, and here Helen Ann and Lucy were blithely carrying on intimate chats with him behind her back. Mr. Herbert had told his wife that Mrs. Coco didn't have an ice cube's chance in hell if she tried to sue the CP on her own. He advised them to drop the matter entirely and not make fools of themselves, but Maud Herbert had been able to interest Mr. Herbert's associate down the hall, Donna Lee Keely, who was concerned about the CP's alleged brutality toward black women. Although Mrs. Coco wasn't black, Maud Herbert planned to emphasize her minority status as a woman and an Italian. With her Dasypodidae bone Mrs. Coco would be the star witness of the investigation.

"Lucy, you must promise me to keep away from the mayor tonight. Don't you realize what a slimy—"

"Your hands are trembling. Look."

"I've got a very demanding solo to play. Now please, dear, go away."

The Barber went off without a hitch, a pleasant surprise for Mrs. Coco since she was prepared to forgive herself if she missed some of those awful leaps on the A string with her too-small, tortured left hand. Granted, she was a little annoyed when she faded from a double forte to a mystical resignation to suffering on the final C and the dancer kept on going, finishing a few seconds later, but no one in the audience seemed to mind, and Mrs. Coco got a big hand on her solo bow. Pleased that she had had this opportunity to introduce Samuel Barber to Tula Springs, she smiled graciously upon Heidi, who had come backstage to congratulate her. Heidi was looking decidedly healthier since her confinement in the hospital, and not quite so jumbo-sized, although this might have been because Mrs. Coco was in her spike heels and Heidi in sandals.

"Hi," George Henry said, standing a little behind Heidi. He had shaved his moustache and sideburns off, a definite improvement, and the diet Heidi had him on was beginning to show some results.

"Hello, dear. Have you seen Lucy?" Mrs. Coco rubbed the aching callus on her thumb. "I'm not going to stay till the end of this silly thing."

"You look so beautiful," Heidi said. "That dress—I can't get over it."

Since it was an evening gown that Mrs. Coco had made herself—the material was what the inept upholsterer had left over from the chaise longue he had re-covered in her bedroom—Mrs. Coco was especially pleased with the compliment and wished Lucy, who had laughed at the dress, were here now to take note of it.

"Oh, it's nothing," Mrs. Coco said, interrupting Heidi, who had gone on to another topic. "Just a little something I stitched together myself."

"You made it?" She reached out and fingered the sturdy fabric. "George Henry, did you hear that?"

"Your dress is very nice, too," Mrs. Coco said. A little cheap-looking, but tasteful nonetheless.

"Say, Ma," George Henry said, "what's with Duk-Soo? Is it true you fired him?"

"My love, don't," Heidi said, glancing anxiously at him.

"Duk-Soo is very busy these days trying to finish his dissertation. I told him it might be in his best interest to concentrate on one thing at a time."

"So you did fire him. That's great. I hope you feel nice and pure now."

"Come on," Heidi said, tugging on his arm. "Let's go see Connie."

It was a shame how George Henry always ruined his chances with her, Mrs. Coco thought. If he had just kept his mouth shut, she would probably have asked him and Heidi over for a nightcap. But then he had to go and stick his nose where it didn't belong. Well, too bad.

Mrs. Coco had to change ears. Her right ear was tender from so much talking, and yet Alfred just didn't know when to quit. She had been in the bedroom slapping rosin off her evening gown when the phone rang. To her dismay it turned out to be Alfred, Ray Jr.'s father, whom she had spoken with a few times before, but never in person. Alfred had shown up on the scene just when, after much time and effort on her part, she had finally succeeded in finding a home for Ray Jr. at a halfway house in Ozone. Dr. Jewel had done everything he could to block this move, even going so far as to notify the Parish Mental Health Center that Ray Jr. was too competent and self-sufficient for state funds to be expended on his behalf. But Mrs. Coco had outsmarted him by paying a visit to his former boss at Norris State. Dr. Lily Oustelet turned out to be a sensible woman who was delighted to have this opportunity to put Dr. Jewel in his place. Using her pull, she made it clear that Ray Jr. was in need of professional guidance and got him admitted to Dove House. Now apparently Alfred was causing trouble with the Dove House personnel, trying to get permission for Ray Jr. to come and live with him in New Orleans. Not making any headway with them, he had somehow gotten ahold of Mrs. Coco's name and from time to time would call to plead his case.

"I told you, Alfred, it's really not up to me. If the parish authorities say no to you, there's nothing I can do."

Alfred had a high, squeaky voice that didn't quite fit her image of a professional wrestler, his career at the moment, but did seem appropriate for a costume designer, which was what he was studying to be at night school. "Now Ethyl Mae, honey, you're not hearing me, are you? I told you, they promised they'd wipe out my felony record after five years—they do that if it's only drugs and nonviolence-like crimes. And my parole officer, he don't even look at my arms no more. I mean I could have tracks running right across my forehead and he'd trust me, that's the kind of relationship I've built up with him. Did I tell you he's got an in with this bank in New Orleans? I'm pretty sure he can get me a job there as a guard—it's like in the bag. All I got to do is get bonded, and that's a piece of cake once the felony's wiped out. See, I'm getting too old for this rasslin', so I told them I'm going to settle down with a bank job and get me and Ray Jr. a nice little pad in the French Quarter, and then I'll finish up school. You know I've already got myself a grant. I'm good at fast-talking these grant people, they're sort of impressed with the way I can get along so well with my peers. I got my courses all picked out for next semester. Want to hear?"

"Alfred, I've really got to go now."

"Victorian interior design, graphology, and squash. You only get a half credit for squash, but see, it's one of them lifetime sports. I want to get into a lifetime sport. Then I'm taking graphology because I'm interested in becoming a well-rounded individual. The main thing, though, is my costume design. See, I sort of got into it with the rasslin'. I make my own outfits and then I was friends with this guy who turned out to be a jerk, but anyway he could get me sequins wholesale. I'm off sequins now, they don't do nothing to me anymore. There's only two things I dig—musquash and sweater sets. Did I tell you, I'm fixing to make you something you won't believe."

"No, please, don't."

"It's this Orlon cardigan with leather shoulder—"

"Alfred, do not make me anything, understand?"

"You're still pissed, huh?"

"What?"

"You're pissed at Ray Jr. I can tell by the way you intone. Well, you ask me, that isn't very fair. The kid can't be responsible for everything he does. See, he's mixed up a lot of the time and needs someone around who'll show him what's what. That's what I told one of them bastards at the halfway house, and you know what he said to me—why don't you go take a bath? I would've decked him if I wasn't into non-violence."

"I don't know why you think I'm mad at Ray Jr. That's absurd."

"Come on, Ethyl Mae. I know why you sent him to that stupid lovey-Dovey place. All because of your dog. Now don't get me wrong, I'm into loving canines, too. That's cool. It's just that I think human individuals should be on a higher level of love and all."

"Dog? I don't have a dog."

"Hey, hold on. There was this little chihuahua, right? That Korean guy, he told me all about it, how Ray Jr. got scared that night out in front of your house. The mutt comes tearing out after him and he thinks it's a rat and lays it out with a stick. Now he thinks y'all put him away as a punishment 'cause he killed the rat."

Mrs. Coco's eye began to twitch. So Tee-Tee had not run away; he had been killed, and Duk-Soo, knowing the truth all along, had deliberately lied to her. The nerve of that man. After everything she had done for him, coaxing and coddling his dim, defective sense of music, trying to make him feel normal, and this was the thanks she got. "Alfred," she said, "go over that again. Tell me exactly what Duk-Soo said."

"OK, like Ray Jr. was hanging around your— Whoa! What time is it? I got me a tag team tonight."

"Don't hang up," she said, her knuckles white on the receiver. "Hello, Alfred? Please talk, there's plenty of time."

"Got to split. Catch you later, doll."

A little dazed, Mrs. Coco sunk to the bed to sort out her thoughts. In one pile she placed all her anger at the ingrate Korean who had willfully allowed her to get involved with Maud Herbert's CP investigation. In another, smaller pile, like a tangle of unmatched socks, were her dismay and confusion about Ray Jr.'s innocent crime. And finally, the largest pile of all: those unwieldy king-size sheets that no amount of mental laundering could clean, that insidious tenderness she felt for the boy, more than affection, more than pity, something not quite proper that would not let her forget him, no matter where he was. She tried hard to sort all this out in her mind, but her anger at Duk-Soo got confused with anger at the boy, at herself, until she ended up where she had begun, in a general muddle.

"I think you're behaving like a child," Lucy said, entering so abruptly that her mother gave a start.

Whether she was afraid that Lucy might one day begin writing poetry that people could understand, or whether it was something more basic in their chemistry, Mrs. Coco secretly feared this daughter who, though darker in coloring, so closely resembled her. When she had come across the term *superego* in her Freud, Mrs. Coco, who had a tendency to make everything as concrete as possible, had immediately conjured up a certain look of Lucy's, the look that was now being directed at her.

"Leave me alone, please. I've got important things on my mind," Mrs. Coco said.

Lucy had not returned from the pageant with her mother

but had come home later, inviting her brother and Heidi in for drinks. They in turn had invited Connie to accompany them, and they were all downstairs now, celebrating Connie's award for Second Runner-up, two free lube jobs at C&W Body Shop.

"Do you realize how silly it is to stay up here and sulk? Heidi is leaning over backwards to be nice to you."

"I was extremely kind to Heidi this evening. It's not her, anyway."

"You mean Connie? Is that why you're not coming down?" Lucy sat down on the bed and took her mother's hand. "I want you to repeat after me. Say, I am a red-neck bigot from Mississippi. Go ahead, say it, Mother."

Mrs. Coco yanked her hand free. "Don't talk nonsense. If Connie wants to make a fool of herself, at her age . . ."

"Weren't you Miss Swimsuit or something once? Dad told me—"

"Nonsense," she said, and while Lucy went on to contradict her, Mrs. Coco brooded about Ray Jr. and the chihuahua. This was just awful. What would she say to the Concerned Citizens Committee now?

"Lucy, why can't you leave your mother in peace? I'm very tired."

"If it were just me, I would. But it really hurts me to see George Henry trying so hard. Sam and me, it doesn't seem to bother us so much, the fact that we're ignored and unwanted. In fact, I'm sort of glad you don't love me much. I think children who are loved too much end up in trouble. Just look at Larry and spoiled little Nancy with her cashmere sweaters."

Too weary to take the bait, Mrs. Coco let her have her say.

"But George Henry," Lucy went on, "he's so sensitive. He really needs to know that you love him, poor thing. I think it's sort of touching that he won't get married without you.

Any normal mother would be thrilled to death by such a devoted son."

"All right, all right," she said, getting up with a theatrical sigh, "I'll go downstairs. But only for a minute. I'm just too tired to— What's so funny? Why are you giggling like that?"

"Nothing. It's just that when you stand beside the chaise longue in that dress . . ."

"Do you want me to go downstairs or not? OK then, stop. And come over here a minute. I think I came unhooked in back."

15

In Carrel 3G of St. Jude's Wright Memorial Library, Duk-Soo adjusted his earplugs, hoping to get rid of the seashell-like roar that was almost as distracting as the assistant librarian's phone conversation with a gravel company that had poured too much gravel in her driveway. The last chapter of his dissertation, "*Heim, Haims, Heimr, Hām: The Semantic Obfuscation of the Tourist's Ultimate Destination,*" was riddled with queries from his faculty adviser, many of which he simply couldn't read. But he hated the idea of going back to Dr. Barnes and asking him to decipher his prescription-like handwriting, especially since Dr. Barnes himself was often puzzled by his own impatient abbreviations.

"Ultimately, if one renders this logic in Hegelian terms"— Duk-Soo read his own words dispassionately, hoping to find some clue to what Dr. Barnes was objecting to—"the sign 'home' is synthesized into a state of apatheia where one is so acclimatized to one's environment that one fails to perceive anything at all. The tourist, having launched out on what we have earlier concluded was a voluntary exile involving a praxis of unfamiliar sights, sounds, and tastes impacting upon him, is now ready to complete the circular paradigm by returning home. Needless to say, the 'ideal' home is one in which one is so comfortable that one is not aware of oneself at all, i.e., one is totally un-self-conscious: The self has dissolved. What is this 'home' we are talking about, then? Is it not, when we factor in the above, quite simply *der Tod*?"

Next to "this logic" Dr. Barnes had scrawled, or at least Duk-Soo thought he had scrawled, "What logic?" How was he supposed to answer a question like that? It was the logic he had been following for the entire chapter, the entire dissertation. Now was no time for Dr. Barnes to question that. The whole problem stemmed from the fact that Dr. Barnes had made him cut the *Unheimliche* chapter, which would have explained how he, Duk-Soo, had been able to forge the subconscious link between "home" and "death." After all, Freud had demonstrated the intimate connection between *heimlich* ("homely"), *heimisch* ("native"), and *heimlich* ("concealed, secret, private"). Dr. Barnes simply must allow him to restore this passage of Freud's: "If this is indeed the secret nature of the uncanny *(das Unheimliche)*, we can understand why linguistic usage has extended *das Heimliche* ('the homely') into its opposite, *das Unheimliche*; for this uncanny is in reality nothing new or alien, but something which is familiar and old-established in the mind and which has become alienated from it only through the process of repression." With this passage restored, Duk-Soo was convinced, Dr. Barnes would be able to see the logic that led from the uncanny to Freud's quotation of an old proverb: "Love is home-sickness." Now, Duk-Soo reasoned, "love" and "death" had been equated numerous times—he had a whole battery of examples—so that one might replace "Love is home-sickness" with "Death is home-sickness." If Dr. Barnes was too thickskulled to understand this analogy, then he missed the whole point of the dissertation. It was all so clear: tourism was but a metaphor for our sojourn on earth, and home but a metaphor for death. What was the problem? Why couldn't Dr. Barnes just accept this and give him his doctorate? All this quibbling was wearing Duk-Soo out.

Lunch at the cafeteria featured a tostada with Veal Patty Parmigiana and homemade biscuits. Sitting at a table by himself in the echoing hall that could hold one and a half football fields, Duk-Soo scanned an article in the *Annals of the Association of American Geographers,* which was not supposed to be taken out of the library. At the next table a fat priest—Hawaiian? Filipino?—tried to keep a conversation going with some morose-looking students, who didn't seem to have much to say about either the weather or the Seattle Mariners. Duk-Soo proceeded methodically from course to course, not noticing much difference as he read, and wound up the meal with a dish of choc-van-straw ice cream.

Clutching his combination-lock briefcase, he headed through the peculiar noonday fog to the Animal Husbandry Building, where Dr. Barnes, the victim of an office shortage in the Sociology Department, was installed. He had made up his mind that if Dr. Barnes did not understand why "home" meant "death," he would go over his head and complain to the Dean of Humanities. And if the Dean wouldn't listen, he would set up an appointment with the Vice-President, who had claimed on the radio the other day that his door was always open.

A lady clutching a dead or drugged rooster informed Duk-Soo that Dr. Barnes was out testing his new ultralight, so Duk-Soo got up and left.

"Mr. Yoon, there's a message," Mrs. Hicks said when he walked into the lobby of Jervis C. Mawks, where he currently resided. Having refused to take back Ray Jr. after he had run away, Duk-Soo had been threatened with the sheriff, and then Dr. Jewel had evicted him from the Spanish house. Shortly afterwards Duk-Soo had discovered a parking ticket on his motor scooter. If this was the dreaded reprisal from the sheriff, it was a small price to pay for finally getting free of the boy. And furthermore, the dorm wasn't so bad a place to live now that Bruce LaSteele had moved out. He was sharing an apartment in town with eight other gentlemen.

"Are you sure this is for me?" Duk-Soo asked after examining the pink slip Mrs. Hicks had handed him. PROCEDE URGENTLY TO MUSIC BDLG, she had typed out. MANSON.

"Mr. Yoon, please," she said, continuing to paste gold stars on an intramural chart. "Can't you see I'm busy?"

"Did this Manson say who he was?"

"I don't know why everybody expects me to know everything. I'm not God."

The music building? He had no business there now that he had quit taking violin lessons. And Manson? He didn't know anyone called Manson.

"You're making me nervous," Mrs. Hicks said, prompting Duk-Soo, who had been standing there staring into space, to make up his mind.

The brownish mural in the lobby of the music building was something Duk-Soo had never really looked at before, even though it covered an entire wall, floor to ceiling. He had always assumed it was a semiabstract rendering of a concert of some sort, but now as he loitered uneasily in the nearly empty lobby, looking for a possible Manson, he noticed upraised swords and strewn corpses.

"So you got canned, huh?"

It was E.M., sans earring. E.M. never wore his earring in the music building because of his father.

"Hello," Duk-Soo said, trying not to look at his own reflection in E.M.'s mirror glasses.

"You know, Donald, George Henry's real pissed at the old lady. He told me he's going to get you back in, he's going to make Mrs. High Octane take you back. The way he sees it, it's immoral that you got dumped. That's the word he used, *immoral*."

"George Henry can save himself a lot of trouble. I wouldn't go back to the Pro Arts for all the Chinese tea. Let her come crawling on her hands and knees, it won't do a bit of good, I assure you."

Surprised by how bitter he still felt, Duk-Soo struggled to sound aloof and indifferent. He had thought that he had finally mastered his feelings, but now he realized that his hatred for her was as intense as ever. He would never forget the day she had taken him aside after rehearsal and, in an almost offhand manner, informed him that he would be happier if he stopped trying to play the violin. When he had protested, she had had the effrontery to say that she was doing this for his own good, that as far as she was concerned, it would be more convenient if he remained with the Pro Arts. And all the while she was talking, she was clutching a brand-new volume of Haydn trios to her chest.

"She really gets on my nerves," E.M. said. "Got to boss everyone around. You let her boss you too much, that was your mistake. See, people in America, they don't buy this polite business. To us it's just a sign of weakness."

"Emmanuel."

Looking up, they saw E.M.'s father leaning over the balcony, a violin in each hand. Dr. Miller was a very intense man who lifted weights and was eager to get Duk-Soo into the gym to find out just how good he was at this jujitsu business, as he put it.

"Just a minute, Dad. I'm coming."

Duk-Soo gave a half wave to Dr. Miller, his ex-teacher.

"You're better off getting fired," E.M. said, slouching against the mural.

"You better go," Duk-Soo said.

"Anytime you two ladies are through gabbing," Dr. Miller called down.

After E.M. dragged himself upstairs, Duk-Soo looked around again for a likely Manson and then wondered if perhaps Manson was Mrs. Hicks's rendering of Emmanuel. It wouldn't have been the first time that she had garbled a message. But if it was E.M., what was so urgent about telling him that George Henry was on his side?

"Did you see her?"

"Oh, hello, Meg," Duk-Soo said, pausing on the granite steps of the music building. Meg was the pert young cellist who was head of the committee that had accused the Vice-President of hiding from the faculty.

"See who?"

"Ethyl Mae," Meg said, looking harried. "She was waiting for you in my office, but I think she went to a practice room. Got to run."

So, she *had* come crawling. Did she actually think, though, that it would be this easy, that all she had to do was summon him and he would appear and accept her apology? Did she have any conception of the pain she had inflicted, how much he had gone through trying to forget her? Not once in the past six weeks had she called to ask how he was doing, and she knew, too, how much she meant to him. No, that was it; he was through with women forever.

"Sit down," she said after he knocked on the practice room door and was admitted. The cello between her legs, she took the bow and played a few phrases, obviously at a loss for words. But Duk-Soo, who had not sat down, but stood looking coolly at the soundproof walls, was in no mood to help her out.

"Well, sir, what have you got to say for yourself?" she said finally, a rather odd way to begin an apology.

"Me? Perhaps *you* might want to tell me why you didn't give your name in the message. These little games of yours, childish."

"I didn't want to leave my name with that woman in your dorm, Mr. Yoon—for obvious reasons. So I used Meg's."

Meg? Of course, Meg Hanson translated into Hicksese would be Manson.

"Any more questions?" Her eyes squeezed shut as she inhaled deeply on a nonfilter cigarette. "If not, perhaps you could answer a few of my own. First of all, do you have any idea of the pain and embarrassment you have subjected me to?"

A tepid glow of satisfaction almost made Duk-Soo smile. So she had suffered, too.

"If this were just a private affair between you and me, that would be one thing. But the fact that you have allowed an entire town to become involved . . . I'd like to know what you expect me to do now. Tell me." She regarded him with a frank, somewhat aggressive air, her left hand fingering a silent scale on the rosin-speckled fingerboard while smoke curled from the cigarette in her right.

"Do? For one thing, Mrs. Coco, I don't see how I am responsible for what you call our affair becoming public. And if you think you can salve your conscience by asking me to come back and—"

"I'm not asking. I'm demanding."

Although he was flattered by her eagerness, he wished it could have been expressed a little more graciously.

"Wednesday at three-thirty, to be precise. The Bessie Building, third floor, Room 301."

"Is that where you rehearse now?" he asked, disturbed by the self-righteous anger written all over her face, an anger that properly should belong to him now. "Well, I'm not sure I can make it."

"You can make it, all right," she said, loosening her bow. "Brother, you better believe you're going to make it. And I haven't the slightest idea what you mean by rehearsal. This is the CP, Mr. Yoon. Maud Herbert is holding a hearing to investigate the CP."

Suddenly it dawned on him what must have happened.

"You talked to Alfred?" he asked from the piano bench, where he had decided to sit, after all. The week before he had been forced to give Alfred the facts about the chihuahua because Ray Jr. had been blabbing about Communists and rats, both of which Duk-Soo was accused of being while having his arm twisted by Alfred in St. Jude's newly remodeled Social Sciences Study Center. Apparently Alfred was jealous of Duk-Soo, resenting the fact that Ray Jr. had referred to him as Dad.

"You tried to take Ray Jr. away from me, didn't you?" Alfred had said, digging his wrestler's paws into Duk-Soo's trapezius while Dr. Butters, the monitor that evening, pretended to knit on the other side of the room.

"He loves *me*, you understand," Alfred said, leaning close enough for Duk-Soo to be able to read the tiny tattoo on his cheek: *don't touch this body.*

"Yes, he loves you," Duk-Soo whispered.

"What's that?"

"Oww, oh, please, yes, he loves you," Duk-Soo said, feeling Dr. Butters's dim, inquisitive eyes upon him.

"I'm supposed to get up in front of Maud Herbert and her committee on Wednesday," Mrs. Coco was saying, "an open meeting, by the way—the press is invited, and there's some black caucus from New Orleans that will be coming—I'm supposed to get up and tell them how innocent I am when right in my own front yard the chihuahua was . . . Oh, Duk-Soo, how could you? Keeping all this from me, and yet you're perfectly willing to tell everything to a demented drug addict."

"Now look," he said, "I never said a word to Heidi."

"Alfred—I'm talking about Alfred."

"He's an addict?" If so, he had to be the healthiest-looking drug addict Duk-Soo had ever seen, with a neck the size of a tv starlet's waist.

"Heidi, by the way, is not an addict. She happens to be a very sweet young lady who has had some unfortunate experiences in life. I never knew before, but she told me the other night that she was born in a displaced persons' camp in Belgium and her mother cooked nothing but beans every night and her father ran away to Brazil. He was part Arab and they never have heard from him once in all this time."

"I've always liked Heidi, too," he said, momentarily distracted by a baritone's rendition of "Mi chiamano Mimi" in the adjacent soundproof room.

"So what about Tee-Tee? What am I going to tell them about Tee-Tee?"

"Tee-Tee?" he said. If her name was indeed Lucia, then why in the world *did* people call her Mimi? he wondered while Mrs. Coco explained who Tee-Tee was.

"Well, tell them the truth," he said. "Tell them he's passed away."

"No, you tell them he's passed away; then you explain what you did with the body."

"I didn't do anything."

"What did happen to it then?"

"Ray Jr. must have . . . Listen," he said, getting to his feet, "why should I have to testify? Why should I do you a favor? To tell you the truth, Mrs. Coco, I think this discussion has just terminated."

"Please listen," Mrs. Coco said, following him out a side door of the music building. Duk-Soo had made a grand exit from the practice room but almost ruined the effect by glancing over his shoulder to make sure she was behind him. "I did not fire you. I simply suggested that you might like to have more time to work on your dissertation. Isn't that the most important thing in your life right now?"

"You could have called. Not one phone call."

At their best in the height of summer the campus palms still looked yellowish, anemic, but now in the chill autumn fog the folly of trying to extend the tropics this far north was apparent. Duk-Soo snapped off a bedraggled frond, giving Mrs. Coco, who was wheeling her cello, a chance to catch up.

"You've been moving around so much, how could anyone get ahold of you?"

"You didn't seem to have much trouble today," he said coldly.

"What's going on?" she asked, conveniently skirting the issue. "Why did you move out of that nice little house? I thought you hated the dorm."

Now that he could finally tell her the truth, that the real reason he had lived with Ray Jr. was because he was provided with a furnished house, rent free, he balked, thinking this might make him sound rather crass. Also, he didn't want to mention the sheriff's involvement, not to someone as nosy as Mrs. Coco. It was probably wiser to let sleeping dogs lie, or occasionally growl with a parking ticket or two.

"It was too big for one person. I didn't have time to do all the housekeeping and cooking. Those were things Ray Jr. looked after, you know."

"He did do a lot for you, Duk-Soo. You really owe it to him to clear things up about that chihuahua. That's the least you could do. Alfred told me Ray Jr. thinks he's being punished for killing a rat. You've got to let him know that Dove House isn't a punishment—it's a wonderful new home for him."

Duk-Soo paused at a sign, Walk With Light. Ever since his blowup with Ray Jr.—the boy had hidden Funck-Brentano in a family-size bag of caramel corn—he had been troubled by an obscure guilt, obscure because he knew that no one in his right mind could be expected to live a normal life with a pseudo-schizophrenic. But the guilt nagged at him nonetheless, unconvinced by reason.

"Look, Duk-Soo, it's only a few minutes from here. Why don't you drive out with me now? I know it would do him so much good."

"Well," he said, hating himself for not having the willpower to walk away from her, for hoping that she might yet relent and ask him back to the Pro Arts. "But this doesn't mean I'm going to testify on Wednesday, understand?" he added, wondering why she couldn't leave Ray Jr. alone. She was always prying into the boy's affairs when it was really no business of hers at all.

"We'll cross that bridge when we come to it. This way, hon. My car is over here."

"Ray Jr., it's me," Mrs. Coco said, walking over to the bunk bed where he lay. Duk-Soo hung back at the entrance to the room, thinking it strange that there were no monsters or station wagons on the wall, just a few posters of black rock stars. Through the curtainless window he could see sheep in the distance grazing peacefully around a satellite dish. It was comforting to find out how rural Dove House was, but he thought the plainclothes Franciscan brothers downstairs could make more of an effort to get their wards out into the fresh air and sunshine. Most of the boys were sitting around watching tv or fooling with a video game.

"Look who's come to see you," she said as Ray Jr. yawned and rubbed his eyes. "Lazybones, it's Mr. Yoon."

"Hi," Duk-Soo said, approaching the unpainted metal bunk bed that Ray Jr. shared with a roommate who was downstairs now.

"You tell that blood I ain't moving," Ray Jr. said. "This is my fucking bed. Better keep his motherfucking hands off my towel, too."

"Let's talk nice," Mrs. Coco said, picking up the pillow he had tossed at Duk-Soo's head. Her cheeks were scarlet.

"That nigger touch my towel, I kill him. I don't buy nigger lies, you dig?"

"It's so pretty out," Duk-Soo said. "Why don't we go for a nice walk?"

"What a good idea," Mrs. Coco said in a singsong, fairy-tale tone of voice. "Come on, Ray Jr. How can you lie in bed on a fine day like this?"

"Hey, momma, don't hand me none of that jive. I ain't movin'. That motherfucker steal my bed."

As they were riding back to St. Jude after a visit that turned out to be much briefer than they had expected, Mrs. Coco broke a long silence with a comment about how nice Brother Michael was, the man who had shown them the kitchen facilities.

"Very nice," Duk-Soo said, still hurt by the fact that Ray Jr. hadn't said a word to him. It was as if he hadn't been in the room at all, except for the pillow thrown at him.

"Of course, you can't expect those poor brothers to be responsible for everything," she added vaguely. "There seems to be a rough element to deal with, some of those boys, their language."

"Do you think he understood when we told him about the chihuahua?"

"To be frank, Duk-Soo, I think you might have gone overboard. I mean, after all, it *is* wrong to kill."

"But I thought we were trying to help him feel less guilty?"

"I know, but still, it's a fine line. Really, one shouldn't encourage or condone any sort of aggressive behavior in that sort of environment. The staff have all they can handle."

"Well, *pardonnez-moi*," he muttered, wondering if she was ever satisfied. Even in her heaven she would probably be bustling about trying to improve the diction and pitch of the martyrs' songs of praise.

"Don't get huffy, Duk-Soo. You know, that nice blond boy we met in the kitchen, I thought he'd make a much better roommate for Ray Jr. I told Brother Michael to see what he could do about it."

"You mean the boy who had shaved off his eyebrows?"

"He was born without eyebrows, wasn't he? Anyway, there were some very nice-looking boys there. I'm sure once Ray Jr. gets adjusted, he'll have plenty of friends. He needs to be around people his own age. Oh, and do you know what Brother Michael told me? He said he caught Dr. Jewel smoking marijuana in Ray Jr.'s room the other day, so now Dr. Jewel is forbidden to set foot in Dove House. I can't tell you what a relief it is to get Ray Jr. away from that man. And did you know that Brother Michael has a master's degree in social work? What could be better—real professionals who are religious, too. I think it's just wonderful. We're so lucky there are people like that, so devoted. Aren't we lucky? When you think about it, we have a lot to be thankful for." She punched in the car lighter with a faintly trembling hand. "Don't you agree? Just wonderful."

Brooding over the visit, Duk-Soo saw nothing of the countryside they drove through, and when Mrs. Coco dropped him off a block away from Jervis C. Mawks Men's Residence Hall, he even forgot to be disappointed that she had not asked him back to the Pro Arts.

Larry came for Thanksgiving and got the royal treatment, Mrs. Coco lavishing on him all sorts of treats and surprises, secretly thankful that her son had been considerate enough to send his second wife, a somewhat overbearing woman, to her parents' home in Port Arthur. Mrs. Coco had also extended an invitation to Ray Jr., but Brother Michael thought it would be wiser for him to spend the holidays *en famille;* and besides, Duk-Soo had promised to dine with the boys at Dove House that day. This helped lessen her own guilt about the boy. She had been trying to convince herself that there was really nothing wrong with Dove House, that this would eventually work out to be if not a wonderful home for him, at least an adequate one, but the guilt remained nonetheless, a dour ostinato beneath the somewhat frivolous laughs she and Larry shared.

Since for one reason or another none of the other children had been able to make it home, Mrs. Coco was allowed to enjoy the company of her firstborn without worrying about giving equal time to the rest. It would have been even better if Amy, Larry's daughter, had been able to come since she and Mr. Coco, who chose to mope around in the background during his son's visit, were so fond of each other. But Amy was spending the holidays with a friend of hers from U.S.L. whose father knew Crystal Gayle.

The doldrums that always set in after the holidays were particularly depressing this year. Mrs. Coco tried to sail through them with a Pro Arts Trio concert in Lake Charles, an excuse to see Larry again, but even though she was able to get a tentative booking from an elementary school, Myrtice ruined the trip by checking into the hospital. Trying to look on the bright side of things, Mrs. Coco saw that Myrtice had at least provided her with a ready-made excuse when Maud Herbert approached her about the Roast.

"It would be such a nice gesture if the Pro Arts played," Maud Herbert said as Mrs. Coco raked oak leaves into a plastic bag. Since Maud Herbert had declared that she was never going to speak to her again, Mrs. Coco was surprised to see the pillbox hat and something resembling a smile beneath it. In the interest of protecting Ray Jr. from public outrage, Mrs. Coco and Duk-Soo had talked it over and decided that neither one of them should testify at the Concerned Citizens Committee hearing on the Citizens Patrol; Tee-Tee's demise would remain their secret. Of course, Maud Herbert had gone into a tailspin. She simply could not fathom Mrs. Coco's behavior. After all she had done for her, personally taking the bone to the L.S.U. Agricultural Extension Station to get it identified, rallying some of the leading citizens to her defense, and then Mrs. Coco had the gall to phone at the last minute and say she was feeling under the weather and wouldn't be able to testify.

"Maud, excuse me, but I'm not sure what a roast is," she said, anxious to get the leaves out front before the men came.

"It's a banquet where people get up and say funny things about him."

"I'm sure there's plenty of funny things that can be said

about Mayor Binwanger, but don't you think it's rather cruel to make him sit there and listen?"

"You don't seem to understand, dear. It's a testimonial. We're honoring him for all he's done for Tula Springs."

Mrs. Coco stamped on some leaves, smushing them into the plastic bag. From bits and pieces of gossip and vague, elliptical reports in the paper, Mrs. Coco had learned that the Concerned Citizens Committee, which had been formed in order to expose the CP, linking it to shady financial dealings with the mayor and documenting cases of harassment and racial discrimination, had somehow gotten turned around in midstream, so that by the time the hearings came to an end, a special resolution had been passed praising the CP for providing better police protection than any other community's in St. Jude Parish. In fact, during the investigation, from which Donna Lee Keely, the chairperson, had resigned in protest, the committee's Finance Subcommittee, chaired by Maud Herbert, had discovered that the town actually owed the CP for overtime work guarding the hazardous chemical dump on Tula Creek.

"Maud, what about the poor black women?"

"That was all thoroughly gone into, my dear. It turned out that one of them had struck a gentleman from the CP with her purse. In other words, there was unnecessary roughness on both sides. They had both been drinking, you see."

"But should a CP be drinking on patrol?"

"He wasn't officially on patrol. Technically he was off duty."

Mrs. Coco tied up the green bag, hoping it weighed less than eight pounds, while Maud Herbert scraped a puce Nike on an oak root.

"In any case, you can't really imagine that I would want to show up at a testimonial for that man."

"Surely it's the least you could do for the mayor, Ethyl

Mae. After all, you're the one who started this whole thing. I think it's very magnanimous of him to let bygones be bygones. He's the one who suggested the Pro Arts, you know."

"*He* did? The man must be out of his mind. And by the way, it wasn't me who started the investigation."

Maud Herbert hitched up a cheap-looking purse that had *LV*'s all over it and sighed. "How soon we forget. Who was it complaining about harassment from the CP? Who was it that was upset by all the bones in her backyard? Who was it told poor Mrs. Loll that her father was a crook? Now you want to wash your hands of the whole thing."

"I haven't changed my mind about him or his CP, not one iota."

"Then why didn't you testify? You realize, dear, that when you didn't show up that day, you exonerated him completely. I don't have to tell you how embarrassing it was for me, after I had advertised the Dasypodidae bone all over town."

For a moment Mrs. Coco wished that she had gone ahead and perjured herself; at least then the town would have been closer to the truth than it was now. But unfortunately there just happened to be a commandment against bearing false witness.

"I'm sorry, Maud."

"Well, it's going to look pretty odd with your husband sitting up there on the dais with the mayor and you not even showing up."

"What?"

"Surely you know Louis has agreed to speak. All the most prominent businessmen are going to be there, and Louis is sort of their *éminence grise.*"

Mrs. Coco looked grimly in the general direction of McNair's, two blocks away. "It's useless discussing this, Maud. The Pro Arts couldn't play even if I wanted. Myrtice is in the hospital."

"Oh, I'm so sorry. It's not serious, I hope."

"She's always going in for some checkup or other, nothing major. But she definitely won't be able to play. Now if you don't mind, I've really got to get these leaves out front."

By the time Mrs. Coco finished raking, it was already dark. She worked hard, hoping to exhaust herself so that when Mr. Coco returned from the store she would not have the energy to throttle him. Lately things had been looking up for them, Mr. Coco having recovered from his slump, putting in long hours once again at work, so he wasn't always underfoot in the house. Now to learn that he was planning to speak at a testimonial for the man who had seduced his daughter—it was simply too much. There was no doubt about it: he had finally gone around the bend.

"But Ma, Binwanger didn't seduce Helen Ann. They fell in love. And anyway, that was years ago. It's silly to hold that against him."

George Henry was looking especially good in the candlelight, his face not so puffy and red, his hair neatly styled, and his clothes less flamboyant, more fitting for a man his age. Last week he had called her up and asked rather formally, like a boy on his first date, if she would enjoy having dinner at Dick's China Nights, just the two of them. She, of course, knew what was coming but decided she had fought her last battle with him and graciously accepted the invitation. The fact of the matter was, the more she saw of Heidi, infrequent though these glimpses were, the more Mrs. Coco began to realize that underneath it all she wasn't such a bad egg. Foolish, perhaps, but not altogether bad. Furthermore, she was tired of crusading for the Catholic Church. If the infidels didn't want to be saved, then perhaps it was best to just let them be.

"George Henry, that man ruined your sister's life. Look at Helen Ann, almost forty and she still hasn't found anybody to settle down with. Instead she's been squandering her money on crickets and teahouses. No good husband would have let her get away with that." At loose ends after the failure of the teahouse in Australia, Helen Ann had accepted George Henry's offer to help pay the air fare home for a little R and R. She was installed in Sam's room for the time being because her old room had a leak in the ceiling that Mr. Coco was unable to fix properly.

"It's not Binwanger's fault she's a widow."

"In a way, it is. She married on the rebound the first older man she came across, a man with a heart condition. Don't you see, the mayor imprinted on her, like those baby geese that follow mother dogs. Someone that much older, he should have been more responsible. After all, she was just a schoolgirl."

"She was in college."

"Yes, but—"

"Listen, Ma. I'm sick and tired of talking about Helen Ann. That's all you ever think about—something that happened years ago to her. You have other children, you know."

"I'm sorry. You're right, dear."

"Anyway, there's something I've got to say."

Mrs. Coco braced herself. The moment had come to hand over her sword, to accept the inevitable defeat of Right Thinking that this pagan world seemed to require of anyone with any principles. Yes, she would accept Heidi as a member of the family. She would go to the damn wedding—and smile, to boot. Maybe when you came right down to it, it would do her son a lot of good to marry someone who had been raised on a diet of beans. Heidi, at least, never wasted a penny, and she refused to serve expensive red meat.

"Yes, dear?"

"It's sort of hard," he began in a small, choked voice. "I mean like it's hard to admit you were right. I've known all along you were right, and that's what's made it sort of rough between us." He reached out and touched her hand. "See," he said, his voice getting louder, more confident, "the thing is, it's like our family never really says things, the things we feel for each other. Heidi has helped me that way—she's so in touch with her feelings. So I guess what I'm trying to say is"—he wiped away a tear with his knuckle—"I really care for you so much. I want to protect you, not hurt you, because I . . ."

"Heart, it's OK," she said, squeezing his big rough hand and wishing the waiter would stop staring at them. She had tears in her eyes too: to think that he would finally be man enough to admit she had been right all along.

"I love you."

"Yes, of course," she said, wishing he would keep his voice down. "Now let's let bygones be bygones and have ourselves a nice dinner."

"Anyway, I guess you know what I'm getting at," he said after they had ordered. George Henry asked for a Swiss cheese omelette and she an Aloha Burger, which she had a coupon for, clipped from Friday's paper. "I was wondering if maybe the Pro Arts could play at the wedding."

Mrs. Coco's newfound warmth toward her son dropped a degree or two. Was there no satisfying him? Wasn't it enough that she was planning to agree to attend, but now she was expected to perform?

"George Henry, I don't think the Pro Arts would be really appropriate. Isn't it enough that I'll . . . that I'll be there?" There, she had said it. It was done, her sacrifice consummated.

"Well, naturally I assumed you'd come. After all, this was your idea. You were right all along."

"My idea?" She looked puzzled as the gray-haired waiter in a none-too-clean gold jacket set another round of drinks before them.

"You get the martini," the waiter said, putting another

double martini in front of Mrs. Coco, who usually never drank anything stronger than rosé, but who felt the need to fortify herself tonight, "and your husband here gets the ginger ale, right?"

"Uh, I, that's not—no, leave the martini. Fine. That's all."

"George Henry," she said, once they were alone again and their blushes had subsided, "I admit that Heidi seems to have had a good effect on you recently, but that hardly makes it *my* idea. Yes, you have cut down on your drinking and—"

"Cut down? I don't drink at all. And I don't understand why you keep bringing Heidi into this," he added, waving away her cigarette smoke with a frown. He had given up smoking, too, but since she was smoking two packs a day, she didn't feel like mentioning this improvement.

"Well, I assume Heidi is responsible."

"Ma, what are you talking about? Weren't you listening to what I was saying—you were right about her. She and I, I mean we did connect on some very basic level—it was deep and all. But I realize now that when you're in it for the long haul . . . Like all those times we postponed the wedding and I would blame it on you. It wasn't your fault. It was Heidi and me, we were the ones who had the real doubts. We were just projecting everything on you."

"Oh," she murmured, vaguely pleased, yet puzzled.

"You knew all along what was going on, didn't you? Like when you took me to Powell's to see Connie, I was so pissed at you because you were right—deep down I missed Connie so much. I guess the thing that really cinched it, though, was the beauty pageant. When I saw Connie on the stage again, something hit me. It was like I was back in the sixties, that night Connie was crowned Miss Housing Development. She looked the same this year as she did way back then—it was like we weren't really getting old. I was so happy, Ma—and as for Connie, she said when she read in her paper that I was getting married, it really wrecked her. She realized how much she—"

"Wait a minute now. You're not telling me that you and—"

"I know, you're worried about Heidi. But we've hashed it all out, Ma. She understands. See, she admitted she had been sleeping with this therapist at the drug rehabilitation program, she had this thing for him, so she's like really happy now that she doesn't have to be guilty about me anymore. It's not cool, really, all this guilt. Of course, when Heidi first told me about the therapist, I swear I nearly killed her. But all that negative shit is gone now. Heidi and Connie have been working on me. They've helped neutralize all this male chauvinist stuff I was hung up on."

"George Henry, how is it physically possible for you to marry a lesbian?" Mrs. Coco asked, trying her best to sound practical, down-to-earth, but still finding herself turning a little red when she pronounced the last word. Any hint at morals, the Church, or even common decency would, of course, only alienate him.

"Ma, don't say that. She's bisexual, just like you and me and every other person on this planet."

"Dear, I know this may come as a shock to you," she enunciated, trying to counteract the numbing effect of the second martini, "but I am not bisexual."

"You're not sexual, period. That's what Connie used to be like, totally repressed, just like you. I felt like I was going to bed with a Rubbermaid glove, everything always had to be squeaky clean. She was so frightened of herself, you know, but now that she's had this experience—wow, it's just amazing. She's learned so much about her body. I can't believe the difference. And all that guilt she used to have—she realizes now it's no big deal if part of her really dug women. It's not her whole life anymore, like it used to be, and it doesn't poison all her other relationships with guilt."

Mrs. Coco tried not to show too much disdain for her son's

bargain-basement logic, which was cheap and full of holes. "No guilt, you say? Then what about the poor woman she's been living with on the goat farm? I suppose she hasn't the slightest guilt leaving her and running off with you."

"Why should she? Greta's just a friend. Her boyfriend will move in when Connie leaves. As far as Connie's lover goes, well, she broke up with Connie about two months ago. She moved to Chicago to—"

"Of course, those deviants have no sense of loyalty. How can you expect Connie to stay content with you? What's to prevent her from running off like her girl friend for a prettier face?"

"Her girl friend ran off to Chicago to join the Carmelites."

The omelette and burger with pineapple were set before them, giving Mrs. Coco a moment to regroup her forces. Evolution would be her best weapon, she decided; George Henry would be defeated on his own turf with cold scientific fact. Fortunately the Rosary Altar Society had just finished discussing evolution at their last meeting, so she felt confident enough to launch an offensive. Before the meeting Mrs. Coco had always been somewhat depressed by Teilhard de Chardin's noosphere, but then Mrs. Wattels had gotten up and explained what it meant in plain English. The point was that we were all evolving from matter into spirit, losing useless parts like appendixes and wisdom teeth along the way. Mrs. Wattels felt that Asian people were in the vanguard of evolution, since they were on the whole more compact than the average Caucasian. Of course, there was a problem with this since most Asians weren't Catholic, but Mrs. Wattels felt there was a good chance they would all be converted by the time they were so small that you could barely see them, say in a million years or so. In any case, Mrs. Coco was grateful for the talk, since it made her feel less guilty about her general disapproval of large people.

"Ma, what is all this crap you're handing me?" George

Henry said, angered by her dispassionate observations about how homosexuality had no place in the natural scheme of evolution. "What has evolution got to do with me and Connie?"

She was hurt by his response, because she hadn't once mentioned ethics or morality. "George Henry, please lower your voice. All I'm trying to say is that Connie's problem is much more serious than you think. You just can't shrug it off like you have. Any woman who would even contemplate doing what she has done, how could she ever make a fit wife? Don't you see, she's deeply disturbed. She needs intensive psychiatric help."

"For your information, she's seeing a psychiatrist right now, and he doesn't consider her disturbed in the least. As a matter of fact, he's trying to get her to stop throwing her money away on him. He said he's rarely met such an integrated person—those were his exact words. There's just one problem, one thing he can't understand about her."

"What's that?"

"Why she would want to get married into our family again. That's why Connie keeps on seeing him. She's trying to convince him that you won't ruin her life. See, Dr. Jewel thinks any marriage I get involved in will be fucked up because of you. He thinks you and I have a very neurotic relationship."

"Dr. Jewel? You don't mean to say she's seeing that awful quack! George Henry, haven't you heard he was fired from Norris State, and furthermore, you must not use such language around me."

"All I know is that Jane Loll told her he's the best. He specializes in creative types, artists and writers and stuff. Connie is really high on him, so don't go knocking him just because he doesn't think you're a saint. And by the way, Ma, all that bullshit you were trying to dump on me about evolution and what's natural and not natural—that just happens to be something I know about. Take swordfish, for instance."

"I think it's very wrong to use such language in front of your mother," she said, backtracking for a moment. Language like that was probably the root of all his trouble. She had been negligent in not taking a firmer stand before.

"Dr. Jewel told Connie they're real switch-hitters. Halfway through life the male swordfish—or maybe it's swordtails—anyway, the males turn into females and the females into males. And did you know that there's a species of fish that lays its eggs in the eye of another fish? The eye, Ma. Think about that."

But instead of thinking about the fish's eye, Mrs. Coco became intent on extracting an apology from her son for his language. The more she thought about it, the more wrong it seemed to her. George Henry finally apologized, but in so unpleasant a way that she almost felt compelled to demand an apology for the apology. In any case, after dessert and a brief skirmish over natural law, she asked for the check.

"Put that coupon away," George Henry said as he reached for his wallet. "I'm paying."

"I'll pay for myself," she said firmly, forgetting that she had purposely brought no money with her since it was he who had suggested eating in such an expensive place. If it had been up to her, they would have finished up the leftover tuna casserole at home.

As if she didn't have enough on her mind, what with George Henry intent on marrying a swordfish, and Helen Ann, back home now, the stuffing knocked out of her by one financial misadventure after another, needing all the care and attention a mother could give—as if all this wasn't enough, Lucy had to show up, walking from the drugstore where the bus had let her off with a bundle of dirty laundry.

Lucy had come to see her sister and to have her mother take up the hem in one of her dresses for the wedding.

"Careful!" she snapped at her mother. Turbaned with a towel and wrapped in a red silk dressing gown embroidered with birds of paradise, Lucy, with her olive skin, darker than anyone else's in the family, looked a little oriental and despotic. "Well, do you see anything?" She had asked her mother to examine her left eye, which was tearing.

Eggs? Mrs. Coco was thinking as she peered at the eye, reminded now of the conversation the previous evening at China Nights. So what if a fish had eggs in its eye? What was that supposed to prove? If only she hadn't drunk so much at dinner with George Henry, she could have stood firm, showing him that evolution was on her side. But as it was, her brain had gotten a little addled, and she had veered off into the Church's teaching on natural law, which had ruined everything, since the minute George Henry heard the word *Church*, he became totally irrational, claiming that the only reason Asians were smaller was because the Church was starving them to death with its birth-control policies.

"Mother!"

"What? No, I don't see anything. It's probably just a little scratch."

They were sitting on the canopied bed in Lucy's room, preparing to go down to dinner. Mrs. Coco had stopped in to remind her daughter to be specially nice to Helen Ann and not say anything about the way she looked. The last time the family had seen Helen Ann, at Christmas three years ago, she had looked fit and tanned and had made a good impression on two aunts and an uncle, the well-off Cocos from Fort Worth. But since that time Helen Ann had let herself go, the extra weight of too many crumpets and scones sagging kangaroo-like around her middle.

"Aren't you going to put on any of that lipstick I got you?"

Mrs. Coco asked as Lucy unwrapped her turban. "If not, I'm going to have to take it back to the beauty college. They were having a sale."

"You know I don't wear lipstick. And how you can still go there, after all that stuff about their dog. Hand me my brush."

"Why shouldn't I? Just because it ran away . . . I have nothing to hide," she said calmly, without rancor, for she had decided that this chihuahua was the Cross she was destined to bear for Ray Jr.'s sake. It was not exactly the type of Cross she would have picked out for herself—something like being widowed would have been more her style—but the very unseemliness of it was perhaps a lesson in humility. One thing she knew for sure, though, and that was that she would rather die than see the poor boy subjected to any cross-examining by Gyrene and the CP. He had suffered enough at the hands of Dr. Jewel, and she was only too glad to have the chance to spare him any further distress. Of course, the fierceness of her sacrifice—yes, she *would* rather die—sometimes gave her pause, but with Ignatian discipline she was learning not to dwell too long on or probe too deeply into feelings that were best left unexamined.

"Now you promise not to say anything about the way Helen Ann looks?"

"Mother, stop." Lucy stashed her Worth soap away, four dollars a bar. "I don't care how she looks."

"And sug, if you don't mind, let's not worry about being Italian this evening," Mrs. Coco felt impelled to add because at dinner last night Lucy had harangued her father about the psychic damage he had inflicted on his offspring by trying to pretend he wasn't Italian. She informed him that she was proud her grandfather had been a proletarian cobbler, and he ought to be ashamed that his children weren't bilingual. And furthermore, why the hell didn't they ever have spaghetti for dinner? Twenty-six years she had been around this house, and not once had they ever had spaghetti.

On her way downstairs Mrs. Coco noticed something white under the front door. Curious, she stooped and picked up an envelope with the words *Mrs. Coco* and *Eyes Only* scrawled on the outside in purple ink. While opening it she glanced at the brown spot on her hand that didn't look like the other age spots and worried a little about leprosy again.

"Dear Mrs. Big," she read.

This is to let you know that I'm sick of being bossed around. I got my rights, you know. When we played in Opelousas at the baby school, you divided up the lunch bill at the Holiday Inn into three equal parts when all I had was desert and coffee. I told you it wasn't fair to make me pay for what Myrtle and you were eating and for your information I don't happen to need three *square* meals a day since I have my own protein supplement at home. Maybe you forget why all these schools are asking us to play. You think it's because of you and that tub of lard? It's so they can look at me—you know this and I know this, so let's stop kidding ourselves. Thus, you are being notified at this writing that I am tending my resignation.

Sincerely,
E.M.

P.S. Don't try to come crawling because I just joined the union and the rep told me your scale is a joke he wouldn't tell on his mother-in-law. So there!

"What's that?"

Cramming the letter into the pocket of her pants suit, Mrs. Coco smiled up at Helen Ann, who was almost as tall as her father. When she was young, Helen Ann had been able to discipline the boys for Mrs. Coco, but now, sad to see, she had lost her spunk and had acquired from Mr. Coco a

Lamarckian stoop. Overweight, graying, Helen Ann looked almost as old as her mother, but not quite as attractive.

"Are you all right, Mom?" she asked in the Australian accent that Mrs. Coco could never get used to. They walked toward the dining room.

"Hmm?"

"Listen, I hope you've reconsidered about the wedding. It would be so lovely if you came. And after all, George Henry flew me all the way here so the family could be together for it."

"What? I'm fine, dear," she said, feeling a lump in her throat. When she thought of all she had done for that boy, the times she had driven E.M. back to Ozone when his father couldn't come and pick him up, the banana bread she had baked for rehearsals, hoping to fill him out, the set of strings she had bought for his birthday—and this was the thanks she got. But what was worse was the feeling that she had been through this once before and would continue to endure the same ingratitude over and over again.

"Well, we all have so much to be thankful for," Mr. Coco said mechanically, from force of habit, when everyone was seated at the table. His stylist at the Tiger Unisex had convinced him that his hair would look fuller if he parted it on the right instead of the left, a disconcerting change that made his wife think she was viewing him wrong, like a slide put in backwards.

"Helen Ann, you must give me the recipe for this meatloaf," Mrs. Coco said from the other end of the table, which had been set by Mr. Coco with the heirloom china from Mississippi. Beeswax candles, perks from the Rosary Altar Society, were reflected in the polished cherry, and made Helen Ann look a little less marsupial.

"It's your recipe, Mom. I just left out the oatmeal."

"Dear, oatmeal helps extend the hamburger, and it isn't as

fattening. We should all eat lots of oatmeal and watch the pounds melt away. Now Louis, will you say grace?"

"Bless us, O Lord, and these thy gifts—"

"Please, not that again," Lucy said. "Let me. Dear father who felt it necessary to have your own son rubbed out just because some poor defenseless woman wounded your precious ego by eating an apple, I thank you that for once we are finally having meatloaf without oatmeal in it. Amen."

"Lucy Agnes," Mrs. Coco said, "I've had just about enough of your sacrilege. When you're in this house, you can learn to show a little respect for God."

"A little? Is that all? I've devoted my whole life to Her."

"If you call writing sacrilegious poems about your mother being garbed in rayon—"

"You've been snooping. I told you to leave my stuff alone, didn't I? And it isn't sacrilegious—if only you knew how to read, you'd know it wasn't. For your information I believe something extraordinary happened at Fatima, something that touched the real core of what it meant to be a woman, only it got screwed up by a lot of men trying to tell that poor girl what she felt, what it all meant."

"What do you mean, if I knew how to read?" she demanded, her indignation getting the better of her curiosity. What Lucy had just said intrigued her, especially the part about God being a Her. But she was not going to give Lucy the satisfaction of showing off at her mother's expense.

"Your mother is a remarkably well-educated woman," Mr. Coco put in. "Just because she never finished high school . . ."

"I can read as well as anyone."

"You can't, Mother. You're too literal. You have no clue what's going on in real writing. It's not anything like you think, so from now on, I'd appreciate it if you'd keep your hands off anything of mine. And don't call me sacrilegious, either, not unless you're prepared to tell me what Barth and Tillich and Bonhoeffer, Irenaeus, Augustine, and Ruether, Gutiérrez and Schillebeeckx have to say about the Atonement."

"More lima beans, anyone?" Mr. Coco said.

With a timid smile Helen Ann raised her hand. Over at her end of the table Mrs. Coco sat brooding about Schillebeeckx. She thought he might be the one Father Fua had said was censored by the Vatican, but not being sure, she kept quiet, afraid to give Lucy any more points.

"Father," Lucy said, breaking a stony silence that made everyone self-conscious about the way he was eating, "is it true you're giving a speech for Mayor Binwanger next week?"

"It's not really a speech," he muttered, avoiding his wife's eyes. "Say, did someone bake a pecan pie?"

"No," Mrs. Coco said. "Why do you ask?"

"I thought I smelled one."

"Another nasal hallucination, Louis. You better ask the doctor about it."

"What do you mean by another? And this was real. I smelled a pecan pie."

"By the way, Helen Ann," Lucy said, "I was talking to Connie, and she said she hoped you would be her maid of honor."

"Oh, how sweet. But why me?"

"Well, since the Pro Arts refuses to play, Connie felt she needed as much family support as possible."

"Young lady, the reason the Pro Arts won't play is because there is no Pro Arts anymore," Mrs. Coco said, certain now why George Henry had helped Helen Ann come home. It wasn't for Helen Ann's sake at all; it was so he would have one more ally to beleaguer his mother. "They all quit on me, first Duk-Soo and now today E.M. So let's stop talking about why *I* refuse to play. We're extinct, and that's that."

"But you could at least go to the wedding," Lucy persisted.

"Yes, you could," Helen Ann echoed faintly.

"Tell me one other thing I've smelled that wasn't there," Mr. Coco said.

"And Mother," Lucy said, "I meant to tell you. You ruined a whole day of work for me today. I couldn't write a line with you fussing at Dad about Binwanger. Do you realize how immature you sound, both of you? If you must act like babies, you could at least have the decency to wait until I'm gone. I didn't come all the way from New Orleans for this."

"I would appreciate it if you would refrain from mentioning that man's name while I'm eating," Mrs. Coco said. "And Louis, you smelled fudge the other day. You came downstairs wondering if I had made some fudge for you. Fudge. Helen Ann, must you put your elbows on the table? And please, dear, sit up straight. You know, dear, I've been thinking. Jeans are wonderful for some women, but you've got to have a certain kind of figure to bring it off. Besides, at your age I would think . . . Hon, where are you going?"

"I'm not hungry," Helen Ann said dully.

"Now look what you've done," Mr. Coco said after Helen Ann had left the room. "I thought I told you, Mae—lay off her."

"Don't blame me," Mrs. Coco said, pouring herself another glass of the jug wine she felt compelled to keep on hand during Helen Ann's visit. Someone, though, must have been hitting it on the sly. When she had checked the gallon bottle under the sink before dinner, she found it was already two thirds empty. "I'm not the one who's going to make a fool of himself kissing certain people's rear ends."

"Mother, I wish you'd get off this Binwanger kick. It's ancient history by now. There's nothing between them anymore."

"He called yesterday, didn't he?"

"He called me," Mr. Coco said, "about the Roast. Helen Ann just happened to pick up the phone."

"You talk about being Christian," Lucy said. "Why can't you forgive Binwanger?"

"I can't forgive anyone unless they're sorry first," Mrs. Coco said.

"And boy, do you ever want to make him sorry," Mr. Coco muttered.

"What, Louis?"

"Nothing."

"Is it the abortion? Is that why Binwanger makes you so crazy?" Lucy asked.

Looking hastily through Lucy's bewildering Fatima poem this afternoon, Mrs. Coco had come across several new references to what might be an abortion, which made her wonder if the poetess had been talking to her father.

"I thought she had a right to know," Mr. Coco said, meeting his wife's steely gaze. "And Lucy has a point—families shouldn't keep secrets. It's not healthy. Children can always sense when something's wrong."

Lighting up a cigarette, Mrs. Coco inhaled deeply, hoping to master the fluttery panic in her breast. She couldn't stand to think about Helen Ann's abortion and for years now had succeeded in almost entirely forgetting it by reducing it to a vague, abstract guilt that was always with her. "Things were different in those days, Lucy. Helen Ann would never have found a decent husband, any husband at all, really. You have to remember, she was only a child herself, still in school." The idea of Helen Ann bearing that man's child was, of course, unthinkable. When you came right down to it, it was really as if the mayor had raped her. Mrs. Coco had no choice, absolutely no choice at all: she *had* to urge Helen Ann to get that abortion. "I don't think we have to discuss it anymore."

"Why didn't you ever tell me she had an abortion?" Lucy asked.

"Because you weren't born yet. Or if you were, I don't think you knew any English."

"Your mother's right," Mr. Coco said, "things were different in those days. No one would ever think for one second of having a baby without being married. I know things have changed now, there's lots of unwed mothers, but back then . . . By the way, Lucy, I don't think it's really necessary for you to mention this to Nancy or Sam."

"Or George Henry or Larry," Mrs. Coco said, remembering how easy it had been to keep the boys in the dark. Unless it directly concerned them, they were usually not very curious about what was going on.

"What about Father Fua?" Lucy asked. "Have you told him, Miss Right to Life?"

"Excuse me, please," Mrs. Coco said, dabbing at her face with a napkin before getting up. She did not feel it necessary to sit there and listen to such impertinence from a daughter who, despite all her fancy theologians, never did learn page one of the Baltimore Catechism. In any case, Mrs. Coco knew full well that God and Father Fua would forgive her if she could only make it clear what the circumstances had been. But, being no Margaret Mead, she was dubious about translating such sophisticated cultural values for a Samoan who tended to see everything in black and white. And besides, it wasn't she who had had the abortion. She couldn't go around confessing sins that didn't even belong to her. Oh, if only Helen Ann knew what a shambles she had made of everyone's life by carrying on with a married man!

"She *does*," Mrs. Coco heard Lucy say in the dining room. Mrs. Coco had paused in the kitchen, her ear to the swinging door, before going upstairs. "She drinks way too much, Father."

"It's only when you kids are around," Mr. Coco said. "She feels like celebrating."

"I checked the rosé, and it's almost empty. And no one else in this family can drink that garbage, four ninety-eight a gallon, that's what she buys, and then she dumps Sweet 'n Low into it. Did you see how many glasses she had at dinner tonight? And last night I saw her sneak some up to the sewing room after everyone had gone to bed."

On the staircase Mrs. Coco paused again, wondering if it could possibly be true that she had drunk all that rosé herself. No, Lucy was just out to get her. Surely Helen Ann had been dipping into the jug without telling anyone, and Mr. Coco, too. But when she reached the top of the stairs, going slowly, clinging to the banister, she was surprised to find that she had ascended into nowhere, a dead end of fleur-de-lis wallpaper; perhaps, after all, she had had just a bit too much of that rosé.

17

In the distance he could see one of the refineries that lined the banks of the Mississippi below Baton Rouge, the bright towers rising glibly, somewhat abstractly, like a B-movie set for the City of Tomorrow. Duk-Soo turned from the window and checked his tie and hair in the shard of mirror taped above the men's room sink. Norris State always made him feel that something was wrong with him, that his fly was unzipped perhaps, or his tie loose, his face smudged. When he walked through the overheated green halls, he often stumbled against things he should have seen—a wheelchair, a baseball bat—or while trying to second-guess people coming around the corner or out of the elevator, would bump into them. The smell of the place, a peculiar odor that reminded him of both dentists and exterminators, made him light-headed, anxious, as if he were waiting for something necessary to happen. He had thought long and hard about the boy and was forced to conclude that while Ray Jr. was not an especially likeable or agreeable companion, he did leave one feeling—after he was gone, at least— that one had loved him in some dim, obscure way. It was for this reason that Duk-Soo had ventured onto the grounds of Norris State.

When he finally was admitted to Dr. Lily Oustelet's office after having been kept waiting a good twenty minutes in an anteroom with a snobbish cat that wouldn't let him pet it, Duk-Soo experienced a ripple or two of relief. Youngish, in her late thirties or early forties, stylishly dressed, and smiling, Dr. Oustelet was not the old battle-ax Dr. Jewel had conjured up in his mind. She apologized for keeping him waiting and then asked if he'd care for a chocolate. Duk-Soo declined.

"Yes, it's nice to have a river to look at," she said after he commented about the view from the window of her sparsely but tastefully furnished office. An array of diplomas and certificates behind her desk was balanced on both sides by two symmetrical shelves of books, arranged, it seemed, according to the size and color of the bindings. *Über Unzucht mit Kindern und Pädophilia erotica* caught his eye as he settled into an oversized leather chair that, like the substantial green-shaded brass lamp beside it, would have fit nicely in an exclusive men's club.

"Are you sure you won't have a chocolate, Dr. Yoon?" she asked, holding out the elegant box once again. Perhaps he should, he thought and, nodding, took one. It was so satisfying to hear her call him Dr. Yoon. Of course, the degree wouldn't be officially conferred until the commencement ceremonies in the spring. But Dr. Barnes had finally approved the dissertation, though still unconvinced about the equation of "home" with "death," a willfully perverse analogy, the professor had declared. After a prolonged interrogation in Dr. Barnes's office, Duk-Soo, realizing that he had no choice if he wanted to get his PhD, had recanted and deleted this analogy. But like Galileo he continued to believe furtively in the truth.

"So, what may I do for you?" Dr. Oustelet said after they had made small talk about asphalt, which Duk-Soo had just noticed was splattered on his good suit trousers. He had

driven on his scooter through what he assumed was a heat
mirage, forgetting momentarily that it was December and
the road might look wavy and unstable for other reasons,
namely, new-laid asphalt.

"Well, actually, Dr. Oustelet, I was a little disturbed to
hear from Brother Michael at Dove House that Ray Jr. has
been transferred to the facilities at Florence. Somehow this
does not strike me as being the most felicitous home for him.
The halfway house seemed so much more amenable for a
youth. You know I visited him there quite often."

"Twice."

"Pardon?"

"You paid two visits," she said, picking up a folder from
her desk. "Once on November thirteenth, once at Thanksgiving."

"I'm sure it was more than that," he said, a little discon-
certed that his visits had been recorded. "Whatever, I have
recently taken it upon myself to view the adult institution at
Florence, and I was rather . . ."—about to say *appalled,* he
edited himself—"curious if a juvenile would be happy
there."

"Ray Jr. is no longer a juvenile, legally speaking."

"Did they have to send him there? What was wrong with
Dove House?"

Dr. Oustelet explained that Ray Jr. had proved to be a
disruptive influence at the halfway house, causing fights and
several hundred dollars' damage to the property. Furthermore, she went on, he had not been involuntarily consigned
to Florence. He had signed himself in. "We weren't anxious
to get into a conservatorship hearing, you understand," she
said. "We would have had to go through a fourteen-day cer-
tification. It was much easier to explain things to him and
let him make his own decision. Quite frankly, he was so unhappy at Dove House there was really no problem getting
him to transfer."

"But did he know what it would be like at Florence?"

"We explained everything, Dr. Yoon. Besides, what choice did we have? He's too old for Norris State. His father—I don't know if you've had the pleasure of meeting Luscious Ray, alias Ivan the Red, Baron von Hecht . . ."

"You mean Alfred?"

"Yes, Alfred was obviously out of the question. And there was no way he could live alone, unsupervised."

"I appreciate your difficulties, Dr. Oustelet, and I assure you I don't mean to sound critical of your procedures." His tongue probed the caramel from the chocolate, which had lodged in a sensitive tooth. "What I would like to propose, well, you see, next month I'll be teaching in New Orleans at a private academy, and perhaps Ray Jr. could live with me for a while, at least until a more permanent arrangement could be worked out. I don't know if you're aware of this fact, but he and I did share a house for a while."

She reached for the crumpled foil candy wrapper he had deposited on her desk; smoothing and folding it, she replied, "A house? Whose house, Dr. Yoon? Yours?"

He gave a tight smile, nodded.

"That's odd. According to Mrs. Phillips, the caseworker, you weren't paying any rent on the house."

"Well, you see . . ." he said, wondering if he should claim that he owned the house. He certainly didn't want to explain about the swindler and the sheriff.

Getting up from her chair, Dr. Oustelet lined up a neat stack of papers so that it was trim with the edge of her polished desk; then, after moving a second stack to balance the first, she perched casually on the edge of the desk, in the exact middle. "A third party was paying the rent," she said, glancing at the folder beside her.

"Rent? There was no rent. Mrs. Phillips must be mistaken."

"Dr. Yoon, do you mean to tell me that you didn't know

that the property at 115 Howard belonged to the Catahoula Corporation, and that the rent was paid on the first of each month by Dr. Nathan Jewel?"

"Well, I . . ." No, he didn't. It made no sense to him. Why would Dr. Jewel want to hide the fact that he had been so generous? Of course, this might explain why he, Duk-Soo, had never been bothered by the sheriff. The sheriff had nothing to do with the Spanish house after all, if what Dr. Oustelet was saying was true. And it did seem to be. She handed him a copy of one of the rent receipts so he could see for himself. There was Dr. Jewel's signature and the Catahoula Corporation, which for some reason sounded vaguely familiar to him.

"It's strange, isn't it—Dr. Jewel going to such trouble and expense for one of his patients? Why don't you tell me about it, Dr. Yoon?"

"Me? I don't . . . well, he was always very kind to Ray Jr."

She looked expectantly at him while he tried not to notice her legs, which were quite shapely and rather close to his face. "Are you aware of the importance of the doctor-patient relationship? It is a special trust that must be handled with the utmost respect and professionalism. If you were a doctor, would you offer your patient a weed?"

"I suppose not," he said, trying to grasp the metaphor; a weed as opposed to a flower?

"Yet this is exactly what Dr. Jewel has done, not once, but several times. Mrs. Phillips reported the odor of marijuana in your house on three separate occasions, each of them shortly after Dr. Jewel had visited Ray Jr. You're aware, perhaps, that I tried to get him fired from Norris State. Would you like to know why?"

"Well, he certainly didn't speak English very well," he said, hoping to sound as innocent as possible. "I noticed a lot of *ain't*s."

"Believe me, Dr. Yoon, that affectation of his, trying to

sound down-home, I could have lived with that, even though I personally found it highly annoying. And maybe even the weeds—if I were sure he was just using them himself. No, what I could not and will not tolerate is his Ferenczi. That's where I draw the line."

"Oh. I thought it was a Mercedes."

"Don't get cute with me, sir," she said, and the smile quickly faded from his anxious face. "Sándor Ferenczi was a disciple of Freud's who tried to make a name for himself by advocating certain unorthodox techniques, including stroking the patient on his lap. Needless to say, he was disowned by every reputable therapist of his day, including Freud himself. Dr. Jewel, though, has allied himself with a chic new theory that Ferenczi was misunderstood. That was his defense at the hearings I instigated when I tried to get him fired. So we all had to sit and listen to him spout a lot of baloney about love, how the analyst must share in the therapy, opening himself up emotionally to the patient, how love is the only cure for psychic trauma—all sorts of crap like that. You understand, of course, that not once, not twice, not three times—four times, Dr. Yoon, four documented times I happened to enter Dr. Jewel's office and found a patient on his lap. Twice it was Ray Jr., once an eight-year-old girl, and once my secretary—she was a patient of his at the time. Dr. Jewel is very clever, though. Somehow he was able to convince a few members of the board that he had done nothing unethical, that he was simply using experimental techniques. You can imagine how distressed I was to learn that after leaving Norris State he was still involved with Ray Jr. But my hands were tied. There was nothing I could do then, even though I was extremely curious about this gentleman Dr. Jewel had dredged up to act as a . . . shall we say, guardian? I take it you're not a relative?"

A bead of sweat stung Duk-Soo's eyes. "Of whom? Dr. Jewel's? No. I hardly know him, just barely. Oh, uh, Ray Jr., he's just an acquaintance of sorts. You know how it is." A plump seagull sashayed across the window ledge with a hoarse, fowl-like squawk that startled Duk-Soo, who was leaning forward in the comfortable leather chair, clasping and unclasping his suddenly oleaginous hands.

"No, I don't. Tell me, just how did you become an acquaintance of Ray Jr.'s?"

"Let's see—I was playing in a Chinese restaurant one evening and—"

"Playing?"

"The violin. I'm a concert artist."

"Oh. That's funny, I thought you were getting a degree in sociology. And by the way, it just so happens that the office of the Dean of Humanities at St. Jude has no record of your being awarded a PhD, *Dr.* Yoon."

Had she phoned while he was waiting to see her? This woman was truly a menace.

"Oh, that, I can explain that. You see, I just found out from my adviser, Dr. Barnes, that I would, uh, my dissertation is approved, but you see, he hasn't gotten around to notifying the Dean's office yet. He's got some sort of flying tournament this weekend, but as soon as he gets back, he'll tell the Dean, and it's the spring, that's when I'll officially get the degree."

"You're a concert artist as well? Tell me, do you perform exclusively in Chinese restaurants?"

"Oh, no, all over, everywhere. I'm a member of a very wonderful quartet, the Pro Arts."

"Pro Arts. That's odd. Could there be two Pro Arts in Louisiana?"

"What? I doubt it."

"Not too long ago I had a talk with a certain Ethyl Mae Coco. She told me she was the leader of a group called the Pro Arts—only this was a trio."

His mouth opened, but nothing came out. He tried again.

"Well, you see, I used to be with, but then my work, you know . . ."

"Are you married, Mr. Yoon?"

"Of course," he said, anxious to prove that he could not possibly be involved in any sexual scandal. "For years and years."

"Years and years—and here in Mrs. Phillips' report you are definitely not married, never have been married. Interesting. Would you care to explain?"

By the time Duk-Soo left the Executive Director's office, he was in need of a fresh shirt. But there wasn't time to return to St. Jude to change his sweat-soaked Geoffrey Beene if he was going to make it to the wedding. He shuddered to think how close he had come to admitting he was married to a Communist. It seemed that Dr. Oustelet could read his mind, catching him in every lie except one, when he claimed his wife was now living in Seoul. Not only did Dr. Oustelet forbid him to have anything more to do with Ray Jr., but she almost threatened to report him to the Dean of Humanities for irregular conduct and going under an assumed name, Dr. Yoon. There was no doubt about it, he mused as he hurried down the green halls, looking for the nearest exit; it was a very big mistake to have let Mrs. Coco offer up his services to her god. Just look what it had led to, when she had insisted that the Pro Arts play for charity at Norris State. Charity indeed. From now on he would think twice about ever feeling sorry for anyone again.

"I told her she was a darn fool, but you couldn't keep that gal in bed for love or money," Mrs. Fitt was saying to Duk-Soo near the indoor mosaic pool with live fish in it, big ones, not just the goldfish type. Not far away, within earshot, her daughter-in-law, Myrtice, was propped up in a one-of-a-kind chair that had been designed especially for the Loll residence in the Beáu Arts Estates, where George Henry and

Connie had just been remarried. Myrtice was supposed to be in the hospital, but when she had learned she would have an opportunity to see the inside of Mrs. Loll's house, she had risen, taken up her pallet, and walked. Mrs. Fitt was going to help sneak Myrtice back into the hospital after the wedding reception.

"She's looking well," Duk-Soo said, observing the paper hospital slippers Myrtice had on, the result of a hasty, mismanaged flight, no doubt. Really, he could not approve of such unauthorized displacement, especially when she was looking so pale. Who knows what she might be transmitting to the other guests?

Decked out in what was rumored to be an eight-hundred-dollar dress, Mrs. Jane Loll stood in a circle of well-wishers, beaming like a newlywed, while Connie, crowned with a garland of wilted daisies, sat in a corner with George Henry, holding hands. Mrs. Fitt, her ninety-two-year-old eyes bright with champagne, was telling Duk-Soo about a male nurse in the hospital who collected miniature license plates, which he made into lazy Susans, but Duk-Soo only half-listened as he studied the Coco children he had heard about but had never met before. This was the real reason he had come to the wedding, to be able to see what Larry, Sam, Helen Ann, Lucy, and Nancy looked like. If it hadn't been for them, he would have gone straight back to the dormitory after the unsettling interview with Dr. Oustelet and crawled under the covers.

Larry turned out to be not quite as good-looking as Duk-Soo had expected from his mother's descriptions. About an inch or two shorter than George Henry, and several pounds lighter, Larry looked more youthful than this younger brother, not just because of a full head of hair, but also because of such boyish mannerisms as draping an arm over people's shoulders and slapping fannies. Unlike George Henry, who bore no resemblance to either parent, Larry had his mother's blue eyes and rather wide mouth. Sam, on the other hand, thin and strikingly handsome, looked very much as Mr. Coco must have looked in his twenties. Duk-Soo had spoken to him earlier, just after the ceremony, asking if his mother was planning to show up.

"She claimed she would have come if it hadn't been here," Sam said in a gentle voice that had a familiar ring to it. "She was afraid the mayor might come. Mrs. Loll is his daughter, right?"

"Yes, I believe so," he said, looking hard at the boy. Why did the voice sound so familiar? It wasn't at all like his brothers' or his father's. "You live in Canada?"

"Banff. I'm into weaving. Say, you don't happen to need a bedspread, do you? Why don't you come on over to our house afterwards, take a look. I'll let you have it for five hundred."

"Well, actually . . ."

"It's not just a bedspread—it's a work of art. I put everything I know into it, but I don't want to fly back with it. And you know how tightfisted Mom is; she won't give me a decent price. Thirty bucks, that's what she offered. Can you believe? I mean it took me months and months. Look, at the Calgary Stampede it'd cost you at least twelve hundred. I'm giving you a real bargain."

"I'll think about it."

"Don't you care about acid rain?"

"Pardon?"

"This bedspread makes a very personal statement about acid rain. The money you give will be like a donation, see. You can take it off your income tax."

"Oh, good. I'll think about it."

When Mrs. Fitt went to report to Myrtice what color the drapes were in the rumpus room—Myrtice was too weak to walk to the other end of the house—Duk-Soo, noticing that Mr. Coco had left his daughters to speak to Maud Herbert,

took the opportunity to introduce himself to the two youngest Coco girls, one of whom, the black-haired one, was inor-
dinately attractive and bore an astonishing resemblance to
her mother.

"Hi," the brown-haired, Irish-looking one with the pixy
nose said. "I'm Nancy, and this is Lucy, who better give me
back my champagne." She wrenched the plastic cup from
her sister's hand.

"I don't mean to be racist or anything," Lucy said, taking
two cups from a tray being passed by a maid, "but I was
wondering, are you by any chance friends or something with
that violinist my mother had an affair with?" She drained
the first cup in a few gulps and started on the second. "I
mean, there aren't that many Orientals in south Louisiana,
and I thought you might have run into him or something."

Duk-Soo looked closely at the wicked child; surely she
knew very well whom she was talking to. "Pardon me, miss,
but I—"

"She never had an affair with him," Nancy interrupted.

"Darling Veronica," Lucy said, swaying uncertainly, "just
ask George Henry. He'll tell you."

"I did. And I don't believe a word of it. It was so mean the
way you threw that in her face last night, Lu."

"Perhaps I might introduce myself," Duk-Soo said futilely.

"Mean—me? What about her? She's being pretty mean to
George Henry, isn't she? Not coming to her own wedding
. . . his. You're such a toady. Someone has to stand up to
Mother. All her preaching, it really makes me ill."

"She's just . . . Oh, Dr. Yoon, I forbid you to eat those
Cheez Doodles," Nancy added, taking the napkinful away
from him. "Can you believe the food at this party? Cheez
Doodles and bean dip, that's it. Do you know how much lard
there is in bean dip?"

"Nancy is our resident nutritionist," Lucy said, handing
Duk-Soo her empty glass. "She's studying food at Columbia

Teachers College, but she refused to make one single thing for her own brother's wedding."

"Look, this is my vacation, honey. You could have fixed something yourself instead of yelling at Mom all morning. I can't believe that you made such a big deal out of Helen Ann's ab— . . . operation. It wasn't Mom's fault."

"If she didn't act so holier than thou. The nerve of her"— Lucy reached out and steadied herself on her sister's shoulder—"playing the big Catholic and then making her daughter get—"

"She didn't make her. No one made Helen Ann do anything."

"Is Helen Ann ill?" Duk-Soo inquired, mystified by Nancy's eyes. Something about the shape, was it?—or the color.

"What?" Nancy said, munching one of Duk-Soo's Doodles. "I'm going to try calling Mom again. I'm worried."

"Leave her alone," Lucy said as Duk-Soo accidentally brushed against her dark bare arm. "She's just not answering the phone, that's all. She's sulking like a baby."

"I don't care what you say, Agnes dear. I'm going to call her."

Nancy strode off past the fountain, pinching her brother Sam on the way and making a slight detour to herd her father away from the food. Left alone with Lucy, Duk-Soo didn't know quite what to say and after accidentally brushing against her arm again, ended up making some obvious remark about the dog pens which were visible through the sliding glass doors.

"People are starving to death all over the world, and that idiot Jane Loll feeds steak to her stupid dogs," Lucy said.

And Doodles to her guests, Duk-Soo thought, his head spinning with hunger. He had counted on a more substantial repast at the party and had not eaten before.

Jostled from behind, Duk-Soo reached out and touched Lucy to steady himself.

"Touch me one more time, mister, and I'll scream," Lucy said, putting the fear of God into him as she walked off in search of another drink.

"Ah, here you are, Mr. Yoon," Maud Herbert said, appearing at his side. "Are you enjoying yourself? I bet they don't have houses like this in Korea. I mean the common people probably wouldn't."

"Umm," he said, keeping an eye on Lucy. There was something about those children. It was as if he had known them all his life, a positively *unheimlich* sensation.

"I've been dying to talk to you," Maud Herbert confided, getting uncomfortably close. He took a step backwards. "I'm so concerned about Ethyl Mae. When she wouldn't come to the mayor's Roast—by the way, it was a tremendous success. And Mr. Coco gave such a charming speech, I was so proud of him. Anyway, I've been trying to get in touch with her. We used to be just like that, me and her," she said, holding up two stout fingers.

The maid appeared, and while Duk-Soo put Lucy's empty plastic cup on the silver tray, Maud Herbert asked her if she could borrow a quarter.

"In case my car breaks down on the way home, I want to be able to phone," she explained, pocketing the coin the disgruntled maid had given her; and then, noticing her two fingers, still held up, she added, "What's this supposed to mean? Oh. Yes. Well, I think the chihuahua episode must have taken it out of her. You know, I think I've finally figured the whole thing out. For a while it did seem to me that Ethyl Mae was guilty, especially when she wouldn't show up for the hearings. But then I heard the most amazing story— my husband told me. Back in the sixties during all the civil rights to-do, there was a very dedicated white minister who was devoted to the cause but who didn't seem to be getting anywhere. So one day he went outside his house with a shotgun and blasted his bedroom window. Then he called the police and claimed that a white vigilante group had tried to kill him. So, you see, of course . . ."

"I'm afraid I don't quite follow you," Duk-Soo said, finding his patience wearing thin.

"That dreadful creature at the beauty college, Gyrene, she's the equivalent of the minister. She killed her own beloved dog in a fit of rage and then blamed it on Ethyl Mae. She just couldn't accept the murderous impulses inside her and had to project them on others."

"But why would she want to kill her own dog, especially if it was beloved?"

"Ah, Mr. Yoon . . ."

"Dr."

"Dr.? Why, no, you didn't! It's simply too amazing. I never thought in a million years . . . Well, sir, congratulations are in order. Now where was I? Oh, yes. It's always those we love best, those closest to us that we end up wanting to murder. My husband has the statistics to prove it, wives shooting husbands, husbands chopping up wives, sons against fathers, Cain and Abel, Abraham and Isaac, Oedipus and Rex, it's an old, old story."

"But still, it doesn't . . ." He stopped himself, realizing that it really wasn't in his best interest to question her theories. "Oh, now I see, yes, yes. You've got something there." To think that he had ever been afraid of this harmless old fool.

"I have a second theory, too," she said, squeezing his arm in an unpleasant, intimate way.

"Umm?" he said, gazing out at the dog pens. The sturdy beasts were quite ferocious-looking, a strange animal for Mrs. Loll to be so fond of.

"That's that you did it."

"I beg your pardon?"

"And Ethyl Mae was covering up for you. See, I think it might have something to do with the time both of you went to the dump. Why would you go to the dump at five in the morning just to throw away an old hot-water heater, which, by the way, still has never been recovered? And the fact that you, Mr. Yoon, refused to testify at the Concerned Citizens Committee hearings. The only trouble with this theory is that there's no motive. I can't figure out why you would want to kill Gyrene's chihuahua. You've never had your hair done at the beauty college, have you?"

"No," he said, taking another step backwards. "I think your first theory holds more . . ."

"Water. Yes, I agree. It's so disturbing, though, that the body was never recovered. If only I had the body to work with. That's what I said to Ethyl Mae yesterday. I was asking her to help me find the body, but she was no help at all. Really, I must say I'm worried about her. She didn't look well—very run-down, I'm afraid. Have you seen her recently? I've got to do something to cheer her up, get her back to her old self again. Do you think she'd enjoy a trip to New Orleans, just the two of us? We could go shopping and have a nice fancy dinner, squid, I want her to try some squid. She's never had any before, you know. Oh, look, I better go talk to Mr. Coco. He looks sort of lost, poor dear."

Gazing out at the pens, Duk-Soo wondered if maybe he should pay Mrs. Coco a visit. But no. It was like an alcoholic saying one little drink wouldn't hurt: one little visit *would* hurt. The only solution was complete abstinence. Actually, when he thought about it, the best thing that had ever happened to him was being kicked out of the Pro Arts. Without that constant distraction he had finally been able to devote himself entirely to his work and transform himself into a bona fide doctor of philosophy—at least in the spring he would be, if Dr. Oustelet kept her big mouth sealed.

"What's she doing out there?"

It was Mrs. Fitt again, returning from the buffet with a tray of Doodles and champagne. Dressed up with heavy rouge, seed pearls, and garnet earrings, the old woman, thanks to her crewcut, looked rather like a degenerate old man.

"Here, let me," Duk-Soo said, taking the dangerously tilted tray from her.

"She's going to get herself bit."

"What's that?"

"Out there."

A hefty woman he hadn't noticed before was sticking her hand through the fence of one of the pens, rubbing the nose of a pugnacious dog while three of its colleagues growled and jostled one another, trying to get near the hand.

"I'm bringing that tray to Myrtice," Mrs. Fitt said. "Here, give it here."

"Who is that?" he asked, hanging on to the tray.

"Out there? That's one of them Cocos, Helen Sue, I think. And if that gal don't watch out, she's not going to have any fingers left. That's the state dog she's fooling with, official dog of Louisiana."

"The state dog, yes . . . Mrs. Loll raises Cali—?"

"Catahoulas they call them. They's bred specially to track down bears and wild boar and stuff. Ugly little buggers, aren't they?"

Looking out at the woman with those dogs, the Catahoulas, Duk-Soo thought for some reason of parking tickets, a bizarre association that nagged at him while the old woman went on talking about a dog she got into a fight with once, when she was a little girl.

" . . . couldn't bark, that dog, something wrong with its throat," she was saying when in some dim part of his mind, the same part that had once equated "home" with "death," Duk-Soo was suddenly able to make a similar equation that explained why these Coco children seemed so *unheimlich* to him. Wasn't *unheimlich* linked, after all, to *heimlich?* He knew everything now, though he could prove nothing yet.

"Are you all right?" Mrs. Fitt asked irritably. "Come on, give me the tray."

"No, Mrs. Fitt. I'll take it to her myself."

Though troubled by all the equation implied, and wondering how he would go about proving it, he had one small thing to attend to first. All afternoon he had done his best to avoid Myrtice, finding it unsettling to talk with someone who was not only very ill but also had let it be known, according to E.M., that she was glad he had been fired from the Pro Arts. But his conscience wouldn't let him keep on ignoring her. He would take the tray over and say a few pleasant words, behavior that he knew was suspiciously Christian, but nonetheless the right thing to do.

Even though it had a window, the room was as stifling as that computer room at St. Jude where she and George Henry had once tried to talk, but the smell here was worse, something like a pine cleaner trying to mask the odor of Army blankets soaked with night sweat. The greasy window, barred with leafless, brittle vines, seemed to be painted shut, for it would not open. But what bothered her the most, more than the window, the random clank of the heating pipes, or the bare walls with scrubbed but still visible graffiti, was the rubber sheet on the bed. There was something about the rubber sheet that made it so difficult for her to pretend—for his benefit, of course—that everything was going to be all right, that it was not all hopeless.

The ward attendant had told Mrs. Coco that Ray Jr. was confined to this room for three days because he wouldn't stop mincing onions. When the chef had tried to take the new electric mincer away, Ray Jr. had applied a full nelson that accidentally cured the chef's bad back, which was no reason why Ray Jr. shouldn't be punished. The boy wasn't supposed to receive any visitors, either, but Mrs. Coco wondered if the ward attendant accepted charitable donations for the hospital—ten dollars, cash—and she was admitted.

Unshaven, his hair longer now, matted and uncombed, Ray Jr. sat in a corner of the bed wearing his olive golf shirt and boxer shorts. Apparently he was under heavy sedation, for his eyes were bleary and unfocused, and sometimes he would smile for no reason at all. It was only yesterday that she had found out about his transfer from Dove House to the state hospital at Florence. She had phoned Brother Michael, and he had not even remembered who she was at first and then had mentioned the transfer in an offhand way, as if this sort of thing happened all the time. The conversation had been so upsetting that she realized there was no way she could go to the wedding. Above all, she must make sure that Ray Jr. was all right. Yes, she told herself, she most defi-nitely would have gone to the Lolls' if it hadn't been for the fact that Ray Jr. needed her more. Even that terrible scene with Lucy wouldn't have made any difference, when her daughter had caught her reading the end of her poem:

> i, a virgin, mother of six
> Shall be crowned Miss Uni-
> Verse 1950 by Pius XII
> so that his okra might be
> Sweeter, his catfish plump, his con-
> Science clear when my Jews are hung on the Con-
> Fraternity of Christian Doctrine O! Lucia,
> lucy, Mimi, whatever they call you these
> Days, pray for me. Let not this
> Fatima, once daughter of Muhammad, be
> turned into a Tri-
> Umph of his will.

Not even that poem, which was about the most revolting trash she had ever read in her life, would have kept her away from the wedding.

Of course, none of them would have understood her real reason for not going. Even Larry had been angry with her, not to mention Helen Ann and Nancy. She couldn't tell them that she was going to visit the poor boy, because charity was something a Christian should always practice in secret. Her family should have trusted her when she told them that she had something more important to do. If they chose to call her a bigoted red-neck, well, it was just one more Cross she would bear for Ray Jr.

"Would you like to draw, Ray Jr.? I could go get you some Crayolas."

"Judy Malony, you smell. You ain't never getting near this body again."

Retreating to the window, Mrs. Coco tried once again to open it. "Ray Jr., you remember who I am, don't you? I'm Mrs. Coco," she said, her heart thumping hard from the exertion. She simply had to get some air or she might faint. "You remember Sergeant Coco; I'm the one who let you stay up as late as you wanted. We had a lot of fun watching tv, didn't we?"

"Tv's dead. I done killed it."

It was no use; the window wouldn't open, and she wouldn't be able to stand this room another minute. She had to get out. She would go talk to the attendant and tell him that if he didn't let Ray Jr. out into the ward this minute, she would raise such a stink. The idea, keeping someone cooped up in a hellhole like this. It was positively medieval.

"Listen to me," she said, crouching down in front of him. "I'm going to be right back. I'm not leaving you. Do you understand?"

His eyes gazed dully past her at the wall.

"I'm not leaving you, understand?" she repeated, more this time for her benefit than his. Because she had to convince herself that she wasn't lying, that she wouldn't find some excuse, once she was outside, not to return.

His hand was surprisingly cold, clammy. No more words, she told herself, pressing his hand against that lump of rayon on her breast, the scapular. No more words, because almost every word she had spoken to him, about him, was a lie. And this was what the lies amounted to, this room with a rubber sheet on the fourth floor of a loony bin. George Henry was right: she, not Dr. Jewel, had been the one who asked Ray Jr. to lunch that day the Pro Arts had played at Norris State. There was something about his eyes, that look he had had when they were playing the Mozart. It had haunted her, reminding her of something beautiful that could have been. Could have, might have—this was the beginning of her despair, her denial. After that she had tried to convince herself that Dove House was where he belonged when she knew full well it was crushing his spirit. Even today, this very moment, she was simply using him as an excuse to herself so that she wouldn't have to go to that wedding. No, it was not charity that had brought her here; it was her own pride, and anger at her muleheaded children.

"Get away, it's Russia. He'll lock you up if you touch this body. You're not supposed to be in Russia. This is a luscious body here. Don't, get away."

His protests were feeble, though, as she lay down beside him—not, of course, for the first time. This was another lie she had been telling herself, that it was Mr. Coco who had snuck into the sewing room back in August, who had frightened her so terribly with a deep, furtive joy. The seventeen-year-old to whom love had meant everything, she was still there, ready to sacrifice everything again, family, friends, the future, because the seventeen-year-old knew that there was no future, no past, only what is. But when the fifty-seven-year-old had awakened, she had to dress up in lies once again, pretending that she was outraged at her husband, pretending that the future and the past were all that mattered.

Ray Jr. did not move, his arms did not even attempt to hug her. But it was enough to have him there beside her, making even the black pumps she had on, her tweed suit, and the purse digging into her hip seem somehow a natural, living part of her. This, of course, was the biggest lie of all, she realized, for she was not, as she had thought when she crawled into bed with him, protecting *him* from the rubber sheet. No, it was the other way around. There never was and never would be a Saint Ethyl Mae of Tula Springs. There was simply a woman who was tired of crying "Unclean" wherever she went, who was hoping finally, after all this time, to be touched.

"Miss Coco, Miss Coco."

She felt a hand upon her shoulder. Jerking awake—oh, Lord, she must have fallen asleep beside Ray Jr., who was snoring lightly, a bare foot draped over her black pumps— she propped herself up, clutching her purse to her breast.

"Get out," she said, a terrible anger and fear choking the words, making her sound hoarse. "Get out of here, you filthy—"

"Now Miss Coco," the mayor said, looking down at her with that bland, handsome face that she had never been able to bear to look directly at before. For years she had carried around inside her an image of the mayor as he looked twenty years ago, so that now, confronting him directly for the first time, she was surprised to see that the face was not as smooth as she remembered, that it was deeply lined, sagging, and discolored beneath the eyes.

"I forbid you to see this boy," she said, putting herself between the mayor and Ray Jr. "You and that degenerate Dr. Jewel—look what you've done to him. Just look. I'm telling you now, Mayor Binwanger, I won't rest till I see you and that doctor friend of yours in jail, both of you."

"Now listen here, it wasn't me who put him in here. I had a good home for him until some meddling fool woman started to—"

The purse caught him on the ear, his right ear, with such force that he staggered back a step or two.

"Get out, you pig! Out!"

"No, Miss Coco," he said, feeling the ear gingerly with one hand, "no, I'm not going, not yet. Not until I've talked to my son. You see, it's time he came home. I want to tell him it's time to come on home."

19

It was a church none of them had ever been in before, a building Mrs. Coco could not recall having seen, even though she must have passed it several times on her way to Baton Rouge. Perhaps it was the sign out front that made her mind draw a blank: Church of Jesus Christ of Latter-day Saints. But now that she thought about it, how peculiar that there were enough Mormons in Tula Springs—it was Duk-Soo who had told her Latter-day Saints meant Mormons, and that not all Mormons lived in Utah—to be able to afford a church—or chapel, according to Duk-Soo—fancier than Our Lady of the Flowers, with cushioned pews and a formidable-looking organ that looked as if it could easily blast anyone who got too comfortable, wide awake.

"Are we supposed to play now?" Mrs. Coco whispered to George Henry, who was getting an A from Duk-Soo. Set up in the loft beside the organ, they could see the bishop, who ran a thriving catfish farm out on the Old Jeff Davis Highway, peering up expectantly at them while the casket, the best money could buy, was rolled up the aisle past the handful of people who had shown up for the service. A choking sound filled the vault of bluish bricks as Dr. Fitt, sitting beside the old woman in the first pew, broke down and began to weep openly.

"We play after he talks, don't we?" Duk-Soo said.

"That's what I thought—but why is he looking at us?"

The bishop gave an impatient flick of his hand.

"Y'all do something," Connie said. She was sitting on a folding chair to the right of the musicians, her legs sprawled out in not the most ladylike manner, the result, no doubt, of her swollen belly. Mrs. Coco had tried to make the bulge seem a little less conspicuous with a beige maternity dress she had picked out for her daughter-in-law from the new line of women's apparel that was being introduced to McNair's. As if Mr. Coco didn't have enough trouble selling men's clothes, this spring he had to see how much he could lose selling women's. Connie was going to act as a special consultant once she had the baby, which was due in another six weeks or so—Mrs. Coco didn't dare count the time too closely since the December wedding; she didn't want to know.

"Well, let's roll," George Henry said, and the Pro Arts launched into the opening bars of the Andante from Mozart's K.421, which was not written for a trio, of course, but they had no choice now. Five bars into it the bishop stood up and began to speak, but the musicians were so engrossed that they didn't hear him at first and had to be silenced by a hiss from Connie.

". . . not only a great asset to us here, but the community as a whole," the bishop was saying. "If there was one word that could characterize her life as a whole, I believe that word would be *involved.* How many of us shut ourselves off in our glass houses and peer out at the world, afraid to soil our hands, our faces? How many of us seem more concerned about what our neighbors think about us than what we are really about?"

While he talked, Mrs. Coco surveyed the backs of the heads below her. There was Mr. Qumquist with one of his daughters, a homely girl who sold driftwood sculpture in the mall. Two pews behind them was someone who looked like Maud Herbert, only it couldn't be, since she had told Mrs. Coco she was too busy to come—what with all the last-minute details for her trip to the Finger Lakes. Closer to the front—surely not a very proper place for a stranger to seat herself—was Duk-Soo's friend, a Finnish girl Lucy had introduced him to last month when he moved to New Orleans. According to Lucy he was quite smitten with her, a disgraceful situation, as far as Mrs. Coco was concerned. Why, this severe, boyish-looking Finn was young enough to be his daughter and could barely speak English, to boot.

". . . filled with an almost awesome enthusiasm for life, each day a new adventure of the spirit . . ."

The bishop paused a moment as Dr. Fitt emitted a peculiar moan, during which Duk-Soo and Mrs. Coco exchanged a glance. To her horror she found herself shaken by suppressed schoolgirl giggles. Nerves, it must be nerves, she thought, trying hard not to look again at Duk-Soo. He had motored all the way from New Orleans as a special favor to Dr. Fitt, who was feeling sentimental about the original Pro Arts. This had given her a chance to talk to him again, a rare opportunity these days, seeing how preoccupied he was with his Finn.

"Yes, the priests seem nice," Duk-Soo had said when Mrs. Coco had questioned him about his job while they were setting up stands before the service. He would be teaching in a Jesuit boys' academy in the fall.

"But you're still an atheist?"

"Of course."

Somehow she had failed, she thought, if after all this time with her he still refused to believe in Christ.

"You know, I was wondering . . ." he began, unfolding a rickety stand.

"Hm?"

"I was wondering if maybe you've heard from . . ."

"Now listen, Dr. Yoon, I want you to be straight with me. Did you know all along?"

"Why do you keep on asking me that? I thought I made it clear, it was only at the wedding. That's when I began to think there might be some connection."

Duk-Soo had already told Mrs. Coco about his experience at the wedding, when he had seen her other children and felt somehow he knew them, especially when he heard Sam's voice and looked into Nancy's eyes. There was something of Ray Jr. in them, nothing obvious, but an unmistakable quality that he was sure couldn't be just a coincidence. In a way this was such a relief to Mrs. Coco herself, finally to discover a reason for those feelings that had tormented her and that she had tried so hard to deny. What she had always thought was an irrational, sinful tenderness that the boy brought out in her could now be conveniently labeled with a sticker that would pass even Father Fua's stiff customs. Of course, this label—maternal affection, as pure as the Virgin Mary's—didn't really describe the contents of the package being smuggled through, but then could any label ever describe it? Like most genuine love, it knew nothing of customs, nothing of boundaries. If Mrs. Coco chose to believe in the label, it was only with a small part of her mind, the part that had to deal with what she called the real world.

Unaware of Helen Ann's abortion, Duk-Soo could put two and two together, a computation that Mrs. Coco, her head clogged by a few too many assumptions, was unable to make on her own. The truth was, Helen Ann had not gone ahead with the abortion. Mrs. Coco had found this out from Mayor Binwanger in December, shortly after she had struck him on the ear with her purse at the state hospital. A peculiar combination of relief and disgust, something like the aftermath of bending over a toilet with a sick stomach, had come over her then—relief because the queasiness that had plagued her for years about the morality of the abortion was finally settled; disgust because that obscenely ubiquitous man, the mayor, was in a way now and forever a part of her family. There was nothing she could do about it.

Twenty years ago, the mayor had explained, Helen Ann had stayed away from Tula Springs long enough to have the baby and give it up for adoption, telling her parents, though, that she had gone ahead with the abortion they had insisted upon. She had been afraid that if she told her mother the truth—Mrs. Coco was practically insane with anger at the time—she would not have been given the money she needed to resettle in Australia with her good friend Louise, an exchange student from Sydney who roomed with her at L.S.U. For her part Mrs. Coco was so horrified by the very idea of an abortion, necessary though it was, that she was grateful that Helen Ann, by staying away from Tula Springs, was keeping everything in the abstract. Afterwards Mrs. Coco put up a mild fuss about Helen Ann's going all the way to Australia to live, but in truth Mrs. Coco would not have objected if her daughter wanted to live on the moon, anywhere far enough away to avoid further contamination from that man.

At first it was impossible for Mrs. Coco to understand how a child of hers could abandon her own baby so easily, but when she confronted Helen Ann after talking to the mayor, Helen Ann told her that there was nothing easy about it. And after all, her own parents had wanted her to get rid of the child, something that Helen Ann, though not a staunch Catholic like her mother—Helen Ann had lost her faith at a slumber party in high school—could not go through with. At the same time, the mayor was frantic that his wife, the President of the Ladies Auxiliary at the Jubilee Baptist Church, might find out about Ray Jr., which would have spelled the end of his career. Mrs. Binwanger was a tough customer, and it was her money that let him play at politics. Still very young, unsure of herself, frightened by what she had done, and embittered by the mayor's cowardice—he, too, insisted that she get an abortion—Helen Ann took the easy way out by running away from everything, hoping that the Lord would somehow provide for the baby.

Although Mrs. Coco always knew that the mayor was hardly fit to call himself a man, she still wondered how any-one with the slightest tinge of natural feelings could allow his son to be adopted by a dope addict. The mayor did his best to explain to her that he didn't really have much say in the matter to begin with. And also, she should keep in mind that Alfred was not born a dope addict. When he had adopted Ray Jr., Alfred owned two filling stations and a fairly successful gymnasium. It was only after his wife had been murdered in a holdup at the Sunoco station that Alfred took to wrestling and then drugs, and by that time Ray Jr. had already been confined to Norris State. "I kept a sharp eye on him there," the mayor told Mrs. Coco. He had made sure that the staff, Dr. Jewel included, was generously com-pensated out of his own pocket for taking special care of Ray Jr. And by pretending that Ray Jr. was a second cousin, something the mayor's wife never looked into since she wasn't on speaking terms with the mayor's relatives any-way, he was able to visit Ray Jr. and occasionally take him out to dinner or a ball game.

This arrangement worked fine until Dr. Oustelet—whom, unlike Dr. Jewel, he didn't trust enough to explain his real relationship to Ray Jr. to—decided that the boy was too old for Norris State. "That's when Dr. Jewel and me put our heads together," the mayor said. He didn't want to see his boy in some crummy halfway house, much less at Florence, which was where Dr. Oustelet wanted to send him. And, of course, the boy could never make it on his own.

"But what about Helen Ann? Why didn't you tell her? She could have done something for him," Mrs. Coco insisted. "Or me? Why not me?"

As far as Helen Ann went, he was still angry at her for doing everything half-assed. She had told him she was getting an abortion but then at the last minute changed her mind and run off, leaving him to cope with all the problems. Did that make her fit to be a proper mother? And as for telling Mrs. Coco herself, that was out of the question then. "I was afraid of you, Miss Coco. I knew damn well how much you hated me, and I knew you'd be unreasonable. You'd tell my wife everything, and between the two of you, I couldn't get myself elected dogcatcher. I don't know if you realize this, but my job means a hell of a lot to me. I've devoted my entire life to public service, and I wasn't about to see twenty-five years of hard work go down the drain."

It had been Dr. Jewel's idea to get Duk-Soo hooked up with Ray Jr. since the Korean seemed to have taken a healthy interest in the boy and was going out of his way to do him favors. As for the living arrangements, the Spanish house in Ozone did indeed belong to a swindler involved in a pyramid sales fraud, but after he fled to the Bahamas, the Catahoula Corporation, a holding company owned by the mayor's daughter, Jane Loll, bought the house at a sheriff's auction. In order to keep the mayor's name out of the whole transaction, Dr. Jewel paid the rent to the Catahoula Corporation, which in turn paid him back in the form of dividends—all of this strictly legal, of course, the mayor assured Mrs. Coco.

"But why did you have to deceive Duk-Soo?"

Because, the mayor explained, Dr. Jewel and he were aware that Duk-Soo was connected with her through the Pro Arts. They had to make sure that the Korean didn't suspect that the mayor had anything to do with the house. It was a little childish of them to threaten him with the sheriff, but they had no other leverage over him. He could have walked out on the arrangement anytime he pleased, as indeed he finally did after a few months. The vague threats were the only thing that was keeping a roof over Ray Jr.'s head. "After all, the Korean was our only hope. There just wasn't anybody else."

So, even though she sometimes had her doubts, Mrs. Coco could believe Duk-Soo now when he insisted that he had not known all along that Ray Jr. was her grandson. She could believe him when he said it was only a hunch, some intuition, that had made him ask her certain questions when she returned from Florence the day of the wedding, questions about her relation to the Catahoula Corporation and why Jane Loll should be involved with Ray Jr.'s welfare. Mrs. Coco had always known that Duk-Soo was a little paranoid, but in this case his paranoia had led him to the truth. And it turned out to be a blessing that he had discovered the truth, because it was only with someone who knew, that Mrs. Coco could have found comfort with that day. After the confrontation with the mayor at Florence, she had found Duk-Soo waiting for her at North Gladiola. The rest of the family still at the wedding, it had been safe for her to break down in his arms, sobbing as messily as a child, while he held her there on his lap in the Queen Anne chair, dabbing at her tears with an antimacassar.

"One thing I'll never understand," she said after the stands had been set up and people had begun to come quietly, in pairs or alone, into the chapel. "How you could allow that doctor to have anything to do with Ray Jr.—I don't know if I'll ever be able to forgive you for that."

"Mrs. Coco," Duk-Soo said, looking her straight in the eye, unabashed, "I never saw Dr. Jewel mistreat the boy, not once. I saw him being kind and loving, that's all."

"But what about what Dr. Oustelet said?"

"What about it? What did she actually see? How much was she imagining?"

"No, Dr. Yoon. I can't agree with you there. Dr. Oustelet is a professional. She knows her business. And when I first met him, I knew there was something funny about him. He's a sick man. There's something truly evil about him." She had to keep on telling, not Duk-Soo, who was tired of hearing it, but herself about Dr. Jewel. It made it much easier to explain her own behavior in the past, which she wasn't too fond of thinking about.

"You still haven't answered my question," Duk-Soo whispered later, after the bishop had been speaking for a good twenty minutes, the last five of which seemed to have more to do with urgently needed flagstones than death. "Have you heard from her lately?"

"Everything's fine," she said, ashamed to tell him that she hadn't heard a word from Helen Ann since she and Ray Jr. had left a couple months ago for Australia. Mrs. Coco had hoped they would stay close to home, where she could help them out, but Helen Ann, when she learned about Ray Jr., was too furious at her mother and the mayor, saying that neither one of them deserved to see her boy again. It hurt so much to be cut off like that, but Mrs. Coco continued to write, and even though her letters went unanswered and her request for Helen Ann's unlisted number was denied, the checks she sent were cashed, which at least gave her some hope.

"Is he happy?" Duk-Soo whispered urgently.

"Hush, y'all," Connie said.

In a pew to the far left of the chapel Mrs. Coco spotted Mrs. Binwanger, without her husband. A surge of bitterness welled up in her as she regarded this prim, overbearing woman tastelessly flaunting a blond mink in spring. This would be the perfect opportunity. She could waylay Mrs.

Binwanger afterwards and tell her everything that she had kept bottled up inside her all winter. And what a service she would be doing Tula Springs, because once Mrs. Binwanger heard about Ray Jr. and all the money her husband had spent on him—no doubt most of it illegally stolen from his wife and written off as some sort of underhanded tax deduction—there would be no chance that the mayor would ever run for another term of office. And why should he? Mrs. Coco was still convinced that something crooked was going on with him and the Citizens Patrol. Perhaps some of that money was even used on Ray Jr.—a disgusting thought.

"I've put my life in your hands," the mayor had told her that day in Florence. "You've got the power now to ruin me, Miss Coco, but I couldn't let my boy stay here. I had to come." So finally, after all these years, she had the power to do some good with her life. It made her strangely exultant when she remembered all that she had suffered at the mayor's hands. There *was* justice after all. One did not have to wait for heaven for Right to win out.

A clatter on the spiral stairs leading to the loft caused a few heads to turn.

"Am I late?" Myrtice whispered as she unpacked her viola. "I just had to get my hair done today, couldn't come looking like I did this morning, and the only people open was the beauty college." Her last visit to the hospital had left her with a little less energy, but aside from this, Myrtice looked pretty much the same as always, except, of course, for the spit curls that someone at the beauty college had apparently talked her into. "What are you staring at? You don't like them? I told Gyrene they weren't me, but she said I—"

"You look fine, hon," Mrs. Coco said. "Come on, let's play."

"Oh, would you look at that. I asked Aunt Sissy to keep Dr. Fitt from crying. It's such a disgrace for a grown man to carry on like that. I know his mother wouldn't have appreciated it one bit. For heaven's sake, she was ninety-three, you know, and she—"

"Myrtice, please! Tune up."

When they played K.421 this time, the quartet Mozart had composed while his wife gave birth, in great agony, to the doomed Raimond Leopold, all the voices were present, complementing one another in such a way that another voice that was neither Myrtice's, George Henry's, Duk-Soo's, nor Mrs. Coco's seemed to emerge from their uncertain performance. It was this fifth voice that Mrs. Coco was, after all this time, finally able to hear as she glanced down at her husband's head, which from this vantage point in the loft was more pink than gray. She was always so used to looking up to him and seeing the gray, but now she realized that he was really as pink as a baby's behind. The voice was, of course, his, the love of her life's, and coming as it did from the other end of the world, one had to be very still inside to hear it, the hush, the silence.

Her umbrella unfurled, Mrs. Binwanger stood in the portico of the chapel waiting for the rain to die down a little before venturing out in her blond mink to her car. In her day she had been known as a beauty, but now she was far too plump, and her otherwise pretty face was spoiled by too much makeup.

"Hello, Mrs. Binwanger," Mrs. Coco said, pausing a moment beside her.

"Hello, Mrs. Coco," the woman said with a hint of condescension.

Mrs. Coco smiled at the hardened face; then, holding an umbrella over her cello, she wheeled the disreputable-looking case to the parking lot, where her husband was waiting in the car, the back door already open.